THE DECEPTIVE
LADY DARBY

Lost Ladies Of London: Book 2

ADELE CLEE

The Deceptive Lady Darby
Copyright © 2017 Adele Clee
All rights reserved.
ISBN-13: 978-0-9955705-8-0

Cover designed by **Jay Aheer**

CHAPTER ONE

A dozen pairs of eyes twinkled in the darkness as Rose Darby raced along the woodland path. The nocturnal creatures stopped foraging and fell deathly silent. She was not the only one who wanted to avoid attracting predators tonight. Perhaps it was best she didn't know what lurked in the foliage. Badgers and foxes made the snuffles and scratches, not men desperate to catch her and drag her back to Morton Manor.

Clutching her linen bag of supplies, she continued through the gloom. A low-hanging branch whipped her face. She caught her foot on the exposed root of a tree and almost went tumbling headfirst into a blanket of ferns.

Oh, why had she not brought a lantern?

She glanced back over her shoulder for the tenth time in as many steps. No matter how many times she blinked to clear her vision, strange shadows danced before her eyes.

Heavens above!

Nicole said it was but a mile from Morton Manor to the main road, a little further to the coaching inn where she hoped to gain a ride to London. By her calculation, it should take fifteen minutes to cover the rough terrain. But she'd run across the boggy field, her feet squelching in her boots and causing blisters. The sodden hem of her travelling cloak dragged the ground. She'd tripped several times in her eagerness to be away from the horrid place, scratched her hands on brambles, ripped holes in her only pair of stockings.

Still, one had to look on the bright side. After spending six months locked in a house at her father's behest, she'd finally broken free.

The rush of elation was brief. How could she celebrate her good fortune when her friend, Nicole, was still trapped inside the manor?

Rose's heart ached at the thought.

Nicole Flint was more than a paid companion. Other than her brother, she was the only person Rose had ever trusted. Even now, as she made a hasty escape, Nicole kept watch on the guard they'd bound and gagged.

The burning pain in her chest returned, and she stopped to catch her breath. The sound of rustling leaves and crunching underfoot forced her to swing around.

"Who … who's there?"

She expected to see Stokes' gnarled face glaring back. His meaty paws lunging in an effort to grab her and carry her home. The guard had caught her once before. He'd given no thought to her gentle breeding when he'd tied her hands so tightly the rope rubbed her skin raw.

But Stokes lay in his sick bed, suffering from a fever. And Nicole would keep the other guard, Baxter, restrained until morning.

Pushing all fears aside, Rose straightened her spine, lifted her chin and continued through the woods. Once out on open ground, she made her way towards the building in the distance.

Despite the late hour, the lamps outside The Talbot Inn glowed. A ploy to entice weary travellers to stop and take refreshment or warm their cold limbs. With the inn situated on the main route to London, the innkeeper accepted patrons both day and night.

But a lady did not enter an inn unaccompanied regardless of the hour.

What if a well-respected family from town had booked in for the night and recognised her? Her only other option was to walk the twenty miles to the city. With luck, she'd arrive mid-morning. But the sore skin on her toes stung with every step. Once the blisters burst, she'd have no choice but to stop and seek—

Four words sliced through the crisp night air to put paid to her plans.

The Earl of Stanton.

The blood in Rose's veins chilled.

What cruel trick was this?

How did her father know she'd escaped?

The male voice came from the vicinity of the courtyard, and so she crept up to the entrance and peered around the stone wall. Two men—a groom and a coachman—conversed as they removed the harnesses from a team of four pulling a coach.

The lump in Rose's throat made it hard to breathe.

She recognised the black and yellow conveyance with red-shod wheels. The irony of the heraldic mark on the door did not escape her. Two black eagles held the golden shield in their talons, neither wanting to relinquish their grip. As the only blonde Darby in the family, her ebony-haired father and brother were always at war over her mistreatment.

"His lordship wants to set off come first light," the coachman said.

Was it too much to hope that her father was heading to London? But why stop at the coaching inn when the manor he owned was but a mile away?

"Why your master wants to visit that godforsaken place is a mystery." The groom's reply sent her heart pounding against her ribs. "Even though it ain't an asylum anymore, folk say they can still hear the cries of the wretched at night."

"I'm not paid to question my master's wishes. If Lord Stanton says he wants to visit the manor, then it's my job to drive him there."

Good Lord!

The men continued talking, but Rose stopped listening. Fate had conspired against her. Once her father reached the manor and found her missing, heaven knows what he would do.

Rose plastered her hand over her mouth for fear the men might hear her ragged breathing. Nicole Flint had taken the job of a paid companion in good faith, only to find herself locked in a rural prison with no hope of reprieve.

No. Despite Nicole's insistence that she should not turn back under any circumstances, Rose had to warn her. It was the only solution her conscience would allow. And if she couldn't persuade Nicole to come with her to London, they would venture north, just for a few days.

Though her feet throbbed at the thought of taking another step, Rose rushed back along the road and crossed the open field into the woods. But what if she met Stokes in the dark? Best to avoid the route leading directly to the manor. Instead, she continued north on the narrow path, the one overgrown, less trodden. If she had her bearings, it veered west and led to the manor's rusty old gates.

Ignoring the pain in her toes, Rose trudged on through the avenue of trees. Slivers of moonlight broke through the green canopy. But as she progressed through the woods a mist descended, casting everything in a silver-white haze. The trees were tall black shadows. Identical. Evenly spaced. The view in front mirrored the view behind.

Rose swung around, disorientated.

Panic flared.

Had she missed the path leading back to the manor?

But then she saw a faint light in the distance. Like a moth to a flame, it drew her forward out into the open air. The sight of the building calmed her racing heart, even though it was apparent this mansion was not the ghastly Morton Manor.

She climbed the stile and limped across the damp grass. If she could just find the stables, wake a groom and beg a ride. The coins in her purse were incentive enough to drag the man from his bed at this late hour.

Rose crept along the walkway, around to the right of the house. The gravel crunched like glass beneath her feet. The sound grew progressively louder no matter how light her steps. But then a woman darted out from the darkness and almost sent her tumbling into the trimmed topiary.

"Move out of my way, girl." The woman glared beneath the hood of her travelling cloak. She gripped a material bag in her hand as though ready to wallop anyone who dared block her path.

Another woman appeared, her breathless pants forming puffs of white in the cool night air. "Mrs Booth. Wait. Please, Mrs Booth."

She was of average height, slender while still appearing sturdy and robust. The long-sleeved brown dress and frilly mob cap confirmed her position as that of a servant. The sight of the silver chatelaine roused visions of Mrs Gripes, the housekeeper at Morton Manor. But while this woman possessed a friendly countenance, Gripes took pleasure from serving food fit for dogs, from hiding the candles and rationing the coal.

"Good heavens," the woman called out to Mrs Booth. "It's the middle of the night. Can you not at least wait until morning?"

"What, and have him persuade me to stay?" Mrs Booth called back as she stomped away. "No. I've made up my mind. I'm not staying another minute in this house."

The housekeeper stopped short at the sight of a stranger lurking in the shadows. She cast Rose an assessing glance and then tapped her on the arm. "You're early. We weren't expecting you until next week. You can explain why you saw fit to arrive in the middle of the night once we've persuaded Mrs Booth to stay. But for now, I need your help."

Rose shuffled on the spot. What should she say? That she'd lost her way and sought a ride back to the isolated manor? No one must know that she, the daughter of an earl, had spent six months locked in an asylum. A place once a home for the insane.

"I fear you're wasting your time," Rose said. "Mrs Booth seems determined to leave. I doubt there is anything you can say to make her change her mind."

The housekeeper stared at Rose, her brows drawn together in curious enquiry. "Was your previous master one of those fussy types? A stickler for educating the lower classes, was he? I worked for a man once who made the staff take lessons in the correct pronunciation of vowels."

It occurred to Rose that the housekeeper referred to her eloquent diction and turn of phrase.

"Erm … yes. The major is an advocate of reform." Rose detested lies, but sometimes they were necessary.

"Well, you'll find the master here has no time to care for himself, let alone the staff." The woman ushered Rose along the path. "If Mrs Booth leaves us, heaven knows how he'll cope."

With her nose thrust in the air, Mrs Booth continued her march towards the front gate while they followed behind. Whenever Rose's toes hit the tops of her boots, she bit back a groan.

"Do you have a limp, girl?" the housekeeper asked. "Because there was no mention of it when the master hired you, and he's too honourable a man to tolerate deceit."

"It's my boots. They've rubbed blisters the size of walnuts."

The housekeeper patted Rose on the arm as they tottered after Mrs Booth. "A miser is he?"

"Excuse me?"

"Your old master. Too tight in the purse to buy his staff a decent pair of shoes."

"Something like that." The Earl of Stanton *was* a miser and a man without a conscience or heart.

Since declaring her affection for Lord Cunningham, her father had lost all use of his faculties. What sane man bundles his daughter into a hired coach and spirits her away to a dilapidated manor?

Poor Lord Cunningham. The man must be beside himself with worry. What must he think of her? No sooner had he professed his love than she vanished without a trace.

"Mrs Booth. Wait. You'll put an old woman in her grave if you don't slow down. Will you not listen to what I have to say?"

Mrs Booth swung around. "Mrs Hibbet, had you endured a week of torture I'm sure you'd be leaving, too. Do you know what I found in my bed this evening?" Mrs Booth didn't give them a chance to ask but pointed to an upstairs window and jabbed her finger. "Toads! Yes, you heard me.

Toads. Not just one of the slimy things, but more than I could count. Hopping about and glaring at me with their cold, lifeless eyes."

"They're just silly pranks. The children adore you." Although the housekeeper wore an affectionate smile, her words lacked conviction.

Mrs Booth straightened. "I'm leaving, and that's that."

"What if I ask the master to increase your wages?" Mrs Hibbet sounded desperate. "With Jane away and three staff sick, we're short as it is." She turned to Rose and patted her arm. "Maybe it's a good thing you arrived when you did."

Rose smiled weakly. She had no intention of staying. A ride to Morton Manor was the only thing she needed.

"His lordship could offer me a chest full of jewels, and it wouldn't be enough."

"The children can't be that bad," Rose said.

"Then you tend to them," Mrs Booth countered. "Let's see if you feel the same when you wake to find your hair sheared and those golden ringlets scattered across the floor."

With that, Mrs Booth swung around with an air of determination and continued on her way.

Mrs Hibbet put her hands on her hips. "Oh, that woman is as stubborn as a mule but only half as handsome."

Rose chuckled, but then a wave of sadness washed over her when she noted Mrs Hibbet's grim expression. "What will you do now?"

"Pray to the Lord for a miracle." A weary sigh left the housekeeper's lips. She shook her head as Mrs Booth disappeared into the distance. "Those poor blighters need constant supervision, and as we're short of maids, I must be the one to mind them."

"Can you not get help in the village?"

Mrs Hibbet put a hand on Rose's back and rubbed

affectionately. "Bless you, dear. But the master will only hire staff from the agency in London. He'll not employ anyone from the area."

"Why? Is the mistress not keen to support those in the parish?"

Mrs Hibbet's expression darkened. "There is no mistress at Everleigh, only his lordship and the two children. No. The master is most insistent."

Only a pompous prig would overlook the local girls in favour of those who'd worked in London's best houses. Then again, if Stokes and Mrs Gripes were examples of the servants one could expect to hire, Rose couldn't blame him for looking elsewhere.

"Come, now. There's no point discussing this out in the cold." Mrs Hibbet scanned Rose's cloak and the linen bag she held in her hand. "Is that all the luggage you've brought with you? My, I'm surprised your previous master didn't confiscate your boot laces. Do you have your references?"

References!

Rose swallowed. "Sorry, no. I have nothing in my bag but a few coins and something to eat." How on earth was she to explain her predicament without confessing all? "I … I thought the major had sent them on."

The lie fell from her lips with ease. Why she kept up the charade was beyond her.

Mrs Hibbet's expression brightened. "Never mind." She put her arm around Rose's shoulder. "Let's get you inside. We'll say someone stole your luggage from the mail coach. Once the master hears you speak, he'll know he's hired quality."

Rose opened her mouth to protest—to tell some semblance of the truth—but no words came out. Since as far back as she could remember, she'd been a disappointment.

While the Darbys were renowned for their rich, ebony locks, Rose wore her golden tresses with shame. After all, her father believed her to be the daughter of the groom or the footman or any other poor soul with whom her mother happened to converse.

"Now, it will be an early start in the morning," Mrs Hibbet continued. "We're so short of staff you'll be the parlour maid, the chambermaid and have jobs to do in the laundry."

The housekeeper hugged Rose's arm. The caring gesture made her heart swell.

Perhaps it wouldn't hurt to help the woman during these trying times. Rose stared at the mansion's imposing facade. When her father reached Morton Manor, Mrs Gripes would inform him that his rebellious daughter had fled to London. No one would think to search this house looking for a maid.

But she had to warn Nicole.

"The major always insisted we take a brisk walk before our daily duties," Rose said.

In the daylight, she'd find her way to the manor, find a way to inform Nicole that the earl was staying at The Talbot Inn and race back before anyone stirred from their beds.

"Good Lord." Mrs Hibbet shook her head. "There's no one awake at five except for the birds."

"Five?"

"I don't know the details of your daily schedule with the major, but your duties here begin at six, sharp." Mrs Hibbet pursed her lips. "A walk is the last thing you'll want after just a few hours' sleep."

At the mere mention of sleep, Rose put her hand to her mouth to stifle a yawn. In a matter of hours, Mrs Hibbet expected to see her awake, dressed and ready to do a full day's work. If she planned on taking a trip to the manor, it would be helpful to know if Mrs Hibbet knew a quicker route.

"A man on the mail coach spoke of an old asylum nearby," Rose said as the housekeeper ushered her in through the servants' entrance. "How far is it to Morton Manor?"

"Saints preserve us." Mrs Hibbet made the sign of the cross. She glanced behind them as they made their way along the corridor as if the ghosts of the mentally deranged followed behind. "We don't speak of that place here. Not ever."

A cold shiver ran down Rose's spine.

She'd spent two hundred nights in that grim house. Yes, the icy breeze often appeared from nowhere. Yes, her heart raced and the hairs on her nape prickled for no reason at all.

"If I go for a brisk walk at dawn, is it safe to venture into the woods?"

Mrs Hibbet opened a door and gestured for Rose to enter the small bedchamber. "There's a path over the stile that leads to the village, though no one's used it for some time. Best not wander too far." She clapped her hands. "Now, I'll go and find you a nightgown, though I can't promise it will fit."

Rose slipped off her cloak, eager to climb into bed and rest her weary bones. "Is there fresh water to wash?"

"You can find it yourself if you follow the corridor to the kitchen." The housekeeper gestured to one of two beds. "Jane's gone home to Abberton to nurse her dying mother and won't be back for a week. You'll have the room to yourself till then."

"Thank you, Mrs Hibbet." Rose forced a smile. Her lids were heavy with the need to sleep, and her limbs felt as though they were no longer part of her body.

"I'll get you some ointment for those scratches on your hand and salt to bathe your feet."

Dawn would be upon them by the time Rose had taken care of her ablutions.

"Do you have a name?" Mrs Hibbet asked. "I can't be calling 'my dear' down the stairs, now can I?"

Lady Rose Darby, daughter of the Earl of Stanton.

"Rose."

The woman's curious gaze searched Rose's face. "Happen your mother chose well. Now try to sleep, dear. You have an early start in the morning. I hope your back is up to the task as you must do the work of two."

The work of two? After the months spent at Morton Manor, she'd learnt to style her hair, make and change a bed, and light a fire with a tinderbox. She'd even punched a man to escape her prison.

Nothing could be more difficult than that.

CHAPTER TWO

Christian Knight, seventh Viscount Farleigh, slumped back in the chair behind his desk, closed his eyes and pinched the bridge of his nose. With any luck, he'd misheard Mrs Hibbet. Or perhaps he was living a scene from a terrible nightmare, and he'd wake in a sweat and with a sudden gasp of relief.

"Did you say Mrs Booth has left?" He cleared his throat to prevent a vile curse from escaping. "Surely not. She's been here but a week."

Mrs Hibbet exhaled slowly. "She found toads in her bed, my lord."

"Toads!" During his reckless youth, he'd woken to find the odd toad in his bed, too, but he didn't tear off into the night and turn his back on his responsibilities. "I assume these particular amphibians didn't hop up three flights of stairs and unlock her door with a key?"

"I've no idea how they found their way in here, my lord." Mrs Hibbet raised her chin. If the house came crumbling down around them, she would never blame the children.

"And where are these slippery creatures?"

"Joseph gathered them up in a basket and released them back into the pond."

Christian sat forward. "And so what are we to do now?"

Mrs Hibbet struggled to hold his gaze. "Is … is there any point hiring another governess? After all, the twins are but seven years old. There's plenty of time for tutoring and the like. And I'm not sure a firm hand is what's needed."

In any other household, the master would chastise the staff for pressing their opinion. But in the two years since Cassandra's death, he'd come to look on Mrs Hibbet as a member of the family.

"As their father, you know I cannot tolerate their constant disobedience." He wished to live in peace and harmony. He wished the house rang with laughter. That all their hearts swelled with nothing but love. "Never mind what happened to Mrs Booth. Mrs Marshall could have broken her neck when she slipped on that sticky substance they smothered over the stairs. How long did she last? Ten days?"

The pain in his chest returned.

His children were his only love, his only failure. Well, not quite. His marriage to Cassandra had been a disaster from the beginning. But that's what came from marrying too young.

Christian rubbed his aching temple. "I don't know what to do to help them. The children tell me everything is fine, yet I sense the pain eating away inside."

Mrs Hibbet shuffled forward. "You don't have to make a decision straight away. Why not leave them for a week or two? Let them spend time without the constant rules and regulations."

"We're minus three maids, a groom and a governess." Christian snorted. "We've barely enough staff to keep the fires stoked let alone tend to two children intent on causing mischief. I need to visit the tenants and assess the repairs to the cottages. And Reverend Wilmslow wants me to attend a meeting to discuss the church roof."

Despite being head of an affluent family, and receiving a three hundred pound a year stipend, the reverend was forever snapping at his heels pleading for funds.

"Then it's just as well I've got news that might make things easier." Mrs Hibbet rushed to the door, yanked it open and summoned the person waiting in the hall.

A maid entered and walked up to his desk. She offered a curtsy graceful enough to appease a king. The grey dress should have made her appear dull, her skin sallow, and yet she possessed a natural radiance that lit up the room.

"This is Rose, my lord, come from London." Mrs Hibbet smiled. "She wasn't supposed to arrive until next week. Happen someone saw fit to send us an angel in this great time of need."

Rose.

He could almost smell the sweet, hypnotic scent.

An angel.

Golden hair framed her face like a halo. If he ripped off her white cap, those tresses would come tumbling down in all their glory.

Good God.

Had Christian been a bystander, one party to these inappropriate thoughts, he would have slapped his own face. The woman was a maid in his household. He blamed his heightened emotions and strained nerves on Mrs Booth's departure. It was not like him to forget his place or his manners.

"Welcome to Everleigh, Rose. I trust Mrs Hibbet gave you a tour of the house and grounds."

Rose smiled. "She did, my lord."

"You may leave your references on my desk, and I shall

attend to them later. As I'm sure you're aware, we are short of staff and must pull together during difficult times."

The maid opened her mouth to speak, but Mrs Hibbet tapped her on the arm.

"As to the matter of references, my lord." Mrs Hibbet blinked too many times to count. "There was a dreadful accident on the road, and someone stole Rose's valise. She arrived late last night with nothing but the clothes on her back. It's why she slept in late this morning."

Christian stared at them both for a moment. Neither met his gaze.

"Indeed." He'd shared a house with Mrs Hibbet for nigh on fifteen years, was just a boy when she took the position. She had lied to him only once before. "What sort of accident?"

"There's only one sort of accident, my lord," Mrs Hibbet replied with a snort. "An unfortunate one."

Christian focused his gaze on the new maid. "You will tell me what happened on the road."

Deceit was a trait he despised, could never tolerate. Short-staffed or not, he'd have the truth from the maid, or she'd be on the next mail coach to London. Perhaps that wouldn't be such a bad idea. Rose proved to be far too distracting, and he'd never had cause to doubt his integrity before.

The apples of Rose's cheeks flushed pink. She swallowed three or four times, sucked in so many breaths there could hardly be any room left in her lungs.

"Well, Rose? What have you to say?"

With wide eyes, the woman stared at him. "There wasn't an accident. I … I lied to Mrs Hibbet because I have no references."

"There, that wasn't too difficult, was it?" He admired the strength it took to tell the truth when one's livelihood was at stake. "And why are you without references when it is a condition of your employment? Surely Mr Burns made that clear at the registry office."

"It's not Rose's fault, my lord." Mrs Hibbet jumped to the maid's defence. "She told me about the references and … well, we're so short of maids … I …"

"You thought it wouldn't matter?"

Was his housekeeper suffering from memory loss? Had she forgotten that he'd thrown a footman out for the part he'd played in Cassandra's charade?

Mrs Hibbet had the decency to hang her head.

Christian turned his attention to the maid. "Were you sent by Mr Burns from the registry office?"

"No, my lord." The maid raised her chin and took on an air of hauteur usually reserved for society's elite.

"Then pray tell me what you're doing here."

"It is all a terrible misunderstanding." Rose turned to Mrs Hibbet and mouthed a silent apology. "I was on my way to Morton Manor but got lost in the woods."

"Morton Manor?" The name filled him with dread. He was aware there were servants at the old asylum, but as yet, no residents had called at Everleigh to make an introduction. "Why were you going there?"

"To work. I was to report to Mrs Gripes, the housekeeper. Indeed, if you would be kind enough to provide an escort, you would have my utmost gratitude."

She curtsied. Not the quick dip offered by maids but a slow, elegant movement that spoke of refinement and good breeding. Her elocution was faultless. Rose had no references because he suspected she'd never worked a day in her life.

"May I see your hands?"

"Certainly."

She offered him her hand. Two red scratches marred the

otherwise porcelain skin. And yet it crossed his mind to bring it to his lips and place a chaste kiss on her creamy-white knuckles. Feeling a sudden flutter of nerves, he took hold of her fingers, ignored the slight tremble and examined the soft tips.

"The position at Morton Manor—" Christian stopped abruptly and suppressed a grimace. He'd survived two years without that name falling from his lips, and yet he'd spoken the words aloud twice in a matter of minutes. "Was it to be your first post?"

"It was."

"And yet no one is in residence."

"No, my lord. There's a housekeeper, a maid and a few other servants."

"And who is your employer?"

The maid hesitated. "It is not for me to discuss his lordship's business."

Christian remained silent while he studied her. Rose had obviously fallen on hard times and had no choice but to work. Everyone in the village complained about the servants at the manor. Some called them rude. Others preferred the term *vicious*. A woman of Rose's delicate nature would be a prime candidate for abuse.

"And what of your history, Rose?"

"My personal affairs are not open for discussion, my lord. Please direct me back to the manor, and I shall leave you in peace."

Peace? This woman's sweet smile and bright countenance would haunt his dreams.

It was as he suspected. A tragic family story had left her with no means of support. Had a brother with a gambling addiction squandered the funds? One thing was certain. He'd suffer eternal damnation before he'd let anyone with half an ounce of decency work in that iniquitous den.

"What is your employer paying you? Perhaps I might match it in the hope you'll accept a position here. After all, we are in dire need of help."

"Paying me?"

"I assume you're not working out of the goodness of your heart."

Rose's bottom lip quivered. "Erm … eighteen pounds."

Christian bit back a chuckle. "Is that not steep for a housemaid with no experience?" He couldn't blame the woman for trying to haggle another pound or two.

"Not for a maid with an excellent education," Rose countered.

He was about to say what use is knowledge when it comes to sweeping the grate, but then it occurred to him that he was also short of a governess. Of course, he'd have to observe the woman carefully before agreeing to unrestricted access to his children.

"Then I offer you twenty pounds per annum to work here, and one new dress and bonnet to wear to church on Sundays."

Mrs Hibbet gasped.

"Rest assured, Mrs Hibbet. I shall increase all other household wages, too." It was the least he could do under the circumstances. None of his staff had complained about the current working conditions. "We shall meet this afternoon and discuss the matter."

"Thank you, my lord." Mrs Hibbet clutched her hands to her chest. "Poor Matilda is struggling to clean the rooms and do the laundry."

"Then the increase in wages will convey my appreciation." He focused his attention on Rose. "Well, will you take a position here?"

Silence ensued.

If she only knew of the horrors that had occurred at the manor, she wouldn't hesitate to agree to his offer.

Rose finally nodded. "I will accept the position on two conditions."

Christian sat back in the chair. Never in all his years as owner of Everleigh had he bargained with a maid. He doubted the six viscounts before had, either. "What are your terms?"

"I ask that a groom accompany me to the manor so I may inform them of my new situation."

Christian nodded. It was a fair request. Had she not asked for an escort, he would have insisted upon one.

"And you will allow me to work for one week without wages." Rose raised her chin and squared her shoulders. It was apparent that the matter was not up for negotiation. "A trial period is necessary to avoid any bad feeling should either of us wish to part company."

Curiosity burned.

The woman had nothing but the clothes on her back. What possible reason could she have for leaving? Then again, a maid this pretty had every right to be apprehensive about the moral character of her master.

"You certainly know how to strike a deal." Perhaps her father had been a wealthy merchant and lost his fortune on a string of poor investments. "Although such a bargain appears to work in my favour."

A coy smile formed on her lips and he struggled to tear his gaze away. "You have yet to witness the quality of my work, my lord."

"As Mrs Hibbet has gone to the trouble of finding you a uniform, then perhaps it's time you showed me."

Christian gestured to the fireplace. The grate was filthy and piled with ash.

"It just so happened there was a dress to fit," Mrs Hibbet added.

Rose wore the grey dress like a second skin. If he didn't know better, he'd suspect Mrs Hibbet had hired the services of London's most coveted modiste. Indeed, the last thing he needed was to give the snug garment covering the new maid's body any further scrutiny.

"You may leave us, Mrs Hibbet. Rose will return with the coal scuttle and lay the fire for this evening." He remembered her request to visit the manor. "Once she's completed the morning chores, you will inform Dawkins he must accompany her to Morton Manor."

"Thank you, my lord." Rose offered him a beaming smile. "I promise to be no longer than an hour."

A deep sense of foreboding gripped him at the thought of her coming within a hundred yards of the place. Evil lingered within its walls. The essence of people's misery contaminated the surrounding air. The asylum closed its doors two years ago, but he could not forget all that had happened there.

"On second thoughts, I shall go with you." He'd get nothing done while waiting for her safe return. "You've lost your way once, and the woods can be treacherous, even by day."

It was not an exaggeration.

A murderer lingered in their midst. He'd suspected so for years.

CHAPTER THREE

The thought of spending any time alone with Lord
Farleigh created a strange fluttering in Rose's chest.
Oh, it was ridiculous. The gentleman possessed such a
commanding presence she really did feel like a lowly maid.
And now he expected her to clean and lay the fire while he
watched.

Her hands were still shaking when she returned to the
study with the brush and pan and knelt down in front of the
hearth.

While locked in the manor with Nicole, they'd had no
choice but to prepare and light the fire in their bedchamber.
Even so, Nicole refused to allow her to attend to the task.

"You're Lady Rose Darby," Nicole often said to raise
Rose's spirits, to remind her she had a life beyond the prison
walls. "You'll not dirty your hands while I'm paid to care
for you."

But her father hadn't paid Nicole anything for her trouble.
She'd given her love and friendship freely. And her reward
amounted to untold days and nights spent with a group of
spiteful rogues. By now the house would be in chaos, Mrs

Gripes' screeches ringing through the cold corridors while
Stokes tore the place apart.

"Are you going to put a rag on the floor to protect the
Persian rug?" Lord Farleigh's words dragged Rose from her
reverie.

"Forgive me, my lord, I ... I'm a little distracted today."

Rose picked up the old sheet and spread it out over
the floor.

Lord Farleigh said nothing, but she could hear his shallow
breath, sensed his penetrative gaze drifting over her while she
swept out the ash and debris. Perhaps that was the reason her
limbs were as heavy as lead, why she dropped the brush and
knocked over the contents of the pan.

They were green, those penetrating eyes that made a
lady's heart race whenever she found the courage to stare into
them. Not the washed-out colour one often mistook for pale
blue, but like a rare piece of jade enhanced with flecks of
emerald. Rich. Captivating.

"You're brushing more ash onto your apron than you are
into the pan."

Rose acknowledged his comment with a nod. She didn't
dare glance back over her shoulder. To meet his gaze would
only make her task more arduous. Trembling fingers were a
hindrance when sweeping.

"Have you cleaned a fire before?"

"A few times." It was a lie. She should have paid more
attention when Nicole performed the task. "Never with
anyone watching me so closely."

The desk chair scraped against the boards. Four long
strides and he was at her side.

Lord Farleigh towered over her. "But you know to wash
the marble hearth and dry it thoroughly with a linen cloth?"

Frustration turned to annoyance. "I can clean the fire

without assistance. I do not need you to stand over me like an overbearing parent."

Rose sucked in a breath. She hadn't meant to sound so rude and disrespectful, but she'd grown tired of subservience. And how was she supposed to concentrate when fears for Nicole's welfare was at the forefront of her mind? Squaring her hunched shoulders, she braced herself for a severe reprimand.

Instead, Lord Farleigh did something far worse. He squatted down at her side, those well-developed thigh muscles almost bursting the seams of his breeches. A whiff of spicy cologne filled her nostrils and journeyed south to tickle her stomach.

"I am merely trying to help," he said in a soft drawl, "though I am aware that my tone can sound condescending at times. It is evident you're used to others doing these tasks for you." A sigh left his lips and breezed past her ear. "What I'm trying to say is that the transition will not be easy."

Rose stared at her dirty hands. "No, it's not."

It wasn't the menial jobs she found distressing. It wasn't sleeping on a lumpy mattress or wearing the itchy dress that clung to her body in all the wrong places. It was the uncertainty of it all that gripped her around the throat and threatened to squeeze.

Was her father liable to appear at the door and drag her back to London?

What had happened to Nicole when the servants had woken to find mutiny afoot?

"I'm a little homesick," she said, turning to face him. Even though home had never been a pleasant place for her, she missed the familiarity that came with waking in one's own bed.

"Is this your first time away?" He stared at her lips and chin.

To offer any explanation would only result in more lies. The intimacy of the moment, coupled with the hint of compassion in those green eyes, proved unnerving. After all, he was a viscount. A gentleman of his status should not be kneeling on the floor offering words of comfort to a maid.

"You must feel a certain sense of peace, my lord, knowing this will always be your home and that no one can take it away from you." She didn't expect an answer. By rights, he should insist she get on with her work.

"One foolish investment and I could lose everything." He dragged his hand through his dark brown hair as his gaze dropped to her mouth once again. "A man must keep his wits if he has any hope of safeguarding his family's future."

Rose imagined the viscount was too intelligent to sink funds into a failing venture. But something kept him awake at night. The shadows beneath his lower lids were a testament to that. While he appeared physically capable of running a mile without stopping for breath, his countenance held a world-weary air.

What plagued his thoughts and haunted his dreams?

When left alone did he lay his head on his desk? Did he close his eyes and pray for salvation?

"Many a drunken sot has gambled away his fortune," she eventually said, aware that she should do something other than stare. "You don't strike me as a man with a weakness for either vice."

Indeed, she doubted he did anything to excess.

"My father taught me to avoid things that corrupt the mind or taint one's reputation." Sadness swam in his eyes. "And now I must set an example for my children."

It crossed her mind to ask about Mrs Booth, about his

inability to keep a governess. But maids did not pry. And with her soft heart, she was bound to offer her services. Her fate lay elsewhere. When the week was up, she would make her way to London, find Lord Cunningham and hope he'd not taken another bride in her absence. Escaping her father's grasp had to be the priority.

"And what a poor example I'm setting," she said, wondering how often he partook in intimate conversations with the maids. "Mrs Hibbet expects me upstairs, and I've not yet laid the fire."

"Then I shall leave you to your work."

"And do you promise not to interfere when I make a mess of things? After all, how's a maid to learn if not from her own experiences?"

"A lady with your manners and education should not be sweeping fires."

"You could always hire me as your paid companion." He looked as though he needed someone to share his troubles, someone to share a drink with and discuss the events of the day.

"Perhaps if you decide to stay at Everleigh, I might consider your proposal."

Rose couldn't help but smile. "After the useless job I've done here, it might be the sensible option."

This time when he looked at her lips, the corners of his mouth twitched. "You have ash on your chin."

Heat rose to her cheeks. And all the while she'd imagined him looking at her for an entirely different reason.

"I'd rather have ash on my chin than on your rug." She used the clean edge of her apron to wipe it away. "Has it gone?"

"No. It's right there."

Rose rubbed a little harder this time. "Surely that's it."

"Here." He removed a handkerchief from the inside pocket of his coat. "Allow me to assist you."

The viscount moved closer and brushed the silk softly across her chin.

Heavens above. Every nerve in her body sparked to life. She couldn't look at his face and instead focused on the picture behind him of a ship sailing across the sea in the moonlight. The lump in her throat grew larger by the second. The heady scent of his cologne made her dizzy. Her breathing grew so shallow he must have noticed.

She cleared her throat.

Lord Farleigh stilled and then jumped to his feet as though the tails of his coat were on fire. "There. One cannot walk about the house with dirt on their chin." His sharp tone was so opposed to the care he'd shown but a moment earlier.

"I thank you for your assistance, my lord." Oh, her voice sounded fractured, so affected by these bizarre sensations rippling through her.

Still kneeling in front of the fire, Rose turned back to the hearth and brushed the grate once more. She heard him retreat, knew the moment he sat back in his chair and dipped the nib of his pen into the glass ink pot.

Channelling the strength of two men, she carried in the coal scuttle and set about preparing the fire. Lord Farleigh never spoke again, but the harsh scratching of the nib on paper conveyed either annoyance or frustration.

With the task completed, she adopted the manner of all good parlour maids and slipped out without a word or glance. Only when safely out of the room did she breathe freely again.

Why did the viscount affect her so?

She had kissed Lord Cunningham and not experienced the same fluttering in her belly. Although, in all fairness, it had been a swift brush of the lips. A chaste kiss that held a hint of promise. Or at least it had until her father spirited her away from London in the dead of night and kept her locked in a rural prison.

"There you are." Mrs Hibbet descended the stairs. "Have you forgotten you were to come and tidy the nursery?"

"I'm just on my way up." She suppressed a groan. Her back ached, and she'd love nothing more than to sit down with a cup of tea.

"It will be a good time to meet the children."

Rose knew nothing of Jacob and Alice other than they were twins aged seven, almost eight, and that they loved to tease and taunt their governess.

"Should I come armed with my pan and brush?"

Mrs Hibbet gave a weak chuckle. "As the maid, you've nothing to fear."

The sound of carriage wheels crunching on the gravel drive brought Foster, the butler, out from his secret hiding place somewhere beyond the stairs.

"Happen it's Dr Taylor and the Reverend Wilmslow," Mrs Hibbet whispered. "They call once a week to tend to those who are sick. The reverend likes a tipple and comes to sample his lordship's best port amongst other things."

"How many servants are ill?" Rose said. It was common to find two maids with a cold, more so to find a footman and a maid suffering from the same symptoms. But their recovery usually lasted no more than a day or two.

So why did Dr Taylor need to visit weekly?

"It varies." Mrs Hibbet sighed. They lingered in the background waiting to catch sight of the visitors. "This week it's two maids and a groom."

"This week?"

"They've not found the source of the infection. Those

who are ill recover in a week or so. But next month another member of staff will take to his bed with a fever."

Before Rose could question Mrs Hibbet further, Foster greeted the new arrivals.

"The gentleman on the left is Dr Taylor." Mrs Hibbet spoke as though the man were a saint sent down from heaven to ease their burden. "The fellow on the right is the Reverend Wilmslow, clergyman of the Abberton parsonage. But don't let that fool you."

There wasn't time to ask the housekeeper what she meant. Foster announced the gentlemen and Lord Farleigh stepped out into the hall to greet them.

Upon seeing the viscount, the little flutter in Rose's belly flew up to her chest and then her throat. His discreet glance in her direction caused the whole process to begin again.

Dr Taylor was of a similar age to Lord Farleigh. With golden hair and a kind smile, it was clear why the man had chosen such a caring profession. The Reverend Wilmslow was a little older, with wisps of white littering the dark hair at his temples. Evidently noting Lord Farleigh's covert gaze, the reverend turned, perused her from head to toe and then smiled.

"A man of God knows it's rude to look away when someone's speaking," Mrs Hibbet whispered.

The transgression was mild compared to most sins, and yet the mischievous glint in the reverend's eye suggested a fondness for his female parishioners. One that went beyond the need to nurture the soul.

Lord Farleigh led the men into his study and Foster closed the door.

Mrs Hibbet exhaled. "Come, I'd best take you up to meet the children. The doctor will want to examine the patients before he leaves and I insist on being present." There was a grave edge to the woman's tone.

"Don't you trust the doctor?"

"Oh, it's not the doctor you need to fear. The reverend likes to say a few words to bring comfort, or relate a biblical story about healing if there's time." The words dripped with cynicism. "Healing's best done with the hands, if you take my meaning."

Rose wanted to pretend that she didn't, for the thought of any man taking advantage of a woman in such a vulnerable state made her feel cold to her bones.

"Then I pray I'm not struck down with the mystery illness."

"No doubt Dr Taylor will give you a restorative. It's helped me keep the devil at bay."

Rose lacked faith in the ability of tonics and tinctures. Once, Mrs Gripes had put an odd herb in her tea to make her docile. Nicole tasted it immediately and refused to take any refreshment unless she'd made the drink herself.

The sudden chime of the long-case clock in the hall drew her back to the present. The eleventh clang was a mocking reminder of her failure to wake in time to warn her friend. The last five hours had passed by in a blur. If she didn't finish the morning chores, she had no hope of venturing over to the manor.

"You'd best wash your hands and meet me upstairs," Mrs Hibbet said. "We'll be working until midnight if we stand here gossiping."

Ten minutes later, Rose climbed the stairs to the second floor.

Although Mrs Hibbet referred to the room as a nursery, it was more a large playroom than a place for children to sleep.

A single wooden desk sat in front of a window too high for a child to look out. A dapple rocking horse with a silver mane and red leather saddle took pride of place in one corner. A doll's house with a facade identical to Everleigh stood on a stand in the other. Scattered about the floor were puppets with tangled strings, wooden soldiers, sticks and odd stockings.

How was such a cold, dull room supposed to inspire a child?

Mrs Hibbet crouched until eye level with the boy and girl with sad eyes and down-turned lips. She held the children's hands, and Rose wasn't sure if the housekeeper was offering comfort or chastising them for a misdeed.

"There now," Mrs Hibbet said as she patted both children on the arm. "Come and meet Rose. She'll help me care for you now Mrs Booth has left."

With a groan and a hand on her lower back, Mrs Hibbet stood and waved the children forward. They came to a stop a few feet away. Rose waited for the boy to bow, the girl to curtsy. It wasn't until Mrs Hibbet cleared her throat that Rose remembered she was the subordinate.

"I'm Rose." She smiled and offered a graceful curtsy. "The new maid."

"Introduce yourself," Mrs Hibbet prompted when the children failed to reply.

"I'm Jacob," the boy said. He held his chin high, his shoulders straight. With thick dark hair and piercing green eyes, Jacob was the image of his father. "And this is Alice. We'll be eight next month and don't need your help."

Alice hung her head. She had the same dark hair as her brother, but her eyes were blue. No one could accuse these children of being the offspring of anyone other than Lord Farleigh.

After hearing Mrs Booth's gripes and grumbles, Rose knew to expect a certain amount of hostility. "Then I pray you take care when working in the kitchen. The plates are hot, and Cook is so busy she forgets to tell you."

Alice chuckled, and Jacob nudged her to be quiet.

"And remember to lay a sheet on the floor when you're cleaning out the fire," Rose continued. "I would have made a terrible mess had your father not reminded me."

Jacob scowled.

"Of course, if you would prefer I fetch your meals and light the fire, I am only too willing to oblige."

"You're not a maid." Jacob narrowed his emerald eyes. The boy was right to be suspicious. "And you can't be the new governess."

"And you are far too astute for your age." Rose noted his surprise upon hearing the compliment. "I'm a lady in need of work as I'm alone and far from home."

The explanation held some semblance of the truth.

"Where's your family?" Alice's sweet voice was devoid of hatred or malice.

"I don't know."

Her father could well be at Morton Manor. Her brother, Oliver, was in Italy, and yet Rose doubted it was far away enough to escape their father's foul temper. A pang of sadness filled her chest whenever she thought of her brother. Once they had been inseparable, had stood together, just like Jacob and Alice, stood strong against the torrent of verbal abuse.

"Is that why you're crying?" Alice said.

Rose dabbed her eyes with the pads of her fingers, surprised to find them damp. "My brother is a thousand miles away, but I would give anything to have him here standing next to me, taking care of me as your brother is eager to do."

Oliver surely knew nothing of her incarceration at Morton Manor else he would have rushed home and fought the guards with his bare fists to free her.

Alice glanced at Jacob with a look of love and admiration.

"Now." Rose inhaled to prevent the water filling her eyes from dripping down her cheeks. "I wish to make a pact with you."

"A pact?" Jacob's eyes widened despite an effort to maintain an impassive expression.

"Indeed." Rose met Mrs Hibbet's wary gaze but turned her attention back to the children. "If you're left in my care, I shall suggest an activity to occupy our time."

"What if we don't like your idea?" Jacob replied.

"Then we will discuss the matter until we can agree."

Mrs Hibbet stepped forward. "We must wait until the master decides who's working up here before we make any plans."

"Of course." Rose was being presumptuous. But, having lost her mother at a young age, too, she understood how grief manifested in other ways. Hostility and hatred were masks often used to hide pain. "Well, I'm sure I'll get to spend at least an hour a day with you."

"Mrs Booth had a strict routine," Mrs Hibbet said. "His lordship won't want the children to grow idle in her absence. Rules keep the mischievous mind out of trouble."

"Did Lord Farleigh say that?"

"No. It was another governess, Mrs Marshall, though I'm not of the same mind."

"All governesses say the same," Jacob said. Clearly, the boy despised women who wore tight top knots and itchy grey dresses.

Rose put her hand to her chest and sighed. "Then thank goodness I'm not one of them. So, do you accept my proposal?"

Jacob turned to Alice and whispered in her ear. The girl nodded, and a giggle escaped as she struggled to contain her excitement.

"We accept," Jacob said in a commanding voice worthy of the heir to a viscountcy.

"Excellent. Perhaps Mrs Hibbet can speak to your father so that I may attend to you for some part of the day."

Both children turned to the housekeeper.

Mrs Hibbet shuffled uncomfortably on the spot. "We'll see what he says. Now, Cook's made shortbread biscuits and said you could both have one if you come straight away."

The children's eyes lit up, and they rushed from the room.

"Don't run down the stairs," Mrs Hibbet shouted after them. After a brief pause, she turned to Rose. "I know you're trying to be kind, but you shouldn't make promises you can't keep. Those tykes have been through enough these last two years, and it's not good for them to get too attached to any one person."

Rose swallowed down the lump in her throat. "The last thing I want is to hurt them."

"I know. I know, dear." Mrs Hibbet patted Rose's arm. "The idea has merit. Happen there's something you could teach them while we wait for his lordship to hire another governess."

"How many governesses have the children had?"

Mrs Hibbet glanced at the ceiling while counting on her fingers. "At least ten, not counting Mrs Booth."

"Ten? Surely someone has sat them down to find out what's wrong."

"They usually leave without giving notice."

Rose shook her head. "I was speaking of the children."

Mrs Hibbet stared at her blankly. Had no one thought to examine why the children drove their governesses away? Had Lord Farleigh not connected the incidents to his wife's death? Perhaps they had but didn't know how to address the problem.

The sound of footsteps on the stairs drew their attention.

Alfred, the footman, appeared at the door. "His lordship needs you downstairs. Dr Taylor and the Reverend Wilmslow want to examine Ann and Jenny, and he's asked that you're present. And they have a tonic for you, Rose, to stop you from catching the fever."

Under no circumstances would she let a drop of the doctor's medicine pass her lips.

"We'll be right down." Mrs Hibbet ushered Alfred from the room. "I'll leave you to tidy the nursery, Rose, and then you'd better call at the manor and inform them of your new position."

Rose shivered at the thought of returning to the old house. Guilt flared, too. While she'd cleaned the fire, and daydreamed about his lordship's dazzling green eyes, Nicole had to explain her actions to Stokes and Mrs Gripes.

But she couldn't worry about that now. The sooner she tidied the nursery, the sooner she could leave for the manor and discover the truth for herself.

"Can I ask you a question?" Rose stared at the cluttered floor.

"By all means."

"Where are the children's beds, and why is the playroom up here?"

Mrs Hibbet raised a brow. "That's two questions, dear." She glanced back over her shoulder. "But I suppose a brief explanation can't hurt."

Something about the housekeeper's expression suggested Everleigh was a house of many secrets.

"Lady Farleigh suffered with her nerves," Mrs Hibbet said. "The noise was too much for her, and she had the nursery moved up here so she could sleep during the day. When she died, Lord Farleigh moved the children's beds to the room next to the master suite, and they've stayed there ever since."

"I see."

Had their mother's illness affected the children's emotional well-being long before her death? Rose knew what it was like to feel unwanted by a parent. As far as the Earl of Stanton was concerned, Rose was another man's by-blow. A legacy left after one of her mother's supposed affairs.

"I'd best see to the reverend before he takes matters into his own hands if you get my meaning." Without another word, Mrs Hibbet hurried from the room.

Rose stared at the mess on the floor. It would take an hour to tidy the children's belongings. But come what may, she had to learn of Nicole's fate before the day was out.

I shall accompany you. The woods can be treacherous, even by day.

Lord Farleigh's words rang in her ears.

But what would she do if she found her father's carriage waiting in the courtyard of Morton Manor? How would she explain the situation to Lord Farleigh? Perhaps she should go alone, say she'd misunderstood his lordship's intentions, that she thought him too busy with the doctor.

Wasn't it better he thought her a little simple? From what she'd heard he had no tolerance for liars, nor did she suspect he had any tolerance for a lady intent on deceit.

CHAPTER FOUR

"You want to search every room in the house?" Christian sat back in the chair and stared at Dr Taylor and Reverend Wilmslow seated on the opposite side of the desk. "For what purpose?"

"To determine if the source of the contagion is inside as opposed to somewhere else on the grounds." Dr Taylor pointed to the long list of names and dates in the leather-bound book lying open on the desk. "At some point or other everyone in the house has been ill. You cannot carry on like this, my lord. Something must be done."

"But you've searched the house twice." Some areas more times than he cared to count. He'd not have them rummaging through the rooms again. "Besides, you said the sickness stems from contact with a poisonous plant."

Dr Taylor had dragged him around the grounds of Everleigh numerous times, examining various species looking for a reason to account for the strange illness.

"Based on the symptoms, lethargy, fever, stiffness of joints, I can think of no other explanation."

Wilmslow took another sip of his tea and placed the cup

and saucer on the desk. "There's a botanist, Hudson, who's just returned from the Indies, spent years studying all manner of species. His theory is that the spores from some plants can get caught in clothes, can hide in all sorts of strange places."

Christian failed to keep abreast of scientific developments. Since Cassandra's death, his children's happiness and the smooth running of Everleigh monopolised his time. Even so, the theory sounded improbable.

"If you're suggesting that there are spores from dangerous plants somewhere in this house I'd have to disagree." The idea was ludicrous. "The illness started almost two years ago. Surely nothing could survive indoors for that long."

And yet Cassandra's restless behaviour and constant fatigue bore a resemblance to the symptoms shown by his staff. If so, it meant that she'd come into contact with the source long before the spate of illnesses began. If only he could be sure. Perhaps he could have prevented her demise. Perhaps then he wouldn't feel so guilty for not loving her as he should have.

Dr Taylor pushed his hand through his mop of hair. "Then we shall have to interview the staff again. We must take our search beyond the perimeter of Everleigh."

"Dare I suggest you seek permission to venture onto Morton Manor's land?" Wilmslow said, despite knowing how Christian felt about the old place. "And perhaps a more thorough examination of the patients might offer a clue. Any sign of a rash or swelling on the chest might help with the diagnosis."

Dr Taylor shuffled uncomfortably in the chair. "Mrs Hibbet assured us that was not the case."

As the youngest son of a baron, Wilmslow went to Cambridge, while Taylor attended Oxford and then studied under the previous doctor of the parish. Consequently, the reverend outranked him and often used the fact to press his point.

As a viscount and master of the house, Christian was grateful he outranked them both.

"Mrs Hibbet is neither a doctor nor a man of God," Wilmslow countered. He turned his attention to Christian. "Was that a new maid I saw hovering at the bottom of the stairs? I don't recall seeing her at church last Sunday."

"Rose joined the staff yesterday," Christian said as his thoughts returned to the moment he'd flagrantly ignored the rules of propriety and brushed ash from her chin.

Damn it all. He'd have to avoid her where possible.

Something happened in the air when they were in the same room. The hairs on his nape prickled sending delicious waves of excitement rippling through his body. When Rose smiled, he felt a tug deep in his core. While every fibre of his being longed for a distraction from the months of misery, he would not degrade himself or his staff by succumbing to the weaknesses of the flesh.

For heaven's sake, she was a maid! Strictly off-limits. Out of bounds. He should be blind to her full lips and beguiling blue eyes.

Guilt flared.

But he was not to blame. He was attracted to the educated lady, to the gentleman's daughter who had no choice but to work for a living. Damn. Rose should not be working as a maid, regardless of her financial struggles. It had taken a tremendous amount of strength not to race to her aid and offer to carry the scuttle, to assist her in the mundane task. Perhaps he should offer her the job of governess, at least until he found a more permanent solution. The position would suit her gentle breeding, and he needed someone to watch over the children. But what decent father would trust his children to a stranger without references?

"My lord?" The sound of Dr Taylor clearing his throat dragged Christian from his musings. "Would you like me to examine the new maid? I suggest she takes a tonic to prevent her from contracting the illness."

The last thing Christian needed was another member of his staff becoming ill. "Rose must give her permission before I can allow you to administer any medicine."

Dr Taylor nodded. "Well, I'm due at the Browns' to check on young Harold's leg. Speak to your maid while I see how the rest of your staff are faring. The illness usually lasts a little more than a week, so I expect both the maids and the groom to be up and about in a few days."

Christian stood, tugged on the bell cord and instructed Foster to find Mrs Hibbet. Since the misunderstanding with Wilmslow and another maid, Jane, Christian insisted on a chaperone.

"Of course, if one believes the gossip, there is another explanation for the bad luck you encounter here at Everleigh." The reverend spoke in the elevated tone of those schooled by the Divine.

Wilmslow referred to the old asylum. They'd discussed the sinister goings-on there many times during the past two years. "I agree there is something morbid about Morton Manor," Christian said, eager to put paid to any lengthy conversation on the subject. "But I do not believe in witchcraft or superstition."

That was not entirely true. He did not believe a house could be evil but often contemplated whether the adverse experiences of its occupants had a lasting effect on any future inhabitants.

"One cannot believe in God without acknowledging the

40

Devil." Wilmslow raised his hands. "I was simply going to suggest that your staff keep a diary of their whereabouts. Perhaps one of them ventured to the manor and contracted the illness there. Regardless of what you believe, many think the place is cursed."

"Then perhaps we are in need of a few extra prayers." Christian gestured to the hall in a bid to hurry the men along. "And yet they do not appear to have helped these last two years."

"Have faith, my lord." Wilmslow rose from the chair. "One must never lose hope. The Lord shall reveal his plan in due course."

The reverend's tone held the same pompous air often used by the righteous to cement their status as preaching windbags.

"Ah, Mrs Hibbet," Christian said as they met the housekeeper in the hall. "Will you show Dr Taylor and Reverend Wilmslow to the servants' quarters. I'll be working in my study should there be anything you wish to discuss."

Dr Taylor turned to him and bowed. "We'll not trouble you when we leave, my lord. I'll give Mrs Hibbet the tonic for the new maid."

Christian inclined his head. "Then I shall say good day to you, gentlemen."

He returned to the study, closed the door and examined the ledger. The monthly expenditure for his house in Berkeley Square failed to distract his thoughts from his impending visit to Morton Manor. Since Cassandra's death, he'd avoided the place. Even so, the memory of all that occurred there was not as easy to ignore.

The clock on the mantel chimed once, and he contemplated whether there was time to eat before Rose knocked to say she'd completed the morning chores.

His thoughts wandered.

How would they get to the manor? Would they walk together in silence? Or would she tell him about the family tragedy that left her alone to fend for herself?

Dipping the nib of his pen into the ink pot, he recorded the bills for the last month into the leather-bound book.

Would they ride there together? Would she sit between his thighs with the wind whipping her hair?

The knock on the door pulled him from his fanciful musings.

Mrs Hibbet entered. "Just to let you know that Dr Taylor and Reverend Wilmslow have left. Both Jenny and Ann should be able to resume their duties in a day or two, and David can return to the stables tomorrow."

"Let them rest until the end of the week." He wondered if the problem with the continual reinfection stemmed from the servants rushing back to work. "But explain that they must remain confined to their room until we're certain the illness has passed."

"Yes, my lord." Mrs Hibbet hovered at his desk, her lips pursed for there was obviously more she wanted to say. "And I … I thought you should know that the children like Rose."

That was a contradiction. Alice liked most people. Jacob despised everyone.

"Rose has asked if she can tend to them," Mrs Hibbet continued, "take them for their afternoon walk and sit with them when they do their sums."

Christian contemplated the request.

"We know nothing about her. By her own admission, she ventured here by mistake."

All the old fears and doubts resurfaced. Trust was not something he gave freely. After his experience with Mr Watson, the previous warden of the manor, it was not something he gave at all.

"People say I'm a good judge of character." Mrs Hibbet straightened her shoulders. "And all I see when I look at Rose is a woman with a good heart who wants to please the children."

"The children cannot afford any more disruption in their lives."

God damn, he was a hypocrite. He was the one who'd hired one governess after another in the hope one of them would help ease their misery. Oh, he'd made a bloody mess of everything.

"Does that mean you won't be hiring a replacement for Mrs Booth?"

"No." The word slipped from his mouth. "You're right. The children need to spend time with those they know and trust. Rose is a stranger."

He wasn't just thinking of the children. For some obscure reason, he didn't want to frighten Rose away, and Jacob enjoyed testing those paid to care for them.

"Perhaps when we know her a little better," he added, noting the disappointment etched on Mrs Hibbet's face. "I'm to escort Rose to Morton Manor. It's only right we inform the housekeeper there of the change in her situation."

As master of the house, he did not need to explain or justify his actions. But as expected, Mrs Hibbet's mouth dropped open.

"You really are going to the manor then, my lord?"

"I am." It was time to put the past behind him. Time to face his demons.

"But I assumed you'd changed your mind." Two deep furrows appeared between Mrs Hibbet's brows. "Rose has already left."

"Left?" Fear trickled like ice-cold water through his

veins. God damn, he'd told her not to go alone. "Did anyone accompany her?"

Macabre images of Miss Stoneway's dead body, sprawled face up in the woods, flashed through his mind. The look of terror in the poor woman's eyes visited him often in his nightmares.

"I don't know, my lord. I presume she asked Dawkins."

Christian shot out of the chair. "That will be all, Mrs Hibbet. I shall be out of the house for the next hour."

Without further comment, he strode from the room and made his way to the stables. One glance inside the stalls, and he could account for all his staff. They must have thought he'd lost his faculties, racing about and mumbling to himself.

"Can I help you, my lord?" Jack stopped brushing the chestnut mare and waited for a reply.

"Saddle my horse and be quick about it. I've urgent business that cannot wait."

Jack set to work straight away. Still, it wasn't quick enough to ease the pounding in Christian's chest.

What in hell's name was wrong with him?

Rose was a maid on an errand. She was not Cassandra, not a woman hell-bent on causing mischief whenever the opportunity arose. And there were no patients at Morton Manor. Not anymore. But then the insane were not the ones they need fear.

CHAPTER FIVE

The ten-minute ride to Morton Manor passed by in a blur. The pressure in Christian's head started as a mild pulsing in his temples, but the dull pain built until it mimicked the pounding of his horse's hooves on the dirt track.

Had he not been galloping at full pace, he would have massaged the back of his neck to ease the mounting tension. And yet the odd sensations plaguing him were so different from those he'd experienced on the night he'd searched for Cassandra.

Fear made him lose his grasp on reality now. Anger had been the only thing driving him then, and perhaps a deep sense of disappointment. He'd known what to expect when he eventually found his wife and the warden. Cassandra stopped arguing about his insistence she receive help for her anxiety. She'd gone from refusing to move from her bed to demanding the maid style her hair in a fancy coiffure. From being too tired to wash to bathing her body in exotic oils and dabbing her skin with expensive perfume.

Christian may have been a fool, but he was not blind.

Had it not been for the children he'd have gone to London, lived separately from the woman he should never have married. But one did not leave those most precious in precarious situations. And so he'd resigned himself to a life of misery. At least until Jacob and Alice were of an age to make their own way in the world.

But then his wife died in tragic circumstances.

Pain sliced through his heart when he thought of his children. To know of such horrors at such a young age had affected their mental well-being. Mrs Hibbet was right. Another governess was the last thing they needed.

But how could he create a life of stability when the house was in turmoil?

As he approached the rusty old gates of Morton Manor, he had no time to contemplate the answer. Instinctively, his horse grew skittish, pulled up and snorted loudly when Christian tried to guide him through the stone pillars.

"There's nothing to fear." He patted the beast and whispered words of comfort. He, too, felt a degree of trepidation. The urge to turn around and ride far away from the eerie place proved overwhelming. But the ghosts of the past informed his view, he reminded himself. And with a horse named Valiant, one expected the beast to have a little courage.

Indeed, his mount snorted once more before stepping across the boundary. Weeds littered the gravel drive. Diseased and gnarled branches lay amongst the overgrown grass on one side of the border. *Death* and *decay* were words frequently associated with Morton Manor.

The house came into view like an ugly blot on the landscape.

He would have looked up at the oddly spaced windows, remembered Cassandra's mocking grin as she watched him depart, but it was the golden-haired ray of sunshine hammering on the front door that captured his attention.

"Rose!" Christian cried out to her, although he'd not meant for the word to sound so sharp. Then again, she had disobeyed his instructions.

Upon hearing the clip of Valiant's hooves, she swung around. "Oh, it's you, my lord."

A range of emotions marred her pretty face. She appeared apprehensive. Sorrow swam in her eyes, and she turned from him once more and banged the door with an air of desperation.

"Were you expecting someone else?"

Obsessed with gaining entrance to the house, she did not reply.

"They've gone. There's no one here." The croak in her voice conveyed the same sense of hopelessness that tainted her countenance. "I've crept around, looked through every window, resorted to rapping the door more times than I care to count."

Christian dismounted and climbed the narrow flight of steps to stand at her side. "Perhaps your employer misinformed you and recalled the staff back to town. Are you certain it was the owner of Morton Manor who hired you?"

Rose nodded, though the look of anguish on her face baffled him.

The chivalrous part of his nature wished for a way to ease her torment.

"Perhaps you're right," she said with a weary sigh. "Perhaps they've all left for London."

"Then there is no need to inform them of your change in circumstances."

She turned and looked out over the desolate landscape,

scanned the ground in front of the house for what he did not know. "Do you think they left in a carriage?"

The question was as odd as her reaction to the occupants' absence, and yet he searched the gravel looking for tracks purely to appease her.

"Servants travel on the mail coach. Only a nursemaid or a paid companion might expect such a luxury."

Rose hung her head. "What have I done?"

"What is it that troubles you?"

"I … I wanted to warn her." The words tumbled from her mouth on a sob. "I should not have waited. I should have come here at first light. It is my fault. Tiredness is a terrible thing."

Usually Christian despised the sound of a woman crying. Cassandra's tears were as fake as her protestations of fidelity, yet Rose's reaction spoke only of sincerity. So much so, he wrapped his arms around her and let her bawl into the folds of his cravat.

It was a mistake.

A pat on the arm would have sufficed along with a few words of encouragement to pull herself together. And yet he was the one who took a measure of comfort from holding her close. It was the pain in *his* heart that eased when he inhaled the sweet scent of her hair, when the warmth of her body penetrated his clothing.

God, it had been so long since he'd felt anything other than bitterness and guilt.

Another heartfelt sob escaped, and her shoulders shook as the dam holding back her emotion came crashing down. No doubt her sadness stemmed from more than her failure to alert the housekeeper of her plans. Christian suspected the tears were for her family, for the unfortunate cards dealt by Fate's cruel hand.

Her hands came to rest on his waist, and a tremor shot through him like a bolt from the heavens.

"Forgive me," she eventually said as her cries subsided. But he'd closed his eyes, couldn't look at her while all honourable intentions were held together by a flimsy thread. "I don't know what came over me."

Christian grabbed hold of her hands and moved them down to rest at her sides. He opened his eyes and took a step back.

"You were obviously distressed." Thick tears coated her lashes. Red veins littered the whites of her eyes. "Though I assume it is your recent misfortune that caused such an outpouring of sorrow."

Rose stared at him, swallowed deeply and blinked. "This is the first time in my life I've been alone."

The comment caused knots to form in his stomach. "I understand," was all he managed to say.

They stood in silence, their ragged breathing filling the air. The need to ease her woes came upon him again. As their eyes locked, he forgot how much he detested the place. He failed to acknowledge that being on the grounds of the manor roused all the old feelings of deceit and betrayal.

In those few perfect seconds, he experienced peace.

"Would you mind escorting me around the perimeter of the house?" She glanced back at the solid front door with its rusty knocker. "I'd like to be certain no one is home before I leave."

Christian inclined his head. "Certainly."

Whenever Rose spoke, he forgot other things too: her status, his morals and ethics. And so, he resisted the need to offer his arm and simply gestured for her to proceed first.

They walked around the manor, peering through every

window, checking inside the outbuildings, trying the handle on the door to the servants' entrance.

The house was still, silent, though in his mind he could still hear the groans and wails of the previous patients, the sound of them banging the windows, pleading for release.

"Have you always lived at Everleigh?" Rose asked as they wandered over to the stables.

"For most of my life, yes." Other than the few years he'd spent in London. "I have a house in town but believe it's better to raise children in the country where the air is clean."

In his youth, he'd been like any other young buck. Trailing from one ball to the next, happy to indulge the pretty widows, to drink copious amounts of brandy, to do anything to annoy his father.

"Then you must remember when the manor housed patients."

"Yes." The word was but a whisper. "I remember."

"Was it as dreadful here as they say?"

Christian contemplated her question as he unhooked the latch on the stable door and peered inside. "*Grim* would be a better word, though the heavy sadness in the air proved to be the most disturbing." Indeed, he could still feel it clawing at his shoulders even though the house lay empty.

"There's no one here," Rose interjected as she glanced over his shoulder. It surprised him that she expected to find people in the stables and not horses. "Perhaps we should head back to Everleigh."

Christian closed the door and gestured for them to return to the courtyard. "I can write to the owner and explain your situation if it will help clear your conscience."

"That won't be necessary."

They followed the path back to the spot where Valiant stood waiting patiently.

"Mrs Hibbet told me that the staff are not to mention the manor in your presence," Rose suddenly said. "Were you acquainted with a patient?"

Christian stopped dead in his tracks. It crossed his mind to tell her that maids should know their place and keep their prying questions to themselves. But no matter how hard he tried to fight the feeling, he did not see Rose as a maid.

A tiny part of him wished the housekeeper had opened the front door and forced Rose to honour her word and accept the position. A life without temptation would be easier if not a little dull.

Perhaps sensing his disquiet, Rose sighed. "I'm afraid I'm not used to guarding my tongue. The conversation flows so naturally between us I often forget my place."

"Life seems to be one constant readjustment," he said remembering the way she clutched his waist when at her most vulnerable. He took hold of the horse's reins and brought the animal to stand at his side. "Do you mind if we walk back to Everleigh?"

He could not allow his maid to ride while he walked. The last thing he needed was to feed the village gossips. And it would only make her transition from gentleman's daughter to hired help all the more difficult. He refused to ride and watch her walk. The only other option was to ride together, but he'd already made enough mistakes, crossed enough moral boundaries.

"No, not at all." She offered him a bright smile. "I've spent months indoors and relish the thought of time spent out in the fresh air."

Christian led Valiant down the gravel drive. For once, the oppressive aura surrounding the manor did not follow him to the gate.

"My wife visited the manor on occasion," he found himself saying. "Well, quite regularly in fact."

Rose glanced at him as they passed between the stone pillars and turned into the narrow lane. "Please, say no more. I did not mean to pry, and I would not want to cause you any pain by reliving the memory."

Christian met her gaze. The rays of the afternoon sun touched her loosely tied hair, the light drawing his attention to the wisps of gold at her temples. Like the warm glow that floods the body when one looks up at the sky on a bright summer's day, Rose's presence brought the same comforting relief.

"I've not spoken about it before, not to anyone."

The truth shocked him. All those hours of silent contemplation and not one word had passed from his lips. Perhaps the only way to banish the ghosts of the past was to confront them. Stepping foot on the grounds of Morton Manor hadn't been as harrowing as he'd imagined.

"Do not feel as though you have to speak about it now."

Most ladies would have relished the thought of hearing secrets, would have squeezed every last drop of information from him in order to share it with their friends.

Rose was different … in every way.

"After the children were born, Cassandra became forgetful, preoccupied," he said, stroking Valiant's nose as they strolled up the lane. "It all started with an addiction to laudanum." One lie had led to another and another until nothing that came out of her mouth made sense. "Reverend Wilmslow brought her to Morton Manor in the hope it might help."

Rose sucked in a sharp breath though tried to disguise it. "Your wife was a patient?"

"No. I would never have left her in that godforsaken

place. But she came to visit for an hour or two each week." The visits were daily near the end. "The warden, Mr Watson, knew how to deal with the delusional, and Dr Taylor and Reverend Wilmslow did what they could to help her."

There was a tense moment of silence.

Rose hung her head as her breathing grew shallow.

Hell, he shouldn't have told her.

"I admire your strength," she suddenly said. "It must have been a difficult time for you. But you kept your wife at home. My … my father once locked me in the house for six months hoping to rid me of my independent spirit. The loss of liberty is suffocating and would be damaging to those with a troubled mind."

Christian stopped walking.

Rose took a few more paces before she realised and then turned to face him.

"Your father kept you a prisoner in your home?" Why anyone would want to suppress the true nature of such a vibrant woman was beyond him. But there were cruel men in the world, men threatened by their own shadow.

"I try not to think of it." She looked up at the blue sky, and the beginnings of a smile touched her lips. "A dear friend once told me that sometimes our greatest teachers are those who cause us the most pain. I believe she was right."

Rose didn't wait for a response, but swung around and continued on her way.

Christian snorted. If Cassandra was his greatest teacher, for the life of him, he could not make sense of the lesson.

He watched Rose glide along the lane, mesmerised by the grace and elegance contained within those precise steps. Her natural poise suggested an inner confidence though it was clear her heart was still healing from whatever trauma she'd suffered.

His heart was healing, too.

Spending a few minutes in Rose's company made him feel invigorated, if not a little reckless. As he hurried to catch up with her, it occurred to him that Mrs Hibbet was right. Rose would be a positive influence on his children. Perhaps if he limited the time she spent with them to an hour or two a day, they might come to accept her. They might decide not to put toads in her bed.

"As it's clear your skills with a poke and scuttle are adequate at best," he began, as an odd surge of excitement raced through him at the thought that she would no longer be a maid, "the role of temporary governess would suit you better. With your genteel upbringing, I'm sure there are numerous ways you can educate the children."

"Governess?" Rose cast him a sidelong glance. "Does that mean I won't need to clean out the fires?"

"No, I'm happy to freeze if it means making the children happy."

And you happy, he added silently, though the thought shocked him.

"And what if I wake to find spiders or toads in my bed?"

A pang of shame filled his chest for his inability to control his children. "I … I don't know why they do that."

"I do." Rose's reply was but a whisper. She cleared her throat. "But I suspect I lack the attributes you require in a governess."

When comparing Rose to the host of other governesses he'd employed, she only lacked the permanent scowl and the deep furrows between her brows. On the subject of the attributes he required, kissable lips and cornflower-blue eyes were now top of the list.

"Often a governess is a lady of equal status in manners and education but lacking in family wealth." He focused on keeping an element of desperation from his voice. "Do you not fall into that category, Rose?"

"I was not speaking of manners or education, my lord, but of discipline. It is not in my nature to punish minors. And I don't believe it does anyone any good in the end."

Again, Christian recalled Mrs Hibbet's advice that the children needed respite from the rigid rules and regulations.

"Children must learn that their actions have consequences." It was a lesson he'd be wise to observe, too. Kissing the new governess would only lead to disaster, regardless of how tempting he found her.

"I agree," she said, and it took him a moment to realise she wasn't talking about kissing. "But are we not more inclined to remember the lessons from those we revere?"

As they approached the gates of Everleigh, Christian decided he had a newfound respect for his maid, for his new governess, for the lady who'd breezed into his life mere hours ago.

Good lord. He'd known her for less than a day and yet could not deny the strange sense of attachment. It was all rather baffling.

Rose stopped at the fork in the path. To the right were the stables, to the left, the entrance to the servants' quarters.

"Thank you, my lord, for coming to my aid at the manor." She tried to disguise the smile that touched her lips as she bobbed a curtsy.

Christian should have used the opportunity to insist she never go there alone again, but he was suddenly captivated by the dusting of freckles on her nose.

"You should not be outdoors without a bonnet."

A frown marred her brow. "But I don't own a bonnet."

How was that possible for a woman of her previous standing?

"Oh, yes. I recall there was an unfortunate accident on the road and someone stole your luggage." It was a ridiculous story, though it begged the question what had happened to her possessions?

"Mrs Hibbet thought you might not hire me without references." Suddenly her countenance grew sombre. It was as though someone had thrown a black veil over her face to dull its brilliance. "In desperate times people often resort to desperate measures."

Curiosity burned. The sudden need to know everything about Rose proved to be overwhelming. But he sensed her retreat. Whatever terrible things had happened in her life, clearly, she had no desire to speak of the events.

The need to rouse a smile took hold, too.

"As the governess, you would have a private apartment."

The corners of her lips twitched, and he felt like the richest man alive. "Is that a ploy to encourage me to accept?"

"Perhaps." He smiled as he struggled to contain the odd sensations filling his chest. "Are you tempted to accept?"

"Not on the basis of the superior accommodation. But if you give me your assurance that I am free to deal with the children as I see fit, you might persuade me."

"I expect some tutoring as part of their timetable."

Rose pursed her lips. "Trust me, my lord. It will be a very enlightening week."

"Only a week?" A mild sense of panic gripped him at the prospect of her leaving. Perhaps he was coming down with the fever. It was the only explanation to account for his erratic emotions.

"We agreed to assess the situation once the week was out," she reminded him. "You might want rid of me by then. Now, I promised Mrs Hibbet I'd be but an hour and she has a list of jobs as long as a bishop's stole." Rose offered a parting curtsy. "Good day, my lord."

"Good day, Rose."

Christian watched her walk away. Something told him she had no intention of staying at Everleigh any longer than necessary. But where would she go? What would force a woman to abandon the prospect of a secure home and a regular income?

If he had any hope of making her stay, he had to find out.

CHAPTER SIX

The private apartment allocated to the many governesses previously employed at Everleigh was located on the second floor, next door to the nursery. Mrs Hibbet insisted Rose move into the room right away. The housekeeper's urgency stemmed from the need to prevent anyone else from catching the strange fever that had affected every member of the household at some point or other in the last two years.

"Rose is to be your new governess," Mrs Hibbet said, "just for the time being."

The children stood in the middle of the nursery and stared, their expressions solemn.

"We don't want a governess," Jacob replied. He spoke with the self-assurance of a boy of twelve, not one swiftly approaching eight. "We want you to be the maid. We want a maid's help that's all."

"What is the difference?" Rose failed to understand the child's point. "Both are merely titles. I hope to be your maid, your governess and your friend. If you will allow it." She turned to the housekeeper. "Thank you, Mrs Hibbet. But I shall be fine on my own with the children."

Mrs Hibbet had plenty of jobs to attend to, and so offered no objection. Once the housekeeper had left the room, Rose crouched down until eye level with the children.

"I know nothing about being a governess and nothing of Mrs Booth's schedule. So we'll literally rub the slate clean and begin again."

Alice tugged her brother's coat sleeve and looked up at him all doe-eyed.

Jacob sighed: an old man's weary exhalation not that of a frustrated boy. "On a Friday, Mrs Booth taught me mathematics in the morning and Latin in the afternoon."

"Mathematics and Latin in one day?" Rose said with a chuckle. No wonder the woman woke to find toads in her bed. It certainly seemed a fitting retribution.

"I'm to go away to school next year."

As soon as the words left the boy's lips, Alice clutched his arm as though the wicked schoolmaster was liable to burst into the room any minute and drag the helpless child away.

At seven, Rose had felt the same unbreakable connection to her brother, even though he was much older and spent the majority of his time at school. Indeed, she would give anything to feel Oliver's secure arms wrapped around her. To hear his words of comfort.

"Will it be Eton or Harrow? Do you intend to follow in your father's footsteps?" In Rose's opinion, a child of eight should receive tutoring at home but who was she to argue with tradition.

Jacob shrugged. "Mama said I'm to go to Eton."

His Mama? According to Mrs Hibbet, Lady Farleigh died two years ago. At six, surely Jacob would have been too young for a mature conversation. Then again, some mothers planned their offsprings' education at birth.

"There are better ways to prepare a boy for school," Rose said by way of a distraction as the mere mention of going away made his lip tremble. And better ways to prepare Alice for his departure. "None of them require sitting at a desk for hours on end."

The boy appeared confused yet equally curious.

Rose ventured over to the window. If she stood on tiptoes, she could just see the tops of the trees standing still, motionless. With the sky absent of clouds, it was a good day to take their lesson outside.

"For our first task, we'll need a few provisions." Rose swung around and clapped her hands together in excitement much to their surprise. "Alice, you will need a jacket and a scarf of some sort. One that is easy to tie."

"You're taking us outside?" Jacob's expression grew grave. He pursed his lips and frowned. "We're only allowed to walk on the path."

"Our lesson today will take place on the lawn."

No doubt the boy's anxiety stemmed from a fear of becoming ill.

"If you wrap up warm, you'll not catch a chill." Rose's words of reassurance failed to appease him. "You cannot contract a fever from breathing fresh air."

"We were sick once before," Alice said in the sweet melodic tone that couldn't help but raise a smile. "Papa sat by our beds and told us stories."

Most children suffered from colds and sniffles. Such things passed from person to person. It was an inevitable part of growing up.

"Was it the same illness that struck down the entire household?" Rose knew nothing about medicine or the nature of disease. Still, the sudden heaviness in the pit of her stomach warned her something was amiss. "Did you both contract the fever?"

The children nodded.

When kept a prisoner at Morton Manor, Rose had suffered from a similar illness. Mrs Gripes refused to send for the doctor and insisted the sweating and delirium would pass. The servants argued for hours. Stokes took the cart to Holdgate, some ten miles south, and returned with fresh provisions. Had Nicole not tended to her day and night, she might not have recovered.

"Dr Taylor cured us." Jacob's comment broke Rose's reverie. "And the reverend helped care for us so Papa could rest."

"Did the reverend tell you stories, too?" After hearing Mrs Hibbet's words of caution, the man struck Rose as someone who used every available opportunity to lecture his flock, purely as a means to repent for his sinful deeds.

"He told me about Lazarus while Alice slept. I couldn't keep my eyes open, so he tidied the room."

Tidied the room? How odd.

"No doubt Mrs Hibbet had a fit of apoplexy when she discovered the reverend working as a maid."

"He only organised the cupboards and straightened the clothes in the drawers," Jacob said.

"And he looked under the beds," Alice added.

Jacob scowled. "Don't tell stories, Alice. You were asleep."

"But I saw him." Alice squinted and peered through the tiny gaps between her lids to recreate the moment. "I saw him stand up and brush the dust off his hands."

Jacob tutted. "But you—"

"I think we've strayed from the original topic." Rose had

no intention of listening to them bicker, even though she would have liked nothing more than to question them both about the reverend's odd behaviour. "Now, let us adjourn to the lawn for today's lesson."

As expected the children played the part of rebels with the skill most mercenaries struggled to master. The previous night, when it was time to sleep, they'd jumped on the beds until the creaking floorboards were liable to snap. Now, when it was time for exercise and fresh air, it took thirty minutes for them to put on their boots.

When they eventually made it out onto the lawn, the children kept looking back over their shoulders at the house, surveying numerous windows before their eyes settled on one situated on the ground floor.

"Papa is in the study." Alice pointed to the window. "If he sees us, he might send us inside."

"No, he won't." Heavens, anyone would think they were trying to avoid catching the plague. "And it's rude to point. Now, hand me the scarf."

Alice dragged her gaze away from the house and handed Rose the red silk scarf. It was an odd choice for a child.

"It belonged to Mama," Alice said as though she'd read Rose's mind. "We keep a few of her things in the trunk in our room. The reverend tidied that up, too."

"No, he didn't," Jacob snapped.

"He did when you were asleep. I heard the lid creak when he opened it."

"Well, it doesn't matter now." Rose drew the soft material through her fingers. A lump formed in her throat. "It's a beautiful scarf. How fitting that we're using something so special to help us learn such a valuable lesson."

A faint sliver of jealousy raced through her as she held the garment in her hand. It was foolish really. But she couldn't shake the image of Lord Farleigh draping the scarf around his wife's neck, tugging at the ends and pulling her in for a deep, passionate kiss.

Instinctively, she glanced at the study, only to find the gentleman in question leaning against the wooden shutter, his arms folded as he watched them. Rose's heart raced. She tried to speak but struggled to form a word.

What was it about Lord Farleigh that affected her so? Not once had she experienced these odd sensations with Lord Cunningham.

The children followed her gaze.

"You see," Jacob said with an air of arrogance unbefitting a child. "Papa will wave at us to come inside."

Alice bit down on her bottom lip to stifle her tears. "But I don't want to go inside."

"Thankfully, once we begin our lesson, you'll be unable to see him."

Who was she trying to fool?

Rose did not need to look at the window to confirm his presence. Every fibre of her being, from the prickles at her nape to the tickling in her tummy, told her he was still there.

"Now, who would like to go first?"

That got the children's attention.

"Well, I'm the oldest by seven minutes," Jacob said, and Rose expected him to press his case. "But Papa told me that a gentleman must let the lady go first."

"And your father is right. That is the gentlemanly thing to do." Rose took Alice's hand and drew her closer. "We're going to play a game. It's a game of trust. I'm going to cover your eyes with the scarf, spin you around and it's your job to catch one of us. When you do, you must examine your prisoner. If you identify them correctly, you win a point."

Jacob glanced back to the study.

"Jacob, you will tie the scarf around Alice. I've never been good at knots." Rose's thoughts flashed to Nicole. She knew how to tie the tightest knots. The guard, Baxter, would never have untied them on his own.

"But I'm scared." Alice stepped away.

"Then you have a choice. Be brave or let Jacob go first. Blind man's buff is not about trusting other people but about trusting your own instincts. It's about ignoring the doubting voices in your head and listening to your heart."

With a soft sigh, Alice looked to her brother, and he gave a nod of reassurance. She turned around, and he tied the scarf.

"Ooh, it smells like Mrs Booth's cloak."

Alice meant musty. At least it didn't smell of their mother's favourite perfume. No one wanted to dwell on sad memories when they were having fun.

Well, they would have fun if they ever got around to playing.

With the blindfold secure, Rose spun Alice around a few times. It took a moment for the child to keep her balance and then, with arms stretched out she patted the air in front of her.

"Have faith, Alice," Rose shouted as she touched the girl's arm and then darted out of the way. "Trust your inner voice and listen for the tell-tale sounds of our approach."

"I can't catch you."

Jacob tapped Alice on the shoulder, and she swung around far too quickly and almost fell over.

The game proved easier when played with a large group.

"This time when we touch you, Alice, we will stand still, and you must make your guess based on nothing but instinct." If Rose didn't adapt the rules, they'd be racing about the garden all day.

Rose gestured for Jacob to step forward. After mouthing silently to the count of three, they both placed the tips of their fingers on Alice's arm.

Alice pursed her lips and then giggled as she grabbed Jacob's hand and called out his name. Even Jacob had the beginnings of a smile on his face.

"Well done." Rose was full of praise and helped Alice tie the scarf around Jacob's head.

"We will give you an extra spin," Alice said, "as you are the oldest."

"Only by seven minutes, and I did let you go first."

Alice giggled again, and after a final spin they ran off in different directions.

Lord Farleigh was still standing at the window. Heat crept up Rose's neck as he watched her skip and dodge around the lawn in a bid to distract Jacob.

Jacob's method of playing involved remaining still as opposed to rushing about with open arms. The boy was astute although far too serious for his age. His tactic worked perfectly for as soon as Rose stepped up to him, he grabbed her and called her name.

"Good heavens, Jacob." Rose put her hand to her chest to calm her racing heart. "You've quick reflexes for a boy of seven."

The compliment brought another weak smile to the child's face. "It's your turn, Rose. I'll tie the scarf."

Why did she get the impression things were about to become a little rough?

She knelt on the grass and held the scarf in place. Jacob tugged on the ends as though trying to drag a stubborn horse from a stable.

"You're tying the scarf too tight," Alice complained when Jacob yanked on the knot so hard he pulled out a few strands of Rose's hair.

"I have to make sure she can't cheat."

"A gentleman never accuses a lady of cheating." Rose rubbed the sore spot on her head, happy to discover she did not have a bald patch. "Surely your father told you that."

"People called Mama a cheat," the boy blurted.

It took a moment for Rose to recover from the initial shock of such a blunt comment, particularly one from a child. Why wait until she wore a blindfold to divulge such an important piece of information? If only she could have seen his face and examined his reaction.

"Then I trust they were not gentlemen," Rose replied.

"No, just the servants."

Rose tried to ignore the sudden sadness filling her heart. "Help me to my feet. I must warn you both I am quite good at this game."

Encouraging a competitive spirit would surely quash their solemn thoughts. Indeed, the children tackled their mission to unbalance her with the passion and conviction of an advancing battalion.

The prod in the back came first, followed by tufts of grass thrown at her neck and face. Culminating in Jacob, for who else could it be, dropping a worm into her outstretched hand.

But his plan to annoy her backfired.

While at Morton Manor she often woke to find a spider on her pillow. The infestation of horseflies proved equally troublesome. It was surprising how one grew accustomed to sharing a house with live creatures.

Instead of screaming and throwing the worm in the air, Rose held it gently between her fingers and chased after the children until they were both squealing in terror, and then laughter.

Without warning, they fell silent, no doubt planning something mischievous amongst themselves.

"Even though I can't see you, I know you're still there." Well, she hoped they were. How foolish would she look if Lord Farleigh glanced out of the window to find her running around the lawn with a worm in her hand?

Alice giggled again, but Jacob urged her to be quiet.

One of them snatched the worm from her grasp, but Rose was too slow to react. Then, with loud whoops, they ran circles around her, patting her arm and back and shouting, "Catch us. Catch us if you can."

Rose twirled round and round until dizzy. With outstretched arms, she stumbled forward desperate to cling on to something solid. The children circled her, tapping her body as they went, their cries of excitement whipping past her ears.

A fog of confusion filled her head. She took two unsteady steps to the left and then she fell. But she did not land on the grass. Wrapped in the vice-like grip of a pair of muscular arms, she landed on a hard body that was most definitely not one of the children.

"Hurray! You caught her, Papa."

Papa?

All the air left Rose's lungs as she lay sprawled on top of Lord Farleigh. She did not dare remove the scarf for fear of swooning under the scrutiny of those mesmerising green eyes.

"Shush," Lord Farleigh whispered. "I cannot release her until she says my name."

Lord Farleigh had got the rules of the game confused. "I am the one who does the catching."

His warm breath breezed over her neck, and a deep

chuckle burst from his lips. "Oh, you've caught me, Rose. Make no mistake about that."

She imagined saying something flirtatious in return, but all thoughts turned to the strange tingling surging through her body. She tried to move, but the feel of his thighs pressed against hers rendered her helpless. And the smell of his cologne. Good Lord. Never had she inhaled something so divine.

"Lord ... Lord Farleigh," she managed to say.

"Rose has won the point, Papa."

"Oh, I don't know," he drawled. "I can't help but feel I am the winner of this game."

"You can let her go now, Papa," Jacob said.

"Yes, I think you're squashing her," Alice added.

The girl was right although the experience was far from unpleasant.

"I would release her, but how can I be sure she won't fall again?"

Rose pulled the red scarf down to the bridge of her nose. White dots flashed in her eyes, and it took a few blinks until she could see Lord Farleigh's handsome face clearly.

Her heart flew to her throat at the sight of his warm smile. It was a breathtaking sight to behold.

"Do you think you can stand?" he said.

How could she stand when her limbs wobbled like blancmange?

"Come, children, take an arm each. Your father is stuck unless you lift me up."

Lord Farleigh looked quite content lying on the grass in just his shirtsleeves. The thought that he'd removed his coat, and that the thin linen was all that lay between her and his bare skin, caused a host of scandalous images to flood her mind.

"Your cheeks are red." Alice stared up at her.

"Are they? Well, it is rather warm out."

Lord Farleigh cast her a sinful grin. "I have to agree. I, too, am rather hot beneath the collar."

Jacob came to assist her, but she found the strength to stand.

In one fluid movement, Lord Farleigh jumped to his feet and set about brushing grass from his buckskin breeches.

Rose averted her gaze, and with trembling fingers fumbled with the scarf. "You are extremely good at tying knots, Jacob."

The boy looked to his father who patted his head and winked.

"Allow me to assist you." Lord Farleigh came behind her and set to work on the knot. The pads of his fingers slipped into her hair, brushing the sensitive skin on her scalp. "I thought you might be in need of rescuing when I saw Jacob dig up the worm," he whispered in her ear.

"Thankfully, I couldn't see it. Besides, I'll take a worm over a bed full of toads."

The scarf fell away in her hands, and she gave it to Alice. Either Lord Farleigh had no idea the item once belonged to his wife, or he found the fact unimportant.

"Now, I happened to notice some delicious smells coming from the kitchen." Lord Farleigh hauled Alice up into his arms. "Shall we investigate?"

"Is it cake?"

Lord Farleigh laughed. "I'm pretty certain it is."

With wide eyes, both children nodded. Lord Farleigh placed his hand on Jacob's shoulder, and they walked towards the house. Rose wasn't sure if she had the strength to take a step.

Lord Farleigh glanced back over his shoulder, then stopped and turned around. "Are you coming, Rose?"

"I … I wouldn't want to intrude." The children's eyes swam with love and affection for their father. They drank in his attention, guzzled every last drop.

Lord Farleigh looked at his children and raised a brow.

Alice spoke first. "I think Rose should have a slice of cake because you almost squashed her."

Jacob glanced at his father and then at Rose. "Anyone who can hold a worm without screaming deserves a reward."

"Then it's settled. Rose will join us on our hunt for cake."

"Oh, oh." Alice tugged on her father's waistcoat. "Can we have a picnic?"

"Not today." Lord Farleigh kissed the child's forehead to ease her look of disappointment. "But perhaps tomorrow we might take a picnic to the lake if the weather holds out. Now, let's go and harass Mrs Bates in the kitchen. Are you coming, Rose?"

Rose stared at them as a strange mix of emotions raced through her. For the first time in her life, a sense of belonging filled her chest. She did not want to address the sensations wreaking havoc with a more intimate part of her anatomy. Truth be told she was rather fond of Lord Farleigh. But feeding a mild infatuation would make leaving Everleigh harder to bear.

"Yes, I'm coming." She ran to catch up with them. "How can I refuse a slice of cake?"

CHAPTER SEVEN

"Where on earth has she got to?" Christian paced back and forth at the bottom of the stairs. He turned to the children standing patiently at the newel post. "Did Rose attend to you this morning?"

Alice opened her mouth, but Jacob spoke first. "Mrs Hibbet laid out our clothes. We've not seen Rose today."

"What if she's run away, Papa?"

"She has not run away," Christian said with a sigh, though the pang in his heart confirmed he suspected the worst. "She would not have left without speaking to me first."

Perhaps he had frightened her away. After all, what innocent woman enjoyed being ogled by the master? Guilt flared when he recalled how he'd clutched her to his chest whilst lying sprawled on the grass. Damn.

"Does that mean we can't go on the picnic?" Alice asked.

"We'll wait for another five minutes." A few seconds ticked by before the need to know what kept her proved too hard to ignore. "On second thoughts, Alice, would you run upstairs and knock on Rose's door? Heaven knows where all the servants are today."

"Yes, Papa."

Alice climbed the first flight of stairs only to bump into Rose at the top.

"Alice, you made me jump out of my skin. No doubt I'm dreadfully late." Rose took Alice's hand, and they descended the stairs together. The child could not take her eyes off Rose's hair and neither could he.

"Forgive me, my lord. When I woke this morning, I did not expect it would take so long to style my hair." Rose stroked the soft curls that skimmed her shoulder. "A shorter cut suits me, don't you think?"

Christian stared open-mouthed. What possessed her to cut her hair?

Alice took one look at his face and sobbed. "Does that mean Rose is leaving now?"

"Leaving?" Rose frowned. "Of course not. Why would you think that?"

Rose glanced at Jacob who found it more interesting to stare at his shoes.

"Rose is not going anywhere." Christian met her gaze. "The shorter style is quite becoming. Would you care to divulge what prompted the change?" He had his suspicions but wanted to hear her explanation before he accused his son.

Jacob sucked in a sharp breath.

"A woman who works for a living has no time to worry about managing her hair. This will be easier to deal with in the mornings."

"So no one forced you to make the decision?" He cast Jacob a sidelong glance.

"Forced me? Not at all. One side looked considerably shorter in the mirror this morning that's all. Now I've evened it up."

One had to admire her level of compassion when it came

to his children. More so when one considered she'd known them for two days. Most women would have insisted he beat the boy, demanded he offer some form of compensation to atone for the misdeed.

Rose simply smiled.

"It's only hair." She put her arm around Alice's shoulder. "If I decide I don't like it, I can grow it back. Now, shouldn't we be on our way?"

She really was a remarkable woman.

Even so, it was time for him to sit down with his children and address their mischievous behaviour. He should not have left it so long. But sometimes the truth proved hard to bear, easier to ignore.

"Had anything untoward happened, you know I could not permit the picnic to go ahead," Christian added purely to make the point to his son.

By rights, he should abandon all plans. But seeing his children smile eased his guilt. And an outing would give him an opportunity to learn more about Rose.

"The only thing untoward is that I am terribly late." Rose picked up the wicker basket sitting on the floor at his feet. "But let's not allow such an oversight to spoil the day. Time away from the house can be a tonic for a burdened mind."

A brief respite from his troubles was exactly what he needed. "Then let us not waste another minute."

They took a leisurely walk to the lake, situated a mile or so north of the house, far from Morton Manor's boundary. The few dark clouds littering the sky did not spoil its beauty. No doubt the water was cold. But he noticed the way the sunlight sparkled on the surface. Birds sang. Dragonflies danced near the lake's edge.

As a child, Christian had spent his summers rowing the boat from one bank to the other while his mother sat beneath her parasol and told stories of medieval knights fighting brave battles. They were amongst the happiest times of his life. And yet his children had never experienced such magical moments spent with a mother who cared.

The thought broke his heart.

He should have noticed the signs in the beginning, the tell-tale quirks that confirmed his wife was a vain, selfish woman who derived gratification from the attention of other men. But he'd been a fool, pressured into marrying based on nothing more than wealth and status.

And his children were the ones paying the ultimate price for his stupidity.

"Where shall we sit?" Rose placed the basket on the grass. She put her hands on her hips and surveyed the area. "What about near those trees? There's shade, and it's still close enough to the water's edge."

"As you've come without a bonnet, anywhere out of the direct sunlight will be suitable." He would speak to Mrs Hibbet on their return and send Rose into Abberton to purchase a few necessary items. He pointed to the cluster of trees in the distance. "I once carved my initials on the trunk of one of those trees."

"Which one, Papa?" Jacob spoke for the first time since leaving the house.

"I can't remember. See if you can find it."

He hoped to have a moment alone with Rose, to thank her for not leaving on the first mail coach to London. To apologise for his son's appalling antics. But Alice gripped Rose's hand and tugged.

"Come on, Rose. The first one to find Papa's name gets the biggest piece of cake."

His children obsessed over sweet treats. In the end, they all hurried across the grass to the copse.

"Here it is!" Jacob cried, thoroughly pleased to be the first to find the markings.

They all gathered around the trunk. The children took it in turns to trace the indents with their finger. It occurred to him that Rose knew him only as Lord Farleigh.

"The letters stand for Christian Knight," he informed her.

With wide eyes, she repeated his name as she perused him from head to toe. "Your surname is Knight? As in the heroes sent to rescue damsels in distress?"

The comment confirmed what he already suspected: she had a romantic view of the world. When Rose loved a man, he imagined she would give everything of herself, hold nothing back.

Christian cleared his throat. "As in a man known for his chivalrous conduct."

"Do you always act with honourable intentions, my lord?"

The question caught him off guard. Was she teasing him or testing him? Should it be the latter, he'd fail miserably. If he told her what he'd thought about as he lay naked between the bed sheets last night, his declaration would prove false.

"Let's just say that I may have a few things to confess at church this Sunday, but on the whole, I try to abide by my principles." The sound of scratching forced him to tear his gaze away from her. Jacob had found a stick and was busy carving his initials, too. "Not too hard. You only want to leave an imprint in the bark not strip it away."

"This will be a record of the day we spent at the lake," Jacob said.

"Write mine, Jacob." Alice tapped his arm. "Put it next to yours. And do Rose's name, too."

Rose snorted. "No, there's no need to carve mine. Just think of the poor tree."

"We were all here together." Christian picked up a stick and handed it to Rose. "You must put your initials else it will not be an accurate representation."

She pursed her lips, took one look at the children's excited faces, muttered a few incoherent words and began carving.

Christian watched with bated breath. The urge to learn anything he could about the new governess burned in his chest. "Is that supposed to be a letter *O* or a *D*?"

"Isn't it obvious." Rose squinted as she studied her craftsmanship. "It's a *D*."

"*D* for what?"

Rose raised a brow. "*D* for don't ask so many questions."

Alice put her hand over her mouth and giggled.

Whatever Rose's reason for secrecy, it didn't matter to him. Lord, he'd locked himself away at Everleigh hoping no one would learn of the scandal involving his family. No doubt people gossiped behind closed doors. When a man's wife died under mysterious circumstances, the husband was always the prime suspect.

"The only way to stop me asking questions is to feed me," he said. "Everyone knows it's rude to speak with your mouth full."

"So you have a healthy appetite, my lord."

The innocent comment amused him, particularly when his mind conjured a lascivious reply. "Sometimes it can prove impossible to ignore one's cravings."

"Then we'd be wise not to make you wait."

After laying out the blanket and unpacking the basket,

they spent the next hour lounging in the sunshine, eating ham and cheese, and fresh bread.

"Can we climb the trees, Papa?" Jacob asked though his lack of enthusiasm suggested he expected the answer to be no.

They were two miles from Morton Manor. The children were in no danger. "As long as you stay where I can see you."

Rose's penetrative gaze searched his face, her eyes only averting when the children jumped to their feet and raced off into the copse.

"What is it about the woods that makes you uneasy?" Rose sipped her elderflower cordial and then studied him over the rim of her glass.

To answer meant revealing his darkest secret. "Why did you protect Jacob when he is the reason you cut your hair?" A sigh left his lips. "By rights, I should have punished him."

"And what good would that do? How many times has he gone to bed without supper?"

"If you're trying to tell me I'm doing a terrible job of raising my children, then simply say so."

Her gaze fell to her lap. "It is not my place to say anything at all. Even mentioning it is overstepping the mark."

He was the only one guilty of crossing boundaries. But when it came to Rose, he couldn't help himself.

"Other than Mrs Hibbet, you're the only person I can speak to in confidence." Christian dragged his hand through his hair. He didn't know why, but this woman's opinion mattered to him.

A tense silence filled the air.

"Do you always take picnics with the governess?"

"Never." He shivered at the thought of sitting opposite Mrs Hanson and counting the hairs sprouting out of her oversize mole. "As I'm sure you're aware, the children go to great lengths to avoid spending time with anyone tasked with their care."

"Children? You mean Jacob. Like all loyal sisters, Alice merely follows his lead."

"Alice wants to make everyone happy," he agreed. Thankfully, his daughter's character was far removed from that of her mother, a woman who took pleasure from creating misery at every turn.

"And Jacob carries the weight of the world on his shoulders." Rose looked up at the sun and squinted. "A brother will try to shelter his sister from the harsh realities of the world. And yet such a burden can become too much for him. I would hate for that to happen to Jacob." She spoke in earnest, from experience.

"You have a brother?"

"I do." A brilliant smile illuminated her face, but it fell away almost as quickly as it formed. "Though I have no idea where he is."

"Where in England?" Perhaps he could help her find her family.

"Where in the world. He was in Italy when last I heard from him."

Italy?

Her father must have been a wealthy merchant if his son had the funds to venture abroad. Or perhaps they were a family of gamblers, and with mounting debts, her brother had no option but to flee the country.

"Enough about my affairs." Rose sat up straight. "If I have any hope of understanding Jacob's motives, you need to be honest with me. Are you worried about the strange illness? Is that what keeps you awake at night, or does your restlessness stem from concern for the children?"

"Me?" He stabbed his finger to his chest. "I thought we

were talking about Jacob. How do you know I struggle to sleep?"

She shrugged. "It's merely an assumption I made."

What was he supposed to say? Through his own stupidity, his children were motherless. His inability to solve the problem with his staff left him questioning his own sanity, cursing his inadequacy. They were pathetic reasons.

In a bid to find a distraction, he sat up and began rearranging the plates and packing them away in the basket. Rose handed him her cutlery, and their fingers brushed.

Christian stilled.

Rose took the cutlery and placed it in the basket and then touched his hand. "You can tell me what troubles you. Your secret will never pass from my lips."

The warmth of her hand penetrated his skin. He was so used to being alone. So used to partaking in silent conversations. Besides, he wouldn't know where to begin.

"You have your own problems to deal with without worrying about mine."

"Currently, your problems are mine." Her hand slipped from his, and he felt cold to his bones once again. "I want to do everything I can to make the children happy."

The words *while I'm here* hung in the air despite never being said.

"O-only the children?"

She swallowed visibly and struggled to hold his gaze. "Shouldn't a governess concern herself with the well-being of her charges?"

"Of course." He nodded. "Of course."

They continued packing the basket in silence. Rose looked at him numerous times beneath hooded lids. He supposed he should have said something but how did one explain the strange occurrences without sounding like a candidate for Bedlam? And no man wanted a woman to see him as weak, particularly not one as beguiling as Rose.

Thankfully, Alice came bounding up. "Can we play the scarf game?"

"Have you had enough of climbing trees?" Christian couldn't help but smile. His daughter's cheerful countenance always brought him a modicum of comfort.

Jacob joined them. "I'm too short to reach the boughs, and Alice wants us all to play together."

Rose sighed. "But we didn't think to bring a scarf."

"What about using my cravat?" Christian sat up on his knees and fiddled with the knot. He'd do anything to prolong their outing. The house reminded him of everything wrong with his life. "It's thin enough and easy to tie."

"If you're sure you don't mind." Rose studied his fingers as they worked the knot.

Once undone he tugged one end, and the silk slipped from around his neck. "The question now is who will go first."

Rose's gaze fell to the base of his throat, and absently she moistened her lips. "Perhaps you should. I know I'd like an opportunity to prod and poke you." She laughed but then caught herself. "What I mean is it will amuse me to watch you wander about, helpless."

A man didn't need to wear a blindfold to feel helpless in Rose's company.

Jacob tied the cravat around Christian's head, and Rose came up behind him to inspect the knot. "We must make sure he cannot peek."

The feel of her hand brushing his hair was almost his undoing. They pulled him to his feet and led him away from the picnic blanket. All three of them twirled him around until his head could no longer keep up with his body.

Alice giggled. "Come and catch us, Papa."

Just like the game he'd witnessed yesterday, they took it in turns to pat his arms. One did not need to be a genius to identify the culprits. Alice tickled, Jacob stabbed and prodded, and Rose brushed her fingers over his arm and across his back. He caught the hitch in her breath whenever she came near.

"Watch the lake, Papa," Alice cried. "You're too close to the water."

"Don't worry," Rose laughed, her breathless pants evidence she was running. "We won't let you fall—" Her high-pitched scream pierced the air.

"Rose! Rose," Alice cried. "Papa. Help."

Panic flared.

Christian yanked the cravat up over his head. The brilliance of the sun's rays forced him to blink rapidly. The white spots disappeared, and then he saw Rose in the lake. With arms flailing, she splashed about trying to keep her head above the water.

"It's not too deep," Christian cried. "You should be able to touch the bed."

"I … I can't swim."

God damn.

Jacob teetered on the edge of the bank, his eyes watery and wide, his face ashen.

"Jacob!" Christian cried, but he was too late.

Without uttering a word, Jacob jumped in, too.

CHAPTER EIGHT

R ose splashed and kicked about in the water.
Something slimy slithered past her legs. Her sodden
dress dragged her down, but thankfully she'd landed where
the water was shallow enough to stand.

The shove in the side had taken her by surprise. They'd
been darting around Lord Farleigh, dodging his outstretched
hands, laughing and screaming. Yes, they'd ventured too
close to the edge. That's how accidents happened. But in her
heart, she knew Jacob had pushed her deliberately.

But then, as if the situation were not troubling enough,
Jacob jumped into the lake.

"I'll save you, Rose!" the boy cried, but his head
disappeared beneath the water.

"Jacob!" Drawing on every ounce of strength she had,
Rose found her feet. The murky ripples lapped around her
shoulders, and she pushed forward in an effort to reach him.
"Can he swim?" she shouted to Lord Farleigh, who was busy
shrugging out of his coat. "It's too deep for him."

Alice waved her hand and cried out when Jacob's head

bobbed above the surface. He spluttered and coughed before disappearing again.

Lord Farleigh threw his coat to the ground and jumped in. Being taller and twice as strong as Rose, he reached Jacob and hauled the child up into his arms.

"You foolish boy," he said, clutching Jacob to his chest and pressing his lips to the child's forehead as if he'd already lost him. Lord Farleigh's gaze shot to Rose. "Are you all right? Can you touch the bottom?"

Rose nodded. The cold penetrated her bones. Her lower jaw sagged, and she couldn't stop her teeth chattering.

Lord Farleigh lifted Jacob onto the grass verge. "Turn him onto his side, Alice, and pat his back." He turned to Rose. "Wait, I'm coming for you." He reached her in seconds. "Good God, your lips are blue. Drape your arms around my neck, and I'll pull you to the bank."

She hesitated but then wrapped her trembling arms around him. Christian slid one strong arm around her waist and pulled her tightly to his body as he waded through the water. Once at the edge, he hoisted her up as though she were a small child, too.

It took a few attempts for her to stand, the weight of her dress made every movement cumbersome. She turned to Christian and held out her hand. "Let me help you up."

His wet hand slipped into hers, palm to palm. Their eyes locked and with a heave, she hauled him out.

Without saying a word, Christian rushed to Jacob's side and dropped to his knees on the grass. "Jacob? Can you hear me? Say something."

Jacob turned his head. His pallid countenance conveyed shock, perhaps something else, too. Indeed, when the boy finally held Christian's gaze, his eyes swam with remorse. "Yes, Papa. I … I'm fine. But what about Rose?"

Rose knelt at Jacob's side and picked green algae from his hair. "It will take a little more than a dunking in the lake to frighten me away." She made light of the situation yet her lips quivered, and her hand shook as she placed it on Jacob's chest.

Lord Farleigh placed a gentle hand on her lower back. Rose wasn't sure what to make of the gesture, but it brought comfort all the same.

"We should get back to the house before we all catch a chill." Lord Farleigh touched his son's brow. "Can you walk or should I carry you?"

Alice suddenly burst into tears. "I hate the lake."

"That's because you're the only one who isn't wet," Rose said, attempting to soothe the child. She stood, scooped Alice into her arms and cuddled her close. "Now we're all the same."

A weak chuckle escaped from Alice's lips.

"I can walk, Papa." Jacob sat up. Water trickled from his hair and down his cheek.

Lord Farleigh helped his son to his feet. "I'll send someone to collect the basket."

They walked back to the house in silence but for the water squelching in their boots. Lord Farleigh held Jacob's hand while Rose clutched Alice's tiny fingers. The heaviness in the air spoke of a range of emotions: sorrow, remorse, regret. Lord Farleigh's arm brushed against hers numerous times, though he did not glance in her direction but kept his gaze fixed firmly ahead.

As they traipsed across the field, their hands touched. They could have attributed the discreet movement to their unsteady gait. But then his little finger hooked around hers, and they continued on their way.

Once back at Everleigh, the house erupted into chaos. Mrs

Hibbet organised warm baths for them all. Lord Farleigh sent for Dr Taylor, eager to know that Jacob would suffer no lasting effects from swallowing so much water.

Rose sat on her bed for half an hour, brushing her hair, her mind a jumbled mess of emotions. Nicole was constantly in her thoughts. Jacob worried her. If his malicious pranks continued, someone could get hurt. And what of the intense attraction she felt towards Lord Farleigh? How ironic that a man with the name Knight was the one in need of saving.

A knock on the door disturbed her reverie, and Mrs Hibbet opened it a fraction and popped her head around the jamb.

"His lordship would like to see you in his study once you feel able." Mrs Hibbet glanced at the brown bottle on the side table. "Perhaps you should drink the tonic Dr Taylor left for you. When the cold seeps into your bones, there's bound to be repercussions."

Rose refused to drink anything without knowing its contents. And if the potion worked wonders why were the servants still ill? One had to question the doctor's competence. Perhaps he charged for his visits and was in dire need of funds. He wouldn't be the first man to maintain a professional facade whilst suffering from a gambling addiction.

"A nip of brandy works better than any tonic I've ever taken."

Mrs Hibbet studied Rose's short locks. "His lordship knows that Jacob cut your hair. The child confessed to the crime."

Rose came to her feet. "Then I had best speak to Lord Farleigh. To punish Jacob will only make matters worse."

Mrs Hibbet opened the door fully. An affectionate smile

lit up her face. "I told the master the Lord sent us an angel in our time of great need. Happen I was right."

Rose knocked gently on the study door. Lord Farleigh called for her to enter. He sat behind his desk in dry clothes although his dark hair curled at the nape where the ends were still damp. Jacob sat in the chair opposite, rocking back and forth and nibbling his bottom lip.

"Ah, Rose." Forgetting himself, Lord Farleigh stood and inclined his head. Even as a governess, he treated her more like a lady than any gentleman of her acquaintance ever had. "Please take a seat. After the incident at the lake, I believe a frank discussion is long overdue."

"Of course." She sat in the seat next to Jacob, reached over and squeezed the boy's hand. "I trust you feel recovered and Dr Taylor has assured your father there's no harm done?"

Lord Farleigh cleared his throat. "Dr Taylor will be with us presently. In the meantime, my son has something to say." He nodded when the boy failed to speak. "Jacob."

Jacob turned to face her but stared absently at a point beyond her shoulder. "I'm sorry, Rose, for cutting your hair." He bowed his head as a sad sigh breezed from his lips.

While she pitied the child, she couldn't lie to him. After what he'd done at the lake, to say nothing was as good as condoning his unconscionable behaviour.

"You hurt me," she said softly. The words brought a tightening in her throat. If her father were here, she would say the same to him, too. "You took something from me without my consent. Why would you do that when I have been nothing but kind to you?"

Jacob shrugged.

"Don't you like me being here? Is that it?" Rose pressed him further.

Jacob finally met her gaze. "I do like you."

"Then you have an odd way of showing it. I could have drowned in the lake." When reinforcing a point, one had to be dramatic. "Had the water been a few feet deeper I might not be sitting here."

Lord Farleigh sat forward. "The lake? Jacob told me what he did to your hair." He shot the boy a hard stare. "I thought you'd slipped and fallen in during our game."

Rose lifted her chin. "I did fall in, with a little nudge from Jacob."

Lord Farleigh jumped to his feet and slammed his palms on the desk. "Is this true? For all the saints, tell me Rose is mistaken."

At that, the boy burst into tears. He nodded. Then his shoulders shook as uncontrollable sobs wracked his body, and he huddled into a tight ball in the chair.

Lord Farleigh marched around the desk. "Why would you deliberately—"

Rose raised her hand to silence him and surprisingly he obeyed. She knelt on the floor in front of the chair and placed her hand on Jacob's back. "Were you trying to get rid of me? Do you want me to leave? You need only say the words."

Lord Farleigh inhaled sharply.

"Tell me why, Jacob?" Rose continued. "I can fetch my cloak and leave here within the hour if it will ease your suffering."

Jacob looked up, his white face all red and blotchy. "D-don't go, Rose. Everyone leaves us." He thrust forward and flung his arms around her neck with such force she almost toppled back.

Lord Farleigh put his hand on her shoulder to help steady

her balance. As always, his touch roused a heat in her belly that spread through her like fire in a hay barn.

Rose kissed Jacob on the temple, eased his arms from around her neck and clasped them tightly. "You must talk to me, talk to us. What do you mean everyone leaves?"

"He knows I would never leave him." Lord Farleigh's defensive tone held a wealth of pain. "Does this have something to do with your mama?"

Jacob fell silent.

"The only way to solve the problem is to talk about it." Rose squeezed Jacob's hands. "Some things make me sad when I think about my father."

"But your father wasn't mean," Jacob blurted.

"Oh, he was." It had taken years before her father's barbed words failed to penetrate. "I've never known anyone be so cruel."

The large comforting hand on her shoulder rubbed gently back and forth.

"Mama didn't want us."

"That's not true." Lord Farleigh came to his wife's defence. "An illness of the mind is a terrible thing to live with. A person struggles to understand what is real and what is not." He sucked in a breath. "But that does not explain why you would hurt Rose."

Jacob's head shot up. "I wasn't trying to hurt her. It was a test."

Lord Farleigh's hand slipped from her shoulder. "A test?"

"When you care about someone you forgive them. That's what Reverend Wilmslow says."

Rose breathed a sigh of relief. It all made sense now. "Then you know that I do care, else I would have left this house within five minutes of waking this morning." The comment left her lips before her mind had time to process what she'd said. She truly did care. Was it possible to form emotional attachments in two days? "Everyone knows a woman's glory is her long hair."

Lord Farleigh's breath breezed past her ear as he leant forward and whispered, "I'm afraid I would have to disagree with the last statement."

While her stomach performed a somersault, she tried to focus on Jacob. "I'm not going anywhere for the time being. But know that when the time comes to leave, my decision will have no bearing on my feelings for you and Alice."

Jacob pursed his lips and nodded. "Everyone's happy now you're here."

Rose put her hand on her chest. It was the nicest thing anyone had ever said to her, and she couldn't help but draw the child into an embrace.

"You're not to blame for your mother's failings," Lord Farleigh suddenly said. "Perhaps none of us are."

"But I ... I stole from her." Another sob caught in the child's throat. "She said she knew it was me and that if I didn't give her what she wanted she'd leave and never come ... never come back."

A suffocating silence filled the air.

"She was not herself when she said those things." Lord Farleigh knelt down at Rose's side. "What did you take? Trinkets? Tokens to remind you of your mother?"

"No." Jacob shook his head and pressed his lips together firmly

"Then what did you take that would see her fly into such a rage?"

Jacob shrugged.

"You'll tell me now." Lord Farleigh stood, the sharp edge to his voice revealed frustration, not anger.

"I can't. You'll be cross."

"Can you tell me?" Rose pressed the child.

Keeping secrets only caused guilt to fester inside. She glanced up at Lord Farleigh's handsome countenance. Perhaps she should tell him the truth about her situation, too. But no doubt his sense of honour would prevail, and he'd be obliged to offer marriage after sleeping under the same roof as an earl's virgin daughter.

"This is ridiculous." Lord Farleigh threw his hands in the air. "You were barely six years old when your mother died. Whatever it is you've taken, no one is angry with you, Jacob."

What reason did he have for keeping the secret? What was so terrible that he couldn't tell his father?

Rose stood. "Does Alice know you stole things from your mother?" Manipulating minors was beneath her, but for the boy's well-being, they had to discover the truth. "Does she know your mother threatened to leave?"

Jacob's eyes widened. "No." Panic infused his tone. "Don't tell Alice."

"What else can we do when you refuse to offer an explanation?" Lord Farleigh said.

"Alice will want to read the letters." Jacob gasped and covered his mouth with his hand.

"Letters?" Lord Farleigh straightened. "What letters?"

The boy hit his leg with his fist. "I can't give them to you. You can't see them."

Something Jacob said earlier flashed into her mind. The servants gossiped about his mother being a cheat. What if the letters contained information that might hurt his father?

Rose turned to Lord Farleigh. "With your permission, I'd like to take Jacob to his room. Let me speak to him in a place he feels at ease."

"God damn," he muttered under his breath. "What sort of

man has no control over his children?" The green eyes that she'd seen sparkle with amusement were dull with pain. "You must think me weak and foolish."

Weakness was not a trait she associated with Christian Knight. Just thinking his name sent a shiver from her throat to her belly.

"Loving your children and trying to protect them does not make you weak," Rose whispered. "Not in my eyes."

He studied her face, his gaze falling to her lips and moving up to her hair. "Who are you?" The words held an air of wonder.

She smiled. "Someone sent here to help you in your great time of need. It seems your troubles are far greater than my own."

Throughout her life, no one had ever taken her seriously. People considered her too pretty to be intelligent, too petite to have strength, too blonde to be a Darby. Lord Cunningham had treated her as a trophy, something to prove he'd won the game. And yet Christian was different. He listened to her opinion as if she were a wise seer, sent from a foreign land with the knowledge others only dreamed of possessing.

"Take Jacob upstairs." Lord Farleigh's voice broke her reverie. "Return here tonight after dinner. There are other things you should know. Things upon which I would seek your counsel."

Rose inclined her head gracefully although her heart pounded against her ribs with the force of a battering ram. The more time she spent in his company, the more her obsession for him grew.

She took Jacob's hand and brought him to his feet. "I may have news of my own when we reconvene."

"I'm sorry, Papa." Jacob's head fell forward, his chin touching his chest.

Lord Farleigh placed a hand on the boy's head. "Go now. Spend time with Rose. Tell her all the things that trouble you. You can trust her. We all can."

The sudden sense of elation she'd felt moments earlier dissipated. Would he still feel the same when she finally found the courage to reveal her identity? Would he say the same when he discovered the full extent of her deceit?

CHAPTER NINE

They climbed the stairs to the first floor, but Jacob tugged Rose's hand and pulled her towards the next flight leading up to the nursery. A mild sense of relief filled her chest. The children slept next door to Lord Farleigh. Visiting their room made for an awkward affair when her mind conjured images of the master lying naked in his large bed.

Jacob stopped outside Rose's room. "What I want to show you is in here."

"In my room?" She opened the door and gestured for Jacob to enter. "I must say, it is all rather mysterious."

He waited for her to close the door before moving to the armoire. Tapping his foot on the floorboards to the left, he found the one he wanted and prised it loose. With his cheek pressed flat to the floor, he ferreted about inside the gap and pulled out a book with a blue cover.

"This is what I stole from Mama's room." Jacob blew dust and cobwebs off the surface and handed it to her. "When a letter came, she always left the house in a hurry."

"Is that why you stole them?" She opened the cover of

what looked like a small ledger. One would need a magnifying glass to read the writing with it being so small. Hidden between the pages, she found a handful of letters. The broken red seals bore no identifying marks. "Did you read them?"

"I tried."

No doubt as his reading progressed so did his understanding of the context.

"May I read them?" Every fibre of her being told her to hand them back, to nail the board to the floor and never speak of them again. "You have my word I'll not reveal their contents without your permission."

Jacob's small hand settled on her arm. "Don't tell Papa. It will make him sad again."

Her heart grew heavy. A child should not have to live with such pressure on his shoulders. A man deserved to have peace in his life, to have some semblance of happiness, too.

With some trepidation, she removed a letter, tucked the book under her arm and scanned the missive. She would have described it as a love letter, except the contents focused on the gratuitous aspects of a physical relationship. A blush rose to her cheeks. Heavens. What would a child make of such vulgar language?

"I understand why you didn't want to show them to your father." Indeed, once she'd gained Jacob's permission, how was she to explain them to Lord Farleigh?

The absence of a signature was not surprising. The gentleman in question thought nothing of sending them to Lady Farleigh's home. In itself, it spoke of conceit and arrogance.

"Mama kept them in the drawer next to her bed."

Oh, the poor mite. How had he kept them a secret all this time? Children struggled to hold their own water let alone something so damning. But of course. The last thing Jacob wanted was to hurt his father.

"Why did you keep them in here? Did you not worry your governess might find them?"

Was that another reason he chased the women away?

"No one would look in here unless the governess was ill."

"And a governess is never in the house long enough to catch the mystery illness." All parts of the puzzle seemed to be coming together. "You could have burned them. Your father knew nothing of the letters."

Jacob's gaze shifted about the room. He stepped forward and whispered, "A lady died in the woods, just like Mama. I think the letters might say why but I don't understand all the words."

Rose closed her eyes for a moment. Two women had died in the woods? She'd assumed Lady Farleigh died of an illness. No wonder his lordship insisted on an escort to Morton Manor.

"What if I read the letters? I shall only mention the important things to your father."

Jacob pursed his lips.

"Is it not better I explain their contents than him reading them himself?" she added. The thought of Lord Farleigh discovering the depth of his wife's deception chilled her bones. "What do you say?"

"Don't make him sad. He likes you. Tell—"

The loud rap on the door made them both jump. Rose placed the letter back inside the book and clutched it to her chest just as Mrs Hibbet entered.

"Here you are. We've been looking everywhere. Dr Taylor is here to examine Jacob."

Dr Taylor hovered at the door. The furrows on his brow marred his usually bright countenance. "I cannot tell you how relieved I am to hear of the child's speedy recovery. But it is wise to be prudent. Perhaps we should retire to the comfort of the child's bedchamber."

"Of course." With a tight grip on the book, Rose took Jacob's hand and followed Mrs Hibbet and the doctor down to the first floor.

They all paused outside the door to Jacob's room.

"Would you care to be present while I examine the boy?" Dr Taylor's gaze drifted over her face before falling to the blue ledger. "Mrs Hibbet will stay of course."

"Thank you, but I must see to Alice. I'm sure she would appreciate a distraction after such a dreadful shock."

Dr Taylor nodded. "Mrs Hibbet will relay any information regarding the child's recuperation, but I advise bed rest. We don't want him to catch a chill." He paused. "I trust you didn't find the tonic too distasteful."

"Not at all." The last thing she wanted was a lecture from the doctor. "Now, if you will excuse me, I must see to Alice."

Rose hurried back to her room and spent a few minutes skimming through the other letters hidden inside the book. The sender failed to comment on Lady Farleigh's character and spoke only of her ability to perform lewd tasks with the skill of a seasoned courtesan. The last words were always the same. To meet in a secret location at the agreed time.

Why any woman would want to take a lover when married to a man as handsome as Lord Farleigh was a mystery. Rose had spent the last two nights imagining his strong arms holding her close.

She scanned the ledger by way of a distraction but had to squint to read the words. The names listed in the left-hand column were barely legible. Miss Emma Perrin and Mrs Mary Drew were two she identified. To the right were various amounts of money ranging from thirty pounds up to two hundred.

Were they fees or repayments of debts?

Perhaps Lady Farleigh enjoyed gambling, and it was a list of her creditors. Or were they simply the names of servants she'd hired over the years. Evidently not, as the wages listed were extortionate even by a king's standards. The only other notable thing was the paper compartment attached to the back cover. Rose peered inside and found it empty.

But she had no time to consider the matter further. Alice was waiting. And so she returned the book to its hiding place beneath the floorboard. In truth, the mystery surrounding those named in the ledger was of no consequence. The most pressing problem was how she would tell Lord Farleigh about his wife's sordid affair.

After a quiet dinner alone, Christian returned to the study where he'd spent most of the afternoon. He poured a glass of brandy and gulped it down. The liquid fire burned his throat, but by God, it felt good. A couple more drinks and he might clear the fog filling his head. How was it he knew nothing about the letters? How was it Cassandra still caused mischief from beyond the grave?

Well, he was done with it.

No more governesses. No more secrets. No more lies.

It was time to bury the past for good.

He removed the crystal stopper from the decanter but hesitated. Brandy wasn't the answer to his problems. Still, one more nip would chase the cold from his bones.

The light rap at the door dragged his attention away from the assortment of spirits. "Enter."

When Rose came into the candlelit room, it was as though the clouds had parted to reveal the hot midday sun. Her smile warmed his heart and dragged him from his melancholic mood.

"Rose. It's good of you to come." Why on earth had he said that? As the governess, she had no choice but to abide by her master's request. "I mean it's late, and you've had a tiring day."

"*Eventful* would be a more appropriate word."

"Indeed." He stared at her, and she pursed her lips while she waited for him to speak. "Would you care for a drink?" Damn. He had brandy and port, nothing else. "I can see if Mrs Hibbet has sherry."

"No. One glass and I tend to ramble. Thank you, but I'd best keep my wits."

Christian chuckled. "You're safe with me. I've yet to take advantage of a governess." Indeed, the thought had never entered his head until now.

Rose swallowed. "My only thoughts are for the children. What if they should wake and call for me?"

Of course she was thinking of the children. That *is* why he paid her. Well, he would pay her once the week was out, and he'd persuaded her to stay.

"Please, close the door. We'll sit by the fire. After a swim in the lake, it's wise to keep warm."

She closed the door and came to sit in one the chairs in front of the hearth.

"Do you mind if I take a nip of brandy?"

"Not at all."

Christian poured the amber liquid into the glass and then sat in the chair opposite. He glanced down at her empty hands resting in her lap. "You recall why I asked you to join me? We were to discuss the letters Jacob mentioned." And he could not deny his growing need to spend more time in her company.

"Yes." Her gaze flicked to the crystal decanters. "Perhaps I will have a drink. Port if you have it as I'd rather not disturb Mrs Hibbet. My brother dared me to try brandy once, but it's so potent it scorched my throat. Then again, I was only twelve."

One did not need to be a genius to know she sought a distraction.

"It's an acquired taste." He poured a half measure of port into the daintiest glass on the tray and handed it to her before returning to his seat. "The first gulp is the hardest to bear."

She watched him over the rim of her glass while sipping her port. Her shoulders relaxed a little. "Jacob gave me the letters."

"And did they make for interesting reading?" Oh, he knew Cassandra well enough to guess the nature of their contents. "I suspect they are not for the faint-hearted."

"*Interesting* is not the word I would use." Rose breathed deeply. "I found them rather sad."

"Sad? For whom?"

"For you."

A heavy silence filled the air.

His heart raced. Not because he gave a damn about Cassandra's antics, or what people thought of him, but because those two words brimmed with tenderness.

"I don't need your pity, Rose." He had to be sure he wasn't mistaken. "I was foolish and naive. Some might call me pathetic for ignoring the matter. But the truth is I'd grown weary of her games."

Christian swallowed the rest of his brandy, but it failed to soothe him.

"It's not pity. I find it sad that you didn't receive the love and recognition you deserved. You're a good father, an honourable man."

"And a terrible husband."

"From what little I know of you, I don't believe that's true."

There it was again. An unnamed emotion lingered behind the words.

"I did not love my wife." He had no idea why he was telling a stranger about his personal affairs. But Rose was easy to talk to, and he had been alone for so long. "That makes me the worst kind of husband."

Rose sat forward. "And it is clear from the content of the letters that she did not love you, either. That's what makes it sad. Two lives ruined, and for what?"

Christian snorted. "To appease overbearing parents."

For a man born with privilege and title, love was bottom of the list when looking for someone to wed.

"Then you should count yourself lucky." A weary sigh left her lips. "At least your father didn't lock you away and deprive you of your freedom."

A woman as innocent as Rose had no idea how destructive a volatile marriage could be. "Marriage was my prison. And while I'm blessed to have two wonderful children, I am not sorry Cassandra's gone."

He exhaled long and deep. God, it felt good to tell the truth, to say the words that had festered in his heart for the last two years.

Rose sat back in the chair. She stared at the crackling flames while cradling her glass between her hands. Was she shocked by what he'd just said? Was it right to feel relief over his wife's death?

"Jacob said his mother always left when a letter arrived. He must have been five when this occurred."

Christian brushed his hand through his hair and squeezed his eyes shut briefly. "It makes me sick to my stomach to think he understood some of what went on." How did a child so young learn to manipulate events?

"Some say children are extremely perceptive." Without warning, she stood and walked over to the window, placing her empty glass on the silver tray as she passed. She looked out at the woods in the distance. "There is something I want to ask you." She paused briefly. "It's dark, and yet you've not drawn the curtains. Why?"

That was not the question that troubled her.

He took a moment to answer. "Perhaps I need to see what's happening outside."

She swung around and raised a challenging brow. "You're not telling me the whole truth."

This woman could see into his soul, could read his thoughts.

"What more do you want me to say?"

"That you have a fear of those you love going into the woods because your wife died there. That another woman died there too, and so you keep watch, waiting for something to happen, but you don't know what."

Christian jumped to his feet and placed his glass on the mantel. "How do you know Cassandra died in the woods?" He crossed the room to stand in front of her. "Did Mrs Hibbet tell you?"

"Jacob told me."

Christian stepped back and perched on the edge of the desk. "That poor boy."

"He didn't mention the details." Rose turned to face him. "Though he believes the deaths are connected in some way. He must have overheard a conversation to assume such a thing. Does it have anything to do with this mysterious illness?"

God, how he wished it was something as simple.

"The woman Jacob is referring to escaped from the asylum. No one knows how Miss Stoneway died. Another woman escaped too, Miss Turner, but to date, no one has found her."

A frown marred Rose's brow. "Do you suspect foul play?"

Christian shrugged. He didn't know what to think anymore. Methods could be quite brutal when it came to ridding the insane of their demons. "The consensus is that Miss Stoneway's mental imbalance somehow contributed to her death."

"I see."

She fell silent.

"Just say what is on your mind, Rose."

She cleared her throat. "If Morton Manor is as horrendous as some suggest, perhaps Miss Stoneway took her own life."

He considered Rose's pursed lips, could almost hear the questions, the suspicions bouncing back and forth in her mind. "And so you're wondering if that's how Cassandra died. Well, it's not. Would you like me to tell you about that fateful night? Would it surprise you to learn that my wife died in the arms of her lover?"

Rose gasped. But instead of stepping back in shock, she moved closer. Of course, she'd read the letters, and probably knew every sordid detail of the affair.

Christian grasped the edge of the desk. "Her lover, Mr Watson, died, too."

"Mr Watson?" The colour drained from Rose's face. "Is that not the name of the warden at Morton Manor?"

"Indeed."

"But … but I heard the warden died in a fire."

She seemed well informed for someone who'd recently arrived in the area. But then servants enjoyed gossiping below stairs.

"He did." Christian stared into Rose's blue eyes, hoping to prevent the horrid vision he'd encountered that night replaying in his mind. "They died together in a cottage in the woods."

Recognition dawned. Her head shot around to the window.

"The property was north of the boundary between Morton Manor and Everleigh," Christian clarified.

The cottage once housed the gamekeeper, when poaching was rife, and the woods provided the perfect place to move about undetected. Now just a few stones remained. The headstones of adulterers.

Rose turned back to face him. "It must have been dreadful," she whispered. Wide blue eyes searched his face, journeyed over his hair. Slowly, and with some hesitance, she cupped his cheek. "I'm sorry you had to experience such a tragedy."

Christian closed his eyes as the warmth of her skin broke through his ice-cold barrier. He couldn't open them for fear of what he'd do if he caught even a hint of affection in her eyes. How was it possible for so gentle a touch to soothe him and ignite a fire in his belly at the same time? He wanted her. More than he'd wanted anything his whole damn life.

"You … you deserve to be happy," she continued breathlessly. "And you look so … so handsome when you smile."

His ragged breath echoed in his ears. He sensed her drawing near, felt her sweet breath breeze across his skin.

When her hand slipped away, and her soft lips touched his cheek, his heart almost leapt from his chest.

"Forgive me, my lord." She broke contact almost immediately. "I—I don't know what came over me."

Christian opened his eyes and knew there and then he was lost. He'd be repenting until the end of his days for what he was about to do. But he didn't care. Surely a man deserved to taste heaven after spending years in hell.

He reached for her hand, brought it to his lips and held it there while he inhaled the floral scent of her skin. *Rose.* So sweet. So delicate. So tempting.

His other hand slid around her waist and guided her to stand between his legs. "I know what it's like to be a viscount with endless responsibilities, to be a father and lord of all he surveys. But I've forgotten what it's like to be a man."

"You're more of a man than anyone I've ever met."

The compliment warmed his heart as well as another part of his anatomy. "Can I kiss you, Rose?"

She exhaled, moistened her lips and nodded.

The touch of her lips was everything he imagined it to be: instantly soothing, deeply arousing. What started as light brushing and chaste nips, soon ignited into something far more powerful and intense.

With a moan of appreciation, he crushed her to his chest, coaxed and teased her lips apart so his tongue could explore her mouth's wondrous depths.

Rose.

She met him with equal enthusiasm. Her hands journeyed up over his chest and around his neck. Dainty fingers tangled in his hair, tugging, holding him in position. Audible pants filled the air as a desperate hunger to taste each other deeply took hold.

He broke contact on a gasp, his body wracked with the need to carry this woman to his bed and make her his own.

"My lord." The whispered words drifted over him as he kissed along her jaw and neck.

"Call me Christian. Let me hear my name fall from your lips."

"*Christian.*" Her head fell back exposing the elegant column of her throat. Damn. He'd never seen a sight as beautiful.

As he worked up to the sensitive spot below her ear, relishing in her little moans and sighs, he opened his eyes and stared out at a sky littered with stars. God, he felt so alive. So blissfully free. Perhaps the Lord had answered his prayers.

But then something caught his attention.

A plume of black smoke crept into his field of vision, swirling higher and growing in density. Another person might have questioned the phenomena, but Christian knew exactly what it was.

"Rose." He clasped her arms and forced her to straighten, kissed her once on the lips as she gazed dreamily into his eyes, purely because he couldn't help himself. "I need to open the window."

A mischievous smile touched her lips. "It is rather hot in here."

He shook his head. "There's smoke in the sky above Morton Manor."

On a loud gasp, Rose swung around. She stepped aside, and Christian rushed forward and raised the sash. The smell of burning wood flooded his nostrils, carried on a breeze from the direction of the house.

"You're sure it's the manor?" Panic infused every word.

"Most definitely."

"Then we must do something." She grabbed his sleeve and pulled him towards the door.

Christian caught her by the arm and forced her to stop. "I'll go. Stay here with the children. I fear if they wake to a commotion it might rouse painful memories of the night Cassandra died."

"But what if there are people trapped inside? You can't tackle a fire alone."

By the time he reached the manor, it would be too late.

"Stay here," he insisted. "I shall return shortly." He took her face between his hands and claimed her mouth in a kiss that could well have to last him a lifetime. "Do not open the door to anyone. Promise me. Promise me you'll remain here."

She hesitated and glanced back at the window.

All the old doubts crept into his mind. What if his nightmare wasn't over? Visions of the future flashed before his eyes. He saw Rose rushing towards him just as the burning building collapsed, leaving her buried beneath the rubble.

"Promise me, Rose. If you care for me at all, you'll stay here."

She rubbed her neck, her pretty face marred by an inner conflict. Her answer would prove telling.

Eventually, she sighed and placed her hand on his arm. "Very well. I shall remain here. You have my word."

CHAPTER TEN

The biting wind nipped at Christian's cheeks as Valiant galloped down the lane leading to the manor. Thick smoke filled the air and half choked him. The scent of burning timber almost made him cast up his accounts, but he forged on ahead.

As soon as they passed through the gates, his horse grew restless and pawed the ground at the sight of the flames licking the walls and devouring everything in its path.

Morton Manor blazed like a beacon. A pyre in memory of all the poor souls who'd perished there. A fitting end for a place once regarded as the sanctum of witches.

Water filled his eyes. But he was not sad or sorry.

He glanced around the courtyard, one last jubilant goodbye.

Good God!

Preoccupied with his own private celebration, he'd failed to notice the gentleman sitting on the ground clutching a woman in his arms. Christian gave Valiant a reassuring pat, dismounted and rushed towards the couple.

"I saw the smoke and came immediately." Christian

pointed to the building. Within hours Morton Manor would be a pile of ash and rubble. "But I can see I'm too late."

The man failed to tear his gaze away from the woman's face. He held her to his chest, brushed loose tendrils of red hair from her brow. Were they the owners, returned after a lengthy trip? Though dirty, the cut of his clothes suggested a man of wealth. Was this the lord who'd hired Rose?

Christian bent down at their side. "She is alive I take it?" At times like this one had to ask insensitive questions.

The gentleman nodded. "Yes, but she's inhaled smoke, fallen somehow and hurt her head." In obvious distress, he continued to stroke the woman's cheek.

"May I?" Christian gestured to her hand, waited for a nod of approval and then checked for a pulse. The steady beat thrummed against his fingers. But he knew the dangers of smoke inhalation. "There's a doctor in Abberton a few miles up the road. I'll ride there at once."

A heavy sigh of relief burst from the gentleman's lips. "We'll wait at The Talbot Inn. I don't care what it takes. Have him come at once."

It crossed Christian's mind to direct them to Everleigh. As the closest neighbour shouldn't he be the one to offer the gentleman and his wife a bed for the night?

"Will you be all right at the Talbot? I have a large house and would offer you a place to stay." If he did, then they would discover he'd stolen their maid. And the injured woman bore too many similarities to Cassandra. "But I have young children who would be … be easily distressed at the sight of …" Christian struggled to finish the sentence.

"Thank you for the thought. The inn is clean and comfortable, and Mrs Parsons is a capable woman who'll know what to do."

Christian nodded. "Then I shall return with the doctor and meet you there."

Time was of the essence and so he did not dally, did not give the manor a second glance, but mounted his horse and galloped down the drive. The ride to Abberton through dark country lanes took fifteen minutes. He'd pushed the horse hard, hoping the wind would blow the smell of smoke from his coat.

"Dr Taylor." Christian rapped the wooden door of the doctor's house three maybe four times before his housekeeper answered.

"You'll be wanting the doctor no doubt." The woman's bulging cheeks swamped her tiny mouth and chin. She blinked rapidly when she recognised him. "My lord, come in. Come in. Goodness. The doctor wouldn't want me to leave you waiting out in the cold."

"I must speak to your master. It's a matter of great—"

"Lord Farleigh?" Dr Taylor appeared at the top of the stairs, wearing a shirt and loose-fitting trousers. "What has brought you out at this hour?" He padded in his stocking feet down to the hall. "Is it Jacob? Is he unwell?"

"No. It's not Jacob." Christian swallowed to catch his breath. "There's a fire at Morton Manor. The whole place is ablaze. A young woman needs urgent attention."

Dr Taylor's face grew ashen. "A woman? But I thought all the occupants had left the manor."

"Who told you that?"

Dr Taylor scratched his head. "I—I can't remember. Perhaps it was Mrs Brown or was it your housekeeper, Mrs Hibbet? Never mind." He turned to his housekeeper. "Fetch my bag from the study and have Carter saddle my horse."

After bobbing a curtsy, the woman scurried off.

"Give me a few minutes to dress, and I'll meet you outside."

Christian sat astride Valiant, staring out into the distance while he waited for Taylor. But it wasn't the disaster at the manor that plagued his thoughts. For the first time in years, he looked forward to going home, to having another private conversation in the study with his governess.

Guilt flared as the image of that sweet, sensual kiss came flooding back. His desire for Rose should have roused a pang of shame. But no matter what position she held in his household, he refused to see her as a servant.

For heaven's sake, he'd never met a more intelligent woman. And regardless of her situation now, she could hold her head amongst the elite of society. Perhaps he should press her for more information regarding her background. But what if his probing questions pushed her away? He'd grown accustomed to having her around. Couldn't bear the thought she might leave.

"Forgive me for keeping you waiting, my lord." Dr Taylor appeared on his mount. "Carter, my groom, grows less efficient as the years pass. Now, where are we headed? I trust someone moved the woman in question to a safer location."

"Yes, The Talbot Inn."

"Ah, we'd best get there before Mrs Parsons mixes one of her tinctures. The woman cooks the best lamb stew for miles around but is lacking when it comes to herbal remedies."

They nudged their horses out onto the lane and set off towards the inn.

Alerted by the clip of their horses' hooves on the cobblestoned courtyard, Mr Parsons rushed out to greet them. "His lordship said you'd be coming. They're waiting upstairs."

So the gentleman was a member of the aristocracy. Damn.

Not only did that present a problem when it came to stealing servants, but there were still those in London who liked to gossip about Cassandra. It was yet another reason for remaining in the country.

They dismounted, and a groom took their horses.

"Take me to her at once," Dr Taylor said, removing the leather satchel draped across his shoulder. "Ensure Mrs Parsons doesn't give her anything to eat or drink until I've made a thorough examination."

"Aye, sir."

They hurried inside. Mrs Parsons appeared and beckoned them upstairs. "I've put the lady in here." She rapped on the door, opened it ajar and peered inside. "The doctor is here, my lord."

"Praise the saints. Show him in."

Christian tapped Taylor's arm. "I'll be downstairs should you need anything." The doctor liked privacy when he worked, and Christian wanted to avoid making polite conversation.

Despite the late hour, numerous people sat around the crude wooden tables in the taproom, supping their drinks. Christian found a spot in the corner near the fire and ordered a tankard of ale. Mr Parsons approached the table, wiping his hands on the apron tied around his waist.

"Terrible news about the lady," he said in a hushed voice. "Although I doubt any of us care what happens to the manor."

"No doubt some of Mr Watson's old patients will rejoice once they hear the news." Christian swallowed a mouthful of ale. "As will I once I'm assured the lady is in good health."

"Oh, we're all hoping for that, my lord." Mr Parsons stepped closer. A whiff of stale sweat wafted past Christian's nose. "His lordship doesn't seem too bothered about losing the house. I know some who'd be crying over the burnt timbers."

"I imagine anyone who's spent a few nights in that place would welcome an excuse to leave." Christian sat forward. "Did he give his name? It's been years since I spent time in the city." Much longer since he'd attended balls and social engagements. "And I must admit, I"m curious as to the identity of the gentleman willing to purchase an old asylum."

"The Earl of Stanton's been back and forth from London twice this week, though that's the first time we've seen him since he bought the old house."

The Earl of Stanton?

Oh, he knew the name but remembered the portly gentleman with white streaks running through his black hair. The fellow upstairs was obviously the son and heir.

"Then I trust the lady is his wife?"

Mr Parsons raised a brow. "If she's his wife, then my aunt Fanny's a bishop."

"I see."

The news banished all feelings of guilt Christian had over keeping Rose at Everleigh. The earl had purchased the manor for his mistress, hence the reason for two visits in one week. One needed brash servants when dealing with the sort of parties held by the members of the demi-monde. As a maid in such a house, Rose would have fallen foul to the rakes and rogues looking for easy sport.

Once again, the need to question his motives pushed to the fore. He cared about Rose. *Bloody hell.* The thought caught him off guard. He shook his head. Devil take him, he did care about her. And the kiss they'd shared was precisely that … shared not forced. Pleased to shake off the label of rogue, he drained what remained in the tankard.

The thud of boots on the wooden staircase caught

Christian's attention. Dr Taylor appeared, scanned the room and raised his chin in recognition.

"I'd best fetch the doctor a well-deserved drink." Mr Parsons hurried off and exchanged a few words with Dr Taylor as he passed.

Taylor came over to the table, released a weary sigh and dropped into the chair. "Never underestimate the dangers of inhaling smoke."

"Were you able to help her?" Christian swallowed. Fire smoke attacked like a silent devil. By the time he'd reached the gamekeeper's cottage, Cassandra had stopped breathing.

"She'll live. Thankfully, his lordship reached her in time. A few days' rest and recuperation will see her right again though the cough and dry throat will last a while longer."

Mr Parsons brought the doctor's drink and placed it on the table.

"Thank you, Parsons." Taylor gave a pleasurable sigh as he downed his ale. As Parsons walked away, the doctor turned to Christian. "Any news on the manor?"

"Put it this way. The place will no longer be a blot on the landscape."

Dr Taylor considered him over the rim of the vessel. After an uncomfortable silence, he said, "And you're all right? No memories come back to haunt you?"

During those first few days after Cassandra's death, Taylor had practically lived at Everleigh, tending to the burns on Christian's hands that thankfully healed leaving no scars. "I'm fine."

"Just fine?"

"What do you want me to say? That seeing the manor ablaze brought back painful memories of the night I tried to rescue Cassandra?"

Dr Taylor shrugged. "The mind is a complicated thing.

What you saw tonight might help you remember what happened in the woods that night."

Christian gritted his teeth. "I remember what happened. I know what I saw."

"Yes, a faceless figure in a long black cloak." Taylor kept his tone even. Had Christian detected a hint of mockery he might have grabbed the doctor by his cravat and shook an apology from him. "One minute it was there, the next it simply vanished. You've told me many times before."

The acrid smoke had made it impossible for him to identify the figure watching from the woods. Blinking made his eyes sting, and his only concern was for the lifeless body he'd pulled from the flames.

"It is of no consequence now." Christian brought his tankard to his mouth but slammed it on the table when he realised it was empty. "But to answer your point, no. Tonight's incident did not rouse memories of the past."

Another patron's cackle of a laugh distracted them both momentarily.

"Your new maid," Dr Taylor began. He paused and shook his head. "Forgive me. I cannot remember her name."

There was no reason why he should. "Rose. Her name is Rose. But she's not the maid. She's the governess."

"Indeed." The corners of the doctor's mouth curled up. "It's clear she has the wherewithal necessary for the position. And with the illness spreading it's wise to move her from the servants' quarters."

Every conversation came back to the strange sickness. "You're still convinced contact with a deadly plant brings about the fever?" He couldn't help but convey a hint of cynicism. It sounded ludicrous.

Dr Taylor raised a questioning brow. "What other explanation is there?"

Christian stared at his empty tankard. The problem began not long after Cassandra's death. Maybe Reverend Wilmslow had a point. Had Cassandra brought something into the house, left herbs in the kitchen or a potion to cure insomnia?

There had to be a rational explanation.

His thoughts drifted back to Morton Manor, to the earl and his mistress lying in the courtyard. At the time, he'd not thought to question the absence of any servants.

"Did Lord Stanton say what happened to his staff? Please tell me no one perished in the fire."

"Stanton dismissed them two days ago."

"Dismissed them? Did he say why?"

"No. His lordship omitted to mention it, and it's not a question a doctor asks. I heard the news from the baker in the village. Apparently, one of them came looking for work."

Christian frowned but said nothing. Thank heaven Rose had remained at Everleigh. The thought drew his mind to the beguiling woman waiting for his return. She'd be pacing the floor, eager for news, fearing the worst.

Christian stood. "I should return to Everleigh. What with the manor being so close, I left the servants with their faces pressed to the window. They'll want my reassurance there's nothing to fear."

Mrs Hibbet wouldn't rest until she saw him cantering up the drive. And what of Rose? A woman with her courageous temperament would not stand at the window and watch events unfold. But she'd given her word that she'd remain at the house. And she would not break an oath.

Would she?

CHAPTER ELEVEN

"Close the window, Alfred. We don't want any smoke in here. We've just had the tapestries cleaned." Mrs Hibbet batted the footman's hands away and pulled down the sash with such force Rose feared the noise would wake the children.

From the first-floor window, they had a perfect view of the drive leading around to the stables. They could see the amber glow skimming the tops of the trees around Morton Manor, the sky above a menacing orange and grey mass.

Two hours had passed since Christian departed, though the agonising wait made it feel like days.

"Surely he should be back by now." Rose placed her hand flat on the window pane. The glass was warm beneath her palm. "What if his lordship has suffered an injury and cannot get help?"

Rose's heart pounded in her chest. She could still taste the essence of the man she'd grown to admire. Could still feel the imprint of his hand where he'd gripped her waist in a moment of pure passion.

"Oh, his lordship knows how to take care of himself never

fear." Mrs Hibbet's confident tone belied the nervous twitch of her mouth.

What if Stokes had started the fire out of spite or for revenge? The beast of a man thought nothing of hammering his fists into the face of anyone who got in his way. What if Nicole hadn't left for London?

"Perhaps one of us should go and look for him?" Rose said. Christian couldn't expect her to keep a promise when his life was in danger.

Mrs Hibbet raised her chin. "The master said to wait here and wait here is what we'll do."

"Rose is right." Alfred glanced at the buttons on his shoes to avoid meeting Mrs Hibbet's hard stare. "His lordship could have burnt his hands like last time. If a man can't grip the reins how's he supposed to ride home?"

Panic flared. An image of Christian lying crushed beneath the glowing timbers flashed into her mind.

"I'll go and speak to Dawkins. Send him to check the lane to see if there's any sign of him." Rose had made up her mind, and so hurried along the landing and down the stairs before Mrs Hibbet could protest.

She had every intention of doing just that, but as soon as she stepped out into the open air, the smoke clawed at her throat. The smell of charred wood clung to her nostrils, and all thoughts turned to Christian. If she could feel the effects of the fire here, then surely those in the vicinity would struggle to breathe.

There was no time to go in search of Dawkins. And so she gathered her skirt and hurried along the path leading to the stile.

So much had changed since the night she'd lost her way and ended up at Everleigh. She'd taken the job as a maid purely to avoid seeing her father and being carted back to the manor. She'd taken the job of temporary governess because she felt an overwhelming need to help the children.

With one leg over the stile, she stopped and glanced back at Everleigh. Her heart melted. She loved how the house sat nestled amongst the trees, hidden away from the world. She loved the connection she shared with the children and Mrs Hibbet. Most of all, she loved the feel of Lord Farleigh's lips when they moved wildly over hers.

Christian.

Her heart flew up to her throat when she imagined kissing him again. How had she ever believed herself in love with Lord Cunningham? But she'd been desperate to escape the clutches of a tyrant. Desperate to live in a house full of love and laughter. Desperate to believe anything.

Despair descended.

Her father would find her, eventually. Would it be a day, a week, a month? She had no idea. All thoughts turned to finding Christian, to making the most of the time left. And so she climbed over the stile and hurried along the path, eager to find the route that led to Morton Manor.

This time, an amber glow illuminated everything within a mile of the manor. The fork in the path proved easy to find. As Rose drew closer to the burning house, the heat from the flames roasted her cheeks. The smoke stung her eyes, and she coughed to clear the dust irritating her lungs.

For a second she thought she saw a black figure moving through the trees. Rubbing her eyes made them water, and she blinked numerous times before glancing up again.

The dark shape staggered towards her.

Rigid with fright, she froze. The knot in her stomach tightened. "Who's there?"

"Miss Asprey?" The figure called out to her as he

stumbled along the path. "Is … is that you, my dove?" He tripped and fell, coughed and spluttered. "God damn."

Despite her fear, Rose stepped forward to help him. Taking hold of his scrawny arm, she assisted him to his feet. From the black marks on his face and the stench of smoke on his clothes, he must have come from the manor.

"Can you forgive a man for his stupidity?" His breath smelt like rotten meat mixed with claret. The man's bloodshot eyes and skeletal features would have scared the Devil away. "I should not have left you in there to perish. Thank the Lord you escaped."

She'd never set eyes on the man before. But for some reason he recognised her. Then again, he did seem delirious.

"You've mistaken me for someone else, sir." Rose batted the fellow's hand away from her arm. "Have you escaped the fire at the manor?"

"Fire?" He appeared dazed, unsteady on his feet. "Oh, the fire, yes." A length of spittle hung from the corner of his mouth. "There's nothing left, you know. But what a clever dove you are."

Clearly, the man had lost all grasp of his faculties. Trauma did that to a person, made them lose all hold on reality.

"Was there anyone else with you at the manor?"

"Only you, my angel. And I'll not make the mistake of losing you again." In a move as swift as it was sudden, he grasped a lock of her hair.

"Ow! Let me go. Have you lost your mind?"

He examined the hair in his fist. "Your hair is as gold as the sun, not red as fire."

The man spoke in riddles. If the manor accepted patients, he would be a prime candidate. "What on earth are you talking about? Release me at once."

"Wait! You're not my dove." Keeping a firm hold of her

hair, he turned and scanned the woods. "Miss Asprey? Miss Asprey, are you out there?"

Rose tried to prise his bony fingers apart but to no avail. But then the sound of snapping twigs caught her attention.

"Listen. Do you hear my dove approaching?" He tugged Rose's hair until her head almost touched her knees.

"Please. Ow! You're hurting me."

A deep growl sliced through the air. "Get your bloody hands off the lady, now!"

Rose tried to look behind but couldn't move her head more than an inch.

"Bugger off. You'll not take her from me again."

"I swear I will drive my fist through your heart if you do not release her this instant." The gentleman spoke more clearly now, and she knew at once it was Christian. Thank heavens he was safe.

"I told you. She's with me now."

"He's not right in the mind," Rose called out. "He thinks I'm someone else. Someone from Morton Manor."

Christian approached them. He grasped the man's hand and squeezed until she heard the crack of bones. "Release her. I'll not tell you again."

The man cried out in pain, but as soon as he let go of her hair, Christian punched him hard on the jaw. The fellow fell back and landed on his backside in the ferns.

Christian turned to her. "Are you all right?" He stroked her cheek, gazed into her eyes.

Rose nodded. "I came looking for you."

"I told you to remain at Everleigh."

Rose didn't have a chance to answer because another man came charging through the trees. Christian stepped in front of her to act as her shield, and she clung to his waist.

"My lord! Where are you? Lord Mosgrove?"

Christian squared his shoulders. "Who are you?"

The newcomer glanced at the man lying amid the foliage, mumbling to himself and rubbing his chin. "I'm his lordship's coachman. He wandered off, and I couldn't find him."

"Then I suggest you drag him back to the hole he crept out of," Christian's hard tone caused the coachman to step back, "else he'll find himself buried in a permanent one."

Rose peered around the broad expanse of Christian's chest. "Was your master at the manor? Was there anyone else there with him?"

The coachman shuffled uncomfortably. "I just do as I'm told. It ain't for me to comment on his lordship's business." The servant reached down and pulled his master to his feet. "Come on, my lord. Let's get you back to the carriage."

"But … but what about my dove?"

"Happen she'll find her way back."

They stood in silence and watched until the coachman and the crazed lord disappeared from view.

Christian swung around to face her. Puffs of white mist drifted up into the air as he struggled to regulate his breathing.

"You swore you'd stay at Everleigh." His hands settled on her upper arms. He scanned her face, his beautiful green eyes holding a look of panic. "You gave me your word. What if I'd not come back when I did? What if Mrs Hibbet hadn't seen you climbing the stile?"

Rose swallowed. "I needed to know you were safe. I needed to know you were not trapped in that burning building." Tears welled, and her heart raced so fast she feared it might burst from her chest. "I just needed to see you."

He stared into her eyes for the longest time. "Do you have any idea what you're doing to me?"

She didn't know what he meant or how to answer.

"On one hand, you make me feel like the strongest of men," he continued. "I could race up a mountain, climb that damn tree. Punch any man who threatened to harm you. And yet inside …" He paused and shook his head. "Pay me no heed."

She didn't know why, but she stepped closer, wrapped her arms around him and placed her head on his chest. He held her close though said nothing. She could have stayed like that forever: warm, listening to his heartbeat, encircled in his strong embrace.

"I don't know what's happening to me, either," she muttered into his chest for she daren't look into his eyes.

Oh, what a terrible friend she was. She should have been looking for Nicole. But every fibre of her being lived to hear his voice, craved his attention, his tender touch. This obsession would pass. A woman deprived of love surely latched on to any display of kindness. Genuine sentiment took months, even years to form.

So why could she not step away? Why did thoughts of kissing him fill her head?

"It's my fault," he said, breaking the brief silence. "If I'd just left you to your work. If I'd done the honourable thing and—"

"Don't say that." She looked up at him. "I have never met a man with more integrity."

He gave a mocking snort. "Rose, when I'm with you my thoughts are far from moral."

Heat rose to her cheeks. She wanted him to dream about kissing her. She did not want this fantasy to end.

A weak chuckle escaped from her lips. "When I'm with you my thoughts are far from moral, too."

Christian clenched his jaw as his breathing grew shallow. Energy sparked in the surrounding air. Blood pumped molten hot through her veins. He lowered his head, and she came up on her tiptoes, eager to meet him.

He stopped a mere inch from her mouth, and stared at her lips as if they were the most wondrous thing he'd ever seen.

His hands drifted down her back, daring to delve lower to cup her and cage her in his embrace. The first touch of his lips sparked a fire deep in her core. She clutched the lapels of his coat, pressed her aching breasts against his hard body. With light sweeps of his tongue, he teased her lips apart. Her eager tongue touched his, each stroke causing a strange pulsing between her legs. Heavens, his mouth was so warm, so wet, so utterly addictive. A growl resonated somewhere in his throat as their tongues tangled. Their ragged breathing obliterated all other sounds.

"We should not be doing this," he whispered, kissing her throat, nipping the sensitive skin below her ear.

"No, we shouldn't." A delicious shiver raced through her body, leaving her mind in a cloudy haze of lust and desire. "Don't … don't stop, Christian."

He claimed her mouth in the same masterful way he did most things. Oh, she could not taste him deeply enough to satisfy the hunger clawing her belly. He balled the material of her dress in his fists. A cool breeze caressed her legs, and she gasped into his mouth when his hot hands traced a path up over her bare thighs.

"Christian."

His fingers brushed against her most intimate place, once, twice, the third time her knees sagged.

"I've got you, love." One muscular arm gripped her tightly as he continued to pluck a potent rhythm.

She could think of nothing but him, touching his bare skin, devouring his mouth, taking him into her body.

"My lord! Are you in there?" The words echoed through the woods. "Rose? Lord Farleigh? Can you hear me?"

"Bloody hell." The muttered curse revealed his frustration.

Being slightly detached from reality, it took a few seconds for her to realise someone else had entered the woods. Christian released his grip, straightened her dress and stepped away. She wobbled, struggled to gain her balance.

Christian cupped her elbow. "Alfred is coming." His gaze drifted over her lips and hair. "I'm afraid we shall have to explore our mutual attraction some other time."

Her heartbeat pulsed hard in her throat. It amounted to more than exploring an attraction. That word made the whole affair sound superficial. And though she thought him the most handsome man of her acquaintance, her desire to be with him came from her heart as well as her loins.

But guilt flared.

How could she be so selfish? She'd pressed him for more kisses rather than information about the occupants of Morton Manor. At some point, she would have no choice but to leave him, leave Everleigh. If he discovered her identity, he'd offer marriage. But it would be a marriage based on a lie. Another marriage doomed out of a need to conform to society's rigid rules.

And what of the children? They did not need any more disruption in their lives.

"My lord." Alfred caught sight of them and hurried forward. "Mrs Hibbet sent me to help you find Rose."

"Thank you, Alfred." Christian placed his hand on her back and guided her through the foliage and onto the path. "I found her near the boundary."

Rose forced a smile although her head was a jumbled mess of contradictions. Should she stay another day? Should she run? "I thought someone should check that his lordship was unhurt."

Alfred glanced at a point beyond their shoulder. "Mrs Hibbet said there'll be nothing left of the place after this."

"Mrs Hibbet is right. Come the morning Morton Manor will be a pile of ash."

Rose looked back over her shoulder. "Thank heavens the occupants left when they did." Then again, the fool in the woods said he'd come from there. Either way, it didn't matter. Her father couldn't send her back to the manor now even if he wanted to.

"Oh, there were people staying at the house. If you didn't know already, the Earl of Stanton is the gentleman who employed you to work at Morton Manor."

"The house was occupied?" Rose swayed as the ground seemed to slip away beneath her feet. "By whom?"

"Well, I say the earl, but in truth, his mistress has taken residency."

"His mistress?" Rose blinked, but her head whirled. Her father despised women who sought affairs out of wedlock. Woe betide he ever discovered Lord Farleigh had ravished his daughter in the woods. "The Earl of Stanton doesn't have a mistress."

Christian turned to her and frowned. "You mean you were unaware he hired you to keep house for a courtesan." He paused and glanced at the footman. "Walk on, Alfred. I've no intention of spending the rest of the evening gossiping in the woods."

With a curt nod, Alfred strode back along the path, and they followed.

"I … I trust the occupants escaped un-unharmed." She despised her father but couldn't bear the thought he'd perished in the fire.

"Both the earl and his mistress are staying at The Talbot Inn. Dr Taylor is with them. Stanton's mistress is suffering from the effects of the smoke but should be up and about in a few days."

Relief coursed through her. But what of Nicole? "And the servants escaped too?" What if Stokes or Mrs Gripes came to Everleigh looking for work? Her father would pay handsomely for news of his runaway daughter.

"Apparently there are no servants." He offered his hand as they approached the stile. Rose gripped his fingers for fear her knees might buckle. These new developments only added to her confusion. "By all accounts, he dismissed them a few days ago although I wonder how the earl and his companion managed on their own."

Dismissed? It came as no surprise. Her father refused to tolerate incompetence.

"But the gentleman in the woods said he'd come from the manor?"

Christian jumped over the stile and fell into a slow pace at her side. "Perhaps the earl has stolen the man's mistress, and he refuses to accept the fact. What woman wouldn't opt for a younger gentleman?"

"The earl is hardly what one would consider young." Rose snorted but then caught herself. "S-someone told me he's approaching sixty."

"Sixty? No. The gentleman I met didn't look a day over twenty-five."

How was she to argue without revealing too much?

Rose cast him a sidelong glance as they approached the house. "And you're certain you met the Earl of Stanton?"

"Undoubtedly. Now I come to think of it I recall reading that the old earl died. No doubt the fellow I met was the heir."

Rose stopped abruptly.

Her father was dead!

How could she not know? Christian's words echoed over and over in her head. Her heart lurched. Bile bubbled in her stomach and rose to burn her throat. But Oliver was the heir to the earldom.

"I would have brought them here," Christian continued, "but with the woman's vibrant red hair she bore a striking resemblance to Cassandra."

Rose gasped. Nicole? Were Oliver and Nicole the two people who'd escaped from Morton Manor?

Christian stopped and turned to face her. "Is something wrong? Your face is deathly pale."

She clutched her throat. Her father was dead! She blinked back tears of sadness, of regret. Now it was too late for him to make amends. Now his last cruel act would forever define their relationship.

"Christian," she whispered as a black cloud descended to obscure her vision. And then she crumpled to the ground, sucked into a dark oblivion.

CHAPTER TWELVE

"Heaven save us, my lord. What on earth happened?" Mrs Hibbet rushed to his side, her frantic gaze scouring Rose's face and body as Christian held her in his arms. "Was it the fire? Is it the dreaded illness?"

"I've no idea." Panic grabbed him by the throat leaving him barely able to breathe. He came to an abrupt halt at the bottom of the grand staircase. "One minute we were discussing the fire, the next her legs gave way, and she fell to the ground."

Mrs Hibbet touched Rose's head. "There's no evidence of a fever. She feels cold and clammy. If this is the start of the sickness, we can't risk anyone else catching it."

"There's every likelihood she's caught a chill." Hell, Jacob had pushed her into a lake, and she'd swallowed a mouthful of murky water. She'd raced into the woods without a coat or shawl and inhaled the thick smoke, only for a deranged lord to attack her in a case of mistaken identity. "Perhaps the events of the day proved too much for her."

"Still, we should move her to the servants' quarters as a precaution."

Everyone who slept below stairs had suffered from ill effects on more than one occasion. "No. The governesses here have never been ill. We'll take her up to her room." He bit back a groan as he considered carrying her up the stairs.

"Beg your pardon, my lord, but a governess never stays long enough to contract the illness."

Mrs Hibbet had a point. As such, they'd never found cause to search that particular room. "Send Joseph or Dawkins to The Talbot Inn and ask Dr Taylor to call here on his way back to Abberton."

"I'll see to it at once, my lord. Poor girl, she should have drunk the tincture as the doctor ordered." Mrs Hibbet scurried off along the corridor, muttering to herself as she went.

Christian mounted the stairs. Rose's petite frame made the task less arduous. The door to her room stood ajar, and he kicked it open and placed her gently on the bed.

"Rose." Christian perched on the edge of the bed, stroked her cheek and checked beneath her lids in an effort to wake her. "Rose. Can you hear me?"

A faint moan escaped from her lips, and her eyes fluttered although she didn't open them straight away.

He sat patiently waiting. What else could he do other than hold her hand and whisper words of encouragement? Releasing a weary sigh, he pushed his hand through his hair.

Morton Manor was not the only accursed house in the parish. Everyone who dared set foot in Everleigh suffered in one form or other. Perhaps he should move away, take the children to London, at least for the time being. Perhaps he should give the reverend and Dr Taylor free rein to inspect every blasted corner of the house.

A weak moan drew his attention to Rose. Beneath her closed lids, he could see a sign of activity. Her body jerked as her breath came quick.

"Get out of here. Go before it's too late." Her muttered ramblings were barely coherent. "Fire ... fire at the ... the manor."

"Rose." Patting her hand helped as she opened her eyes once and then squeezed them shut. "You're safe. You're at Everleigh. We're waiting for Dr Taylor."

Her eyes flickered, and she opened them again. Thin cornflower-blue irises rimmed dilated pupils. She stared through him as if watching a terrifying scene unfold.

"Wake up, Rose." With a gentle hand, he stroked her brow.

At the touch of his fingers, she sucked in a ragged breath. "Christian?" She scanned the room, her gaze coming to settle on him. A weak smile touched her lips. "I'm at Everleigh. Thank heavens." Her breathing settled, and she exhaled slowly.

"I think the horrendous events of the day have taken their toll." No wonder every newcomer stayed no more than a week. "Dr Taylor will be along presently. Mrs Hibbet fears you've contracted the fever."

She glanced at the tiny brown bottle on her nightstand. "No. If anything, I feel cold to my bones."

"No doubt the dip in the lake, coupled with the cold night air, has given you a chill. A nip of brandy will work wonders if you're able to stomach it."

Rose nodded. "I need something to settle my nerves, although I'm not sure that will help the pounding in my head."

A light knock on the door brought Mrs Hibbet. His housekeeper hovered at the threshold. "Can you spare a moment, my lord?"

From her grave expression, it was evident she had

important news to impart. God, he hoped the woman at The Talbot Inn hadn't taken a turn for the worse. He turned to Rose. "I'll be back in a moment with a glass of brandy."

Once out in the hall, Mrs Hibbet pulled the door closed. "I sent Dawkins to the inn to fetch Dr Taylor," she whispered. "He said someone's been asking after Rose."

Christian jerked his head back. "Someone? Who? What did they say?" Was it that lunatic from the woods? If so, he'd get more than a punch on the jaw.

"Well, the fellow never used her name, but he was looking for a slender woman with golden hair. A pretty thing, he said." Mrs Hibbet glanced at the closed door. "He said she's been missing from the area for a few days."

"Was it one of the staff from Morton Manor?" The earl must have sent a man out looking for the missing maid. Or was Rose's dissolute brother in need of funds and somehow knew she'd taken work with a wealthy lord?

"No, he'd not come from the manor. But Dawkins said the fellow knew his way around a stable."

"I trust Dawkins said nothing about Rose."

"No, my lord. Dawkins knows not to speak to strangers about household business."

There was one saving grace in this whole debacle. His staff were loyal to a fault. "Leave it with me. If the man should call again, direct him to the house."

Perhaps the earl knew Rose had arrived on the mail coach, had heard talk of the mysterious deaths in the woods and feared for his servant. While people knew Miss Stoneway was a wealthy orphan driven insane by the death of her parents, a few feared foul play.

By rights, he should speak to Lord Stanton and explain the situation. But what was the point? After the fire, the earl had no use for a maid. No doubt his only thoughts were for the health and happiness of his mistress.

"Will you remain here, my lord?"

"For the time being."

"What shall I do when the doctor arrives?"

"Send for me at once."

Mrs Hibbet nodded and moved towards the stairs.

"Could you have a decanter of brandy and two glasses sent up to Rose's room?" They both needed a drink. His day had been just as taxing. God damn. If only Jacob had told him about the letters. Then he might have understood the reason behind his son's malicious antics.

Everyone leaves us?

Those words had blown a hole clean through his heart. Yes, Cassandra always left, didn't give a damn about anyone but herself. But the governesses left because Jacob drove them away. A saint would struggle to forgive some of the terrible things the boy had done.

And yet Rose had taken it all in her stride. Not once had she blamed his son. Never had he met a woman with such a kind heart. Indeed, her inner beauty enhanced her appeal. *Appeal* was a mild word for what he felt. By God, he couldn't get the woman out of his mind. She stirred something in him, something deep inside, something long forgotten.

Truth be told, he needed her. She made his world of chaos a bearable place. Even the children behaved differently around her. He'd known from the first glance she was special. He'd felt drawn to her, to her smile, to the sound of her voice. And her lips, heaven help him. From his experiences in his youth, he thought he knew passion. But those fleeting dalliances were nothing compared to the powerful tremors that wracked his body when he was with her.

And yet he could not shake the feeling that their time

together would soon be at an end. Was he as pessimistic as his son? Was Mrs Hibbet right? Had the Lord sent an angel to help them through troubled waters, to steer them to calmer, safer shores?

Did his son have a point?

Did everyone leave in the end?

CHAPTER THIRTEEN

S livers of sunlight touched her cheek, warming her skin. Rose opened her eyes although the morning sun brought with it an overwhelming sense of trepidation. What must Christian think of her? Only simpering debutantes swooned.

But sometimes the body knew better than the mind when dealing with shocking news. Sleep had been the only way to banish thoughts of her father's death. Any hopes of repairing their fractured relationship were gone. She would be forever the daughter of some other gentleman, even though her father lied about her mother's infidelity out of spite and jealousy. And her father would always be the cold-hearted devil who'd imprisoned her in an old asylum as a means of control.

But she could not dwell on that now. Oliver had come home to claim his rightful place as head of the family. No doubt he'd dismissed Stokes and Mrs Gripes as soon as he'd heard about her mistreatment. And by all accounts, he'd rescued Nicole, too.

The chamber door creaked open, and Mrs Hibbet entered carrying a jug. She tottered over to the wash stand and filled the bowl with clean water.

When the housekeeper turned to the bed, she gasped. "Oh, bless us and save us. I almost dropped the jug. You're awake."

Rose stifled a yawn. "Forgive me. I should have got up to help with the chores. What time is it?"

"Almost nine."

"Nine!" Rose pulled back the bedcovers ready to jump out.

Mrs Hibbet plonked the jug on the washstand, rushed to her side and placed a hand on her shoulder. "Rest, dear. His lordship isn't expecting you in the nursery today. The fall in the lake gave you a nasty chill. Best give it another day before you return to work."

"But you don't have enough—"

"We'll manage." With a gentle push, Mrs Hibbet forced her to lie down. "We've been muddling along for two years. One more day won't hurt. And no doubt the doctor will want to see you again."

Again? She had no recollection of seeing him the first time.

A frustrated sigh left Mrs Hibbet's lips. "Reverend Wilmslow thinks you've got the dreaded fever and insisted on searching your room. Something to do with plants and spores from the Indies, although I fear he's been downing his lordship's port again. I might be simple when it comes to science, but it sounds like poppycock to me."

"Search my room?" Rose shivered, and it wasn't from the cold. "And why would the reverend need to do that?"

Mrs Hibbet straightened the sheets and tucked them around Rose's shoulders. "Oh, he thinks the illness is spread by contact with a poisonous plant. Maybe he should spend his time looking for a cure for restless hands instead of poking his nose into other folks' affairs."

Rose grasped Mrs Hibbet's sleeve. "Don't let the reverend in here. And whatever you do, don't leave me alone with him." Her apprehension stemmed from more than a concern over the reverend's over-friendly nature. Something was amiss. She just didn't know what.

"Have no fear." Mrs Hibbet smiled. "Both the reverend and the doctor felt the sharp edge of his lordship's tongue. Never in all my years have I heard him shout so loud, not with the children in the house." She gave a satisfied sigh. "I doubt you'll see the reverend here again until he's desperate enough to come begging for funds."

"What made Lord Farleigh so angry?" He was clearly a man of strong passions, in every sense of the word. One punch had taken the insane fool in the woods clean off his feet. One heated kiss had made her legs buckle, too.

"He said he's tired of people prying into his affairs. Said he'll deal with the matter in his own way, in a manner he sees fit." Mrs Hibbet's face beamed with pride. "Oh, he reminded me of how he used to be, before …" She paused and shook her head. "Well, when he was a younger man with the world at his feet."

A few days ago, it would have been difficult to imagine Lord Farleigh as anything other than a man absorbed with his own problems. But when they were alone, when he kissed her so deeply her stomach flipped, then she caught a glimpse of the carefree gentleman. The man who held her spellbound. The man who made her heart sing.

"I've seen a lot more of that man lately," Mrs Hibbet said. "Happen it comes from having someone young around. Someone educated enough to converse with him on his level."

Oh, what was she to do?

She felt like two people fighting to claim the same body. On the one hand, she enjoyed playing governess to the children, enjoyed the relationship she shared with Mrs Hibbet. But she had not seen her brother for two years, had feared she'd never see Nicole again. And now they were staying at The Talbot Inn, in heaven knows what state after escaping the fire.

If the battle between being simply Rose or Lady Rose Darby was not enough to contend with, now she had an added complication. In moments of fanciful musings, she imagined herself in love with Lord Farleigh. She imagined herself as mistress of Everleigh, sipping port with him in front of the fire on cold winter nights, indulging in far more than salacious kisses.

"It's nice to see him smile again after all that trouble at the manor." Mrs Hibbet's comment dragged Rose from her reverie. "Happen it will all change again if you leave."

"I'm not going anywhere just yet." Rose gave a weak chuckle merely to mask the lie that had fallen easily from her lips. She had to go to The Talbot Inn. How could she not visit Oliver and Nicole?

"That's what Dr Taylor said. You're not to go anywhere but your bed." Mrs Hibbet put her hand to her chest. "Now *there's* a man committed to his work. He was backwards and forwards between here and The Talbot Inn all day yesterday. Thanks to him that poor girl from the manor will be right as rain in a day or two."

"Yesterday? But the fire was last night."

"Last night?" Mrs Hibbet frowned. "No, dear. You slept the whole day yesterday. Dr Taylor came and examined you, although his lordship insisted I was present for the most part. Oh, you won't remember. You didn't open your eyes once. Dr Taylor said the body knows when it needs to heal." She caught her breath. "He wanted you to drink the tonic, but the bottle was already empty."

Empty?

Rose's gaze shot to the night stand. The brown bottle stood in the same place. Perhaps she had downed the contents. She slowed her breathing, paused and reflected as to whether she felt different. No. If anything, the restorative had given her a new lease of energy.

But to miss one whole day?

"I should get up. I can't stay in bed." Rose kicked the coverlet off before Mrs Hibbet could protest, and swung her legs to the floor. "Besides, after breathing in so much smoke, I could do with a stroll outdoors."

Mrs Hibbet put her hands on her hips. "Bed is the best place for you, dear."

"Please, Mrs Hibbet." After spending six months locked in the manor, the last thing she wanted was to remain indoors. "I don't want to be cooped up in here, not today."

"Oh, the doctor will be none too happy when he hears about it." The woman sighed. "But I suppose a walk won't do you any harm."

Rose jumped up and clutched Mrs Hibbet's hands. "Thank you."

"Mind you wear a cloak now. And keep out of the woods. His lordship's ridden to Abberton and won't be back for an hour or more."

"An hour is all I need." Then again, it would take thirty minutes walking at a fast pace to get to The Talbot Inn.

"Mind you get back before his lordship. Else I've no choice but to tell him you've gone."

The journey to The Talbot Inn took a little longer than Rose expected. By the time she reached the cobbled courtyard she'd rubbed another blister on her toe. Still, the slight tingling was overshadowed by the pounding of her heart. During the last two years, she'd dreamed of seeing her brother again, of ruffling his ebony locks and hugging him until he could hardly breathe. A thousand miles had stood between her and her dream. Now, the only thing preventing a reunion was an oak door and a flight of stairs.

But the sudden rush of excitement gave way to doubt.

It mattered not that a patron might recognise her, not with Oliver in residence. And yet something stopped her stepping forward. She stared up at the inn's stone facade, could almost feel her brother's presence behind the leaded glass window.

Realisation dawned.

If she entered the building, there were only two possible outcomes. Oliver would take her home to London, so pleased to see her that he'd not care where she'd been the last few days. Or he would insist on hearing her tale. Demand Lord Farleigh offer marriage.

But what if she went back to Everleigh and hid there for a few more days? No one knew her identity. No one cared for a maid's reputation. And it would give her more time with Christian. Help her make sense of the strange fluttering in her heart whenever he came near.

She paced back and forth, tapping her fingers on her lips, hoping it would help her reach a decision.

An image of Christian flooded her vision. He sat slumped in the chair, his head buried in his hands as he tried to make sense of her lies and deceit. At some point, she would have to tell him the truth. Was it not better to hear it from her lips? Did the children not need an explanation, too?

With one last glance at the upstairs windows of the inn,

she stepped back until out on the lane. It took every ounce of strength she possessed to walk away. But the invisible thread tying her to Everleigh proved hard to ignore.

Head down she hurried along the road, ignoring the carts and carriages passing by on their way to the city. At the crossroads, she turned left towards Everleigh. Lost in her thoughts, she failed to see the rider approaching until the horse slowed to a trot and stopped beside her.

"Rose?"

She looked up, directly into the handsome face of Dr Taylor. Noting the cut of his coat and the height of his top hat, the doctor clearly kept abreast of the latest fashions.

"It is you." The doctor raised a critical brow. "Did I not confine you to your bed?"

Rose forced a smile. After her experience at the manor, she'd be no one's prisoner again. "Surely a dose of fresh air is exactly what you'd prescribe."

"Perhaps. Had you not fallen into the lake or inhaled so much smoke." He frowned. "Is Lord Farleigh aware that you've left your bed?"

"I have not left my bed. But merely come out for a stroll." She bit back a groan for making such a foolish comment.

A smile touched the doctor's lips. "There is no need to be so defensive. It's just that he seemed overly concerned for your welfare."

What was the doctor implying?

"Like any respectable employer, Lord Farleigh treats all his staff with due care and attention." Heat rose to her cheeks when she considered the less than gentle way he'd devoured her mouth.

"Indeed, he does. Now, allow me to give you a ride." He glanced up at the dark clouds forming overhead. "It's a good thirty-minute walk back to Everleigh, and the last thing you need is to get caught in a rainstorm."

"That's kind, but I would not want to cause you any inconvenience." She struggled to hold his gaze. While his eyes were a piercing shade of blue, there was a coldness about them that worked in opposition to his warm, friendly countenance. "No doubt you're heading to the inn. I hear the patient there is in need of your services much more than I."

"In point of fact, I've just left a patient and am not due at the Talbot for three hours." The doctor shuffled back in the saddle. "I can't promise it will be a comfortable ride but the most important thing for you is to miss the storm."

How could she refuse?

Perhaps sensing her hesitation, he added, "While you may frown at the thought of riding with a gentleman in such close proximity, may I remind you I'm a doctor and have ferried many patients back to their homes. Besides, Lord Farleigh would be most displeased to know I rode by."

With no choice but to accept, she nodded and offered her hand. Placing one foot in the stirrup for leverage, the doctor hauled her up to sit sidesaddle in front of him. Two strong arms hemmed her in as he gripped the reins and turned the horse.

The feel of his icy breath against her cheek sent a shiver all the way to her toes. She expected him to canter away, to ensure she made it home before the weather broke. But he appeared to be in no rush and so they simply trotted up the lane.

"I find it rather distressing that a woman of your good breeding must resort to minding the children of the aristocracy," he said absently. "A woman with such a pretty countenance should have a husband to protect her, have her own house and family to mind."

To quell the nervous pang in her stomach, she laughed. "You should be careful. Some women would take your comment as a proposal."

There was an uncomfortable moment of silence. His strong arms held her trapped, and she could feel the heat of his gaze boring into her. Despite being outdoors, she found it difficult to breathe.

"Perhaps it is a proposal," he said, though his tone held not the slightest hint of affection. "There are few women of your looks and education living in Abberton."

Well, clearly the doctor lacked the time and energy to bandy words. "Had I any intention of remaining in Abberton, I might give the matter some thought." It was better to be polite. When she thought of marriage, only one man's face appeared in her mind.

"You intend to leave Everleigh?" He sounded surprised. "Lord Farleigh will be most distressed to lose another member of his household staff."

Guilt flared. But the sudden shift in topic gave her an opportunity to press the doctor for more information.

"Does it not frustrate you that, despite years of studying medicine, you cannot find the cure for the mysterious illness at Everleigh?"

The doctor cleared his throat. "Have you ever heard it said that sometimes you can be too close to a case to see what is obvious to others?"

No doubt it was his justification as to why he'd failed to solve the problem despite weekly visits.

"As someone newly arrived," the doctor continued, "I wonder if you have a theory regarding the continual reinfection. Does anything strike you as odd?"

"I am not a doctor," she said with a snort. "Indeed, neither am I a very good maid."

"Lord Farleigh appears to have no complaints. But I digress. Everyone can make a judgement regardless of their station. And so what is yours?"

Rose pondered his comment. Perhaps it was unwise to reveal her suspicions. Then again, solving the problem of the illness would help ease Christian's burden.

"It is not so much a theory but more a question."

"Go on."

"If the illness is supposedly caused by a plant in the garden, why is it the staff have been ill these last two years? The shrubs and plants are mature and have been a constant fixture since its design." She knew enough about vast country estates to give an informed view.

"Hmm. You have a valid point."

"And the staff are far too busy to roam idly in the woods."

"So, where would you suggest I look?"

Rose fell silent. It struck her what one deemed a coincidence often amounted to more than chance. "If I had trouble solving a conundrum, I would return to the beginning and start again."

Everleigh's elaborate gates appeared in the distance. Dr Taylor tutted and muttered something under his breath. Evidently, he found the conversation useful.

"Perhaps it all comes back to Lady Farleigh," she continued. "Things went awry shortly after her death. And then there is the case of the other woman found in the woods."

The rumble of thunder in the distance distracted them momentarily.

"You speak of Miss Stoneway?" Despite the evident threat of a storm, he slowed the horse to a walking pace.

"I do."

"There is nothing mysterious about her death. The woman

suffered from what I would call an identity disorder. In the end, it became too much for her to bear. I attended her on a number of occasions at Morton Manor. She attacked the reverend during one of his attempts to save her soul."

Rose considered his comments. No one would argue that people in an asylum were sick. By all accounts, Lady Farleigh's troubled mind was to blame for her demise. Nor did Rose doubt that evil lingered in the air around Morton Manor. Still, she felt a nagging need to probe further.

"I hear both you and the reverend also saw Lady Farleigh during her weekly visits to the manor." Did the doctor know of Lady Farleigh's affair with the warden? Surely he must have had an inkling.

"You know about Lady Farleigh's condition?"

"Only that she suffered with her nerves."

A chuckle left his lips although the sound failed to convey amusement. "Her nerves? The lady's problem stemmed more from her desire to behave like a spoilt child. And as I'm sure you're aware, children thrive on attention and will often go to great lengths to satisfy their needs."

No matter how hard she tried, she couldn't imagine Christian marrying a woman deemed so shallow and uncaring. How could a man with such a noble character live with a woman with such loose morals? Rose sighed inwardly. Perhaps part of her problem stemmed from jealousy. The thought of Christian sharing intimate moments with any other woman sent a stabbing pain straight through her heart.

"Lord Farleigh is a good man, and he deserved better," Dr Taylor continued. "It is part of the reason I continue to visit Everleigh, despite getting no further with the cause of his troubles."

They reached Everleigh's impressive roman-inspired entrance, and Dr Taylor tugged on the reins and brought the horse to a stop. Did his reluctance to enter the premises stem from the heated discussion he'd had with Christian?

"Are you not coming up to the house?" she asked, eager to test her theory.

"I'm afraid Lord Farleigh is a little frustrated with me at the moment," he said honestly as he assisted her to the ground, "and rightfully so. Then again, Reverend Wilmslow's insistence he search the house only hinders those who feel a genuine need to help."

"What does he hope to find?" Her thoughts flicked back to the children's comments. Had the reverend been searching their drawers and cupboards looking for something specific? "Surely not a poisonous plant lurking in the linen cupboard."

Dr Taylor's blue eyes flashed with amusement. "That is a question I've often asked myself. But who are we to question the morals of a man of God?"

Morals? What a strange word to use. It implied Reverend Wilmslow had strayed from the one true path to enlightenment.

"The righteous often have their own agenda," she said.

"Indeed." That one simple word brimmed with cynicism. The doctor's eyes scanned her from head to toe. "I'm sure we'll have an opportunity to speak again. Indeed, I shall look forward to the event." He tipped his hat. "But for now, you should do as your doctor instructed and return to your bed and lock the door. One never knows when the dreaded fever will strike."

Rose wasn't sure how to take the last comment. Was the doctor trying to warn her about something?

He left her at the gate and turned towards the lane but then looked back over his shoulder and called, "Good day to you … my lady."

CHAPTER FOURTEEN

Rose hurried to her room, her heart battering her ribcage. Thankfully, she'd made it back before Christian returned from Abberton. But that was not the cause of her distress.

Dr Taylor knew her identity. Why else would he call her *my lady* whilst wearing an arrogant grin? During the doctor's visits to The Talbot Inn, Oliver must have mentioned her.

She sat on the edge of her bed and recalled the conversation she'd had with Dr Taylor. If she followed her own advice, then the strange incidents all came back to Lady Farleigh.

Believing the letters might hold more information, she lifted the board and retrieved them from their hiding place. After wiping away the cobwebs, she sat on the floor, opened the letters one by one and laid them out in front of her.

None of them were dated. None of them were signed.

That in itself posed two questions. How could they be certain Mr Watson sent them? What evidence did Christian have to suspect Mr Watson and his wife were lovers?

Whoever wrote the letters deliberately used vulgar words,

sexually explicit language. So much so, her cheeks flamed as she scanned the pages. Dr Taylor had been pretty blunt when he'd suggested marriage. And doctors certainly knew graphic terminology when it came to discussing the anatomy.

Return to bed ... lock your door ... one never knows when the dreaded fever will strike.

Was the doctor mocking her or warning her?

Was his subtle hint about Reverend Wilmslow's slip from the wheel of morality a clue?

She turned to the blue notebook.

One notable thing stood out. The writing in the ledger proved vastly different in style to the penmanship shown in the letters. She flicked through the pages of twenty or so names. Bar the odd few the rest were women. Married, unmarried, it didn't matter. The ink had faded, and the writing was too small, illegible in places. In the back, were pages of addresses, mostly places in London: Holborn, Charing Cross, one in Bloomsbury.

Rose stood and moved to the window. She flicked back to the names and held the book up to the light.

"Good Lord." The words burst from her lips. "Miss Charlotte Stoneway." All four columns next to the name contained the figure of two hundred pounds. She tried to recall the name of the other woman who'd gone missing but to no avail.

Perhaps she should find the courage to speak to Christian. Together they might make sense of it all. And if she had any hope of helping him, she had to tackle the matter before Dr Taylor revealed her identity.

The first spots of rain hit the glass pane to draw her mind back to the present. Black clouds amassed overhead, and the light patter soon became a torrential downpour.

Her thoughts turned to Christian. She imagined him

sheltering beneath a tree. A lonely, solitary figure whose shoulders sagged with the weight of his burden. Her heart went out to him. And yet here she was, adding to his pain by lying to him, keeping secrets.

It had to stop, for both their sakes.

She moved away from the window, gathered the letters together, placed them inside the book and went downstairs to wait for his return.

She'd paced back and forth outside his study for an hour before taking the book back to her room and going in search of Mrs Hibbet.

An afternoon spent entertaining the children during the storm distracted her from the dreaded moment when she would tell Christian the truth. She ate an early dinner, tucked the children in their beds and still he wasn't home.

"Happen he's taken refuge from the storm." Mrs Hibbet did not share her concern.

But Rose couldn't settle.

How would it be when she returned to London, to live with her brother and parade the ballrooms with a fake smile and more lies to account for her absence? Would she think of Christian then?

"But the rain stopped an hour ago." Indeed, daylight had given way to a clear sky littered with stars.

"The road to Abberton is a quagmire when the rain comes. But his lordship is capable of dealing with most things."

Except for an unruly son and someone who sought to cause him untold misery?

Guilt flared again.

Another hour passed before Joseph's cry rang through the corridor of the servants' quarters. "His lordship's home and has requested a hot bath."

Mrs Hibbet set to work organising the household, dashing here and there barking orders. Never had Rose been party to the flurry of activity going on below stairs. Above stairs, the staff always conveyed an air of order and control.

Rose returned to her room to wait while Christian bathed and ate his dinner in peace. Curiosity burned. Where had he been? What had kept him in the village for most of the day?

As she passed the children's room, she took a moment to peek inside. They both slept soundly, unaware of the mayhem happening around them.

The sound of footsteps taking the stairs two at a time forced her to close the door quickly and turn around.

"My lord,"—her heart fluttered in her throat—"you're back."

Mud splashes stained his beige breeches. A dark shadow of bristles covered his sculpted chin and jaw. His damp hair curled at the ends, just how she liked it. His equally damp coat clung to his muscular arms. He appeared the epitome of rugged masculinity, a feast for the eyes of any lonely woman with a soft heart.

"Rose." He stopped short, brushed his hand down the front of his waistcoat as if that made him more presentable. "Should you not be in bed?"

"I'm feeling much better. Indeed, when you can spare a moment there is something important I wish to discuss."

His curious gaze searched her face. "I have news, too, and would be grateful if you'd join me in the study a little later."

Her heart skipped a beat. Had he learnt of her deception? Surely not. Those intriguing green eyes held no hint of pain or disappointment. The smooth, rich tone of his voice carried an element of warmth and affection.

"And I wish an intelligent ear to listen to my musings," he continued.

The compliment struck a chord deep within. Oh, in the ballrooms she'd received praise for her elegance and beauty. Lord Cunningham commended her for her kind, forgiving nature. No man had ever cared for her opinion.

The trust Christian placed in her was without warrant.

"I must say, I am intrigued to know where you've been all day." Lord, she sounded like a wife, not a governess.

"Did you miss me?" A mischievous smile touched his lips.

In truth, she'd missed him more than he could know. She'd given up an opportunity to reunite with her brother in order to examine the powerful attraction that existed between them.

"It's just that I've not thanked you for taking me to bed last … the other night." According to Mrs Hibbet, he'd scooped her up in his arms and carried her to her room. If only she could remember him holding her close. "I'm afraid my memory of the event is a little hazy."

His smile turned into a smirk. "Should you have any questions, every second is ingrained in my memory."

Their gazes locked, and the air vibrated around them.

The heavy trudge of footsteps on the stairs caught their attention and Joseph appeared carrying two wooden buckets of steaming hot water.

"Forgive me, Rose." Christian inclined his head. "I must bathe. But I shall be with you shortly."

She thought to ask if he needed any assistance. The vision in her mind's eye proved almost as scandalous as the contents of Lady Farleigh's letters.

"Is there something else you wish to say?" he asked, and she realised her mouth hung open.

"No. I shall be in my room when you're ready."

He arched a brow. "Then I shall not keep you waiting long."

Before she crumpled to the floor in a lovesick heap, she walked away. Climbing the stairs to the upper floor proved eventful when one lacked all feeling in their legs. Christian did not retire to his room immediately but watched her until she disappeared from view.

While she waited patiently in her room, the little devil on her shoulder questioned whether it was right to add more weight to his troubles. Perhaps she should wait to hear his news, to offer advice and guidance in the hope of easing his burden.

Thirty minutes passed.

A light rap on her door brought the footman, Joseph. "His lordship has asked to see you in the study." He kept his expression impassive, but she wondered what he thought of the time she spent alone with his master. Did they gossip about her below stairs? Did they disapprove?

"Thank you, Joseph."

She followed the footman to the study. To her surprise, Joseph knocked and informed Christian of her arrival, as if she were a distinguished guest come for a visit.

Christian stood as she entered. He came around the desk, thanked Joseph and promptly closed the door. The click of the key turning in the lock sent her nerves skittering.

"You wanted to see me."

He came up behind her, his breath breezing across her neck. "I've wanted to see you alone since the moment we were disturbed in the woods."

Rose swallowed deeply as a shiver ran from her nape to

her navel. "I—I think it's fair to say we have many things to discuss."

"Discuss? I hadn't planned on talking." His hand settled on her elbow, hot and firm, and he swung her around to face him. "At least not just yet."

Her mind and body melted beneath the heat of his gaze. Clutching the blue book in one hand, she brought her other to his cheek and caressed the soft skin where he'd recently shaved. She loved seeing him like this ... so playful and carefree.

It broke her heart to think that he might not look at her in the same way once he'd discovered she'd lied to him. Tears threatened to fall, and so she pressed her lips to his because she had thought of nothing but him since that night, too.

As always, a chaste kiss quickly turned into an explosion of passion. She threw the book onto the nearest chair, wrapped her arms around his neck and pressed her body into his.

His warm, wet mouth moved so expertly over hers. The melding of tongues sent jolts of pure pleasure shooting through her. Her breasts ached. A similar ache between her thighs urged her to push against him. When his hands found a way up under her dress to settle on her bare buttocks, her heart almost leapt from her chest.

"Oh, God, Rose." He gripped her tightly, his muscular thighs pressing against hers, the solid evidence of his arousal pushing against her belly. "I've never wanted any woman the way I want you."

Sweet heaven above.

Her head spun as he claimed her mouth. The unique scent that clung to his skin flooded her nostrils. Like a potent aphrodisiac, the essence of him flamed the fire between her thighs. She wanted him to touch her as he had done two nights ago. The way no other man had, and she hoped never would.

On a gasp, Christian tore his mouth from hers. "Come upstairs with me, Rose. Let me lavish you with attention. Help me forget everything but the floral scent of your skin, the soft feel of you filling my palms." He squeezed her buttocks gently, and a whimper left her lips.

"We—we can't," she panted. She knew what he wanted. Heaven help her, she wanted him, too.

A dark cloud of disappointment passed across his face. "You're right. It was wrong of me to suggest it. But a man can dream."

Had this been a battle with swords, his last comment would have been the winning thrust.

"Let's stay here." She gestured to the Persian rug. "I couldn't … not in the room next to the children. Not when the servants are awake."

If one was going to commit sin in the name of love, one should try to hold on to a few principles.

She caught herself. Was this love? Lust could be just as addictive, so she'd heard.

With a tender caress of her cheek, Christian brushed a lock of her hair behind her ear. "You know I'm not one of those men who use women to satisfy their needs." He snorted and chuckled at the same time. "Hell, I can't tell you how many years it's been since … well … I've never met anyone who excites me as you do."

This was a perfect opportunity to change her mind. She could sense a part of him pulling back, perhaps realising the folly of the situation. But she wanted the reckless man. The one willing to break all the rules to have her. The one who saw her as more than a trophy, more than a means to refill the family coffers.

"I have only one request." Her heart thumped wildly, with excitement, with nerves.

"You need only ask."

She couldn't stop the seductive smile forming. "Make this a moment to remember."

CHAPTER FIFTEEN

The significance of the moment weighed heavily on Christian's mind. Not because he doubted his capability to love this woman as she deserved. On the contrary, a fiery passion burned in his chest, one long thought buried. But this amounted to more than dipping a toe in the pool of immorality. God damn, he was ready to strip naked and dive straight into the tempting waters.

No longer could he deny the soul-deep connection they shared. Fate brought Rose to Everleigh. And Fate would see their relationship reach the natural conclusion.

Offering her a sinful grin, he pushed thoughts of marriage from his mind for now. "You're in charge, Rose." He tugged the front of her dress and pulled her closer. "Tell me what you want, and I shall happily oblige."

"Goodness, I wouldn't know where to start." Her nervous chuckle was endearing. "You take the lead."

"Then you must let me know you want this, too." He looked for any sign of doubt. "There is a truth, a pure yet potent bond that exists between us. Don't ever be afraid to say what you're thinking."

With trembling fingers, she reached out to touch him. "Teach me to please you, Christian." The hazy look of desire swam in her blue eyes as her hands drifted up over his chest, grazing his nipples. "Show me how you might please me, too."

Every drop of blood in his body rushed to his cock. The woman of his dreams moistened her lips, and he suddenly feared he would wake to find this was all a figment of his wild imagination. Instinctively, his gaze drifted to the window. Both times he'd kissed her they'd been interrupted. God help anyone who dared disturb them tonight.

Rose glanced back over her shoulder. "Close the curtains. There's nothing outside to interest you."

He crossed the room and yanked the curtains so hard he almost pulled down the pole. After working on the knot in his cravat, he threw it onto the desk, unbuttoned his waistcoat, and it ended up somewhere on the floor. His boots followed, and he came to stand in front of her.

"With the awkward things out of the way, you can remove the rest."

She glanced at the door. "What if someone should knock?"

"No one will disturb us." If the gods were on their side, surely nothing disastrous would happen in the next hour. "I am completely at your mercy."

The comment must have bolstered her confidence for she straightened her shoulders and a coy smile touched her lips. "So this is to be a game of master and servant, only we've reversed the roles."

"You're not my servant, Rose." And therein lay the truth of it. Rose was his equal in every regard. In the space of a few short days, she'd become his friend, his confidante, soon-to-be lover.

Ignoring the tightness in his chest, he took hold of her hand and placed it over his heart. It was a way of saying he cared without frightening her, without forcing her to commit.

"It's beating so hard I can feel it against my palm." A look of wonder sparkled in her eyes, quickly replaced with one of curiosity. Her fingers traced a line down over the hard planes of his abdomen and lingered there. "I was right. You're not one to overindulge."

"Only when kissing you."

With her eyes locked on his, she let her fingers fall to the waistband of his breeches. She grasped the front of his linen shirt, tugged the material free and pushed her hands up over his bare chest. "Your skin is so hot."

Christian chuckled. The woman had no idea how deeply she affected him. "Perhaps that's because there's a fire raging within."

"Undress me." The words tumbled from her mouth as her breathing grew shallow. In his youth, he'd seen the look of desire swim in many a woman's eye, but on Rose it was spellbinding.

The amused grin fell from his face as he pictured every curve, every contour. Rose turned around to show him the tiny row of buttons. Barely able to speak, he set to work, eventually pushing the plain garment off her shoulders until it pooled on the floor.

She stepped out of it and turned to face him.

Heaven help him.

He couldn't help but stare at the valley between her breasts, visible above the neckline of her chemise. He tugged on the ribbons of her stays and unthreaded them to leave her standing in nothing but the sheer undergarment.

"God, you're so beautiful." He dragged his shirt over his head, threw it onto the floor and unbuttoned his breeches so they hung low on his hips. He was so damn hard there was no danger of them slipping.

Rose's gaze came to rest on his chest and followed the line of dark hair trailing from his navel down past the waistband. Watching her intently, he pushed the breeches to the floor to reveal his erection.

She gulped, shifted from one foot to the other, and he imagined her growing hot and swollen between her legs. Perhaps feeling a sudden urge to join him in his nakedness, she drew her chemise over her head. But instead of throwing it to the floor, she clutched the cotton to her chest.

Christian moved closer. "I'll take that." He pulled it from her grasp and placed it on the desk behind her. "We do not have to do this. Just say the word and—"

She crushed her mouth to his in a move that shocked him as much as it excited him. The feel of her soft breasts pressed against him was his undoing.

"I want this," she whispered as she tore her lips away. "I want you."

Christian's hands settled on her buttocks. He bent his knees a fraction, pushed his cock into the gap between her legs, rocked his hips back and forth while he lavished her nipple with his tongue.

"Christian." She moved with him, rubbed against his erection, as desperate as he to ease the ache building deep inside.

"If only we had endless hours alone," he said, kissing the column of her throat. "I want to taste you everywhere. I want to stay buried inside you until dawn."

"We cannot afford such luxury," she panted. "It's only a matter of time before someone knocks the door."

The sudden thought that this dream could be ripped from his grasp caused panic to flare.

He took hold of her hand and brought her down to lie on the rug. He settled at her side, his fingers finding their way into the damp hair between her thighs. Lord, she was wet and ripe for the taking.

It took but a few strokes for a moan of appreciation to leave her lips. Despite the urge to cover her body and drive home, he maintained a steady rhythm. Her rosy pink nipples were crying out for attention. A few flicks of his tongue had her arching her back and rubbing against his hand.

"That's it, love," he whispered. "Trust me. Don't hold back. Never hold anything back from me."

"Christian." Her ragged breaths spurred him on. "I—I never want to hurt you."

Christian claimed her mouth, swallowed every moan and pant that burst from her lips. He knew she was close to release when her eyelids fluttered closed, and then her body shuddered as she cried out his name.

Rose had barely caught her breath when he came up on his knees and settled between her thighs.

"You're sure you want to do this?"

"Undoubtedly."

"Trust me," he said as the tip of his manhood pushed against her entrance. A strange feeling gripped him, as if he'd been waiting for this moment his entire life.

"I do." She grabbed hold of his buttocks and urged him not to hesitate.

Needing no inducement, he entered her slowly, withdrew and continued the motion again and again before pushing past her maidenhead to fill her full. God, she felt divine. Christian stilled and closed his eyes, waited for her to grow accustomed to the feel of him.

"Don't stop, Christian."

He wanted to lose himself in the moment, to forget about

the world beyond his study. He opened his eyes and stared at her intently as he thrust deeper. A satisfied smile played on her lips. By God, the sight touched his soul.

"Hmm ... Rose." Saints above, he would never grow tired of loving this woman.

The words filled his head as he filled her body. She wrapped her legs tightly around him, hugged him close, gripped his back and rocked with him.

He thrust hard and deep. The muscles in her core pulsed around his cock as, once again, she soared on the dizzying heights of her release.

With a guttural growl he couldn't suppress, Christian withdrew and spilt himself across her stomach. Reaching for his shirt, he wiped her clean and then collapsed at her side. Overcome with raw emotion, he gathered her into his arms and drew her close as his erratic breathing slowed.

"You don't know how glad I am that you lost your way in the woods." He kissed her forehead and stroked her back. "You've been here such a short time and yet I daren't think what it would be like without you."

Rose draped her leg across his thigh and cuddled into his chest. "I was supposed to find Everleigh that night. I was supposed to find you."

He fell silent for a moment. "We have a lot to discuss."

"Oh yes. You had important news to impart."

"I was referring to what has just occurred." He gave a satisfied sigh. It had been so long since he'd felt at peace.

"Oh, I see. I thought you were talking about your reason for going to Abberton today."

"I went to see Dr Taylor."

"Was he home?"

"No. That's why I called."

Rose pulled away and looked up at him, puzzled. "If you're trying to confuse me, you're doing an excellent job."

A rush of cold air breezed over them, and Rose shivered.

"Come." He stood and brought her to her feet. Lord, her breasts were deliciously soft and round, and his desire for her ignited again. "As much as I'd like to lie here for hours, I'd hate for you to catch a chill."

"Everything always comes back to the dreaded sickness," she said with a hint of amusement.

"That's exactly why I called at Dr Taylor's house." He walked over to the desk and grabbed her chemise, suppressed a grin when he noticed her staring at his bare buttocks. "I wanted to speak to his housekeeper, to ask who makes the tonics and tinctures he provides."

"And what did you learn? With the doctor's hectic schedule I doubt he has time to make them himself."

"Reverend Wilmslow's wife provides the herbs and plants used in the potions." He helped Rose into her chemise, his fingers grazing her breasts just to tease her a little more. "By all accounts, she is a keen botanist who once tried to convince Mr Watson that natural remedies were by far a better means of treating the mentally challenged."

"Well, that explains the reverend's theory about the illness. Although I can see why he didn't mention it, few men would admit to their wives being so knowledgeable. What do you propose to do?"

"I've told every member of the household that they are not to drink the tonics." He held up her stays, and she pushed her arms through the straps. Christian tugged on the ties, kissed the soft swell of her breasts bulging up from her chemise, before stepping back. "Mrs Hibbet will take control of all medicine brought into the house."

Rose's gaze flicked briefly to his manhood. "Before you

hand me my dress would you mind slipping into your breeches?"

He gave a mischievous wink. "Why? Is the sight proving somewhat of a distraction?"

"You know it is." Moistening her lips, she watched him dress. "You were gone all day. Where else did your curious mind take you?"

"To London."

"London?"

"I took a bottle of the tincture to an apothecary and asked for an analysis. He will write with his findings." He helped her into her dress and fought the urge to strip her naked again. "For the first time in years, my mind is clear. Indeed, I don't know why I didn't think of it before."

"Why would you? Who can one trust if not a doctor or a man of God?"

"That's what I'm struggling to understand." He believed most people were capable of deceit to a certain extent. "Being married to Cassandra taught me to recognise the traits of a liar. But why would I suspect them? What would either man have to gain?"

She blinked rapidly. Perhaps it was uncouth to mention his wife after what had just occurred.

"You do pay Dr Taylor for his visits."

He shrugged. "Taylor is a wealthy enough man in his own right. He received a surprise inheritance a couple of years ago."

"And yet he still works as a doctor?"

"He does it for the love of the work as well as the money."

"One cannot deny that Dr Taylor has a caring, approachable manner when dealing with his patients. Indeed, that was my initial assessment of his character. But I admit to finding him a little arrogant."

"Arrogant? That surprises me." He didn't see Taylor the same way, although that could have something to do with Christian's status in society. "And what of Reverend Wilmslow? Do you find him arrogant, too?"

"After what Mrs Hibbet told me, I think the man is a serpent in the Garden of Eden ... out to deceive, out to make an immoral act seem like a caring gesture."

"You speak of the misunderstanding with Jane."

"Was it a misunderstanding?"

"Wilmslow argued he uses a hands-on approach when it comes to healing." Jane had expressed doubt as to whether the reverend meant anything inappropriate. "There was no evidence to suggest otherwise."

"Talking of evidence, there's something I want to ask you."

Christian took her hand and brought it to his lips. "Ask me anything. I shall keep no secrets from you."

He thought he saw guilt flash across her face, but her gaze fell and then it was gone. "How do you know your wife and Mr Watson were having an affair?"

Christian jerked his head back. "I found them together in their woodland hideaway. I heard rumours in the village. On a few occasions, Mrs Wilmslow mentioned Cassandra's fondness for Watson."

"And that's it? You never saw them together? Mr Watson didn't admit to their adultery?"

"Heavens, no. But I believe he took pleasure from controlling her, that he had something to do with Cassandra's illness. Her condition improved when she returned from their sessions at Morton Manor, but often deteriorated in the days after." He paused. "Why do you ask?"

"I don't know." She moved to the chair near the desk, removed the letters from the book and handed them to him. "These letters bear no signature. How do we know Mr Watson sent them?"

Christian gripped the letters and resisted the urge to crumple them in his fist. "You think my wife had another lover?" By God, when it came to Cassandra anything was possible.

"Perhaps."

He waved the letters at her. "What? Are you saying I should read them? The woman took me for a fool. Why open old wounds? The best place for them is the fire."

"No." Rose snatched them from his grasp. "You must see the logic in what I say."

"Of course I see the damn logic." His wife's depravity knew no bounds. Nothing surprised him anymore. "Not only do I suspect Cassandra was a serial adulterer, but I suspect her lover killed her that night."

Rose gasped and took an unsteady step back. "You don't believe her death was an accident?"

"You'll probably think me a fool, but I saw someone in the woods when I dragged her from the fire. I believe the same person had something to do with Miss Stoneway's death."

"Miss Stoneway?" Rose shook her head. "But you said her death had something to do with her mental condition."

"Then tell me what you make of this." He strode over to the bookcase, removed the green book with the hollow interior he'd made to hide the key to Cassandra's medicine chest. Now another key lay hidden in its place. He took it and opened the top drawer of his desk.

Rose stepped closer.

"I found this a few feet from Miss Stoneway's body." He

removed a brass button and placed it on the desk. "I prised this from my wife's hand on the night she died." He put an identical button beside the first one.

Rose stared at them for a moment. "May I examine them?"

"Be my guest."

She placed the letters on the desk, picked up one button with her forefinger and thumb and held it beneath the candlelight. "Gentlemen often seek specific designs for the buttons on their coat or waistcoat. This is no exception. It has the same intricate detail one would expect from a commissioned piece."

A delicate leaf pattern decorated the entire surface, except for a small circle on the left which resembled the sun. Acorns and flowers covered the outer rim. "I'm sure you'll agree, it is a rather unique design," Christian said.

"Undoubtedly." Rose placed it down carefully and picked up the other button. "It's identical in every way. Have you shown them to anyone else?"

"No." Until Rose wandered into his life, the only person he trusted was Mrs Hibbet. "I spoke to Dr Taylor on the night of the fire, mentioned that I thought I saw a figure in the woods near the cottage. But he's of the opinion the trauma may have led to some confusion on my part."

"Did the coroner rule that Cassandra's death was accidental?"

"Yes, and he ruled Miss Stoneway died from fright."

"Fright?" A deep furrow lined her brow. "Is such a thing possible?"

"According to the Bills of mortality, apparently so."

Rose fell silent. She stared at the floor and tapped her lip with her finger.

No matter how long she stood thinking, Christian knew

the answer would not come. Unsolved problems and unfounded suspicions plagued his every waking thought.

"And the only connection your wife and Miss Stoneway share is that they were both patients at Morton Manor."

"Indeed."

"Then, as difficult as it may be, you must read the letters." Rose pushed the notes towards him. "A jealous lover may well have caused the fire at the cottage. If the letters are not from Mr Watson, then you must discover who wrote the missives."

Christian thrust his hand through his hair. "Are they as vulgar as I suspect?"

She nodded. "They detail intimate relations between a man and a woman, though they bear no resemblance to what we've just shared."

The comment warmed his heart. "You mean the letters lack passion, tenderness, any true feeling or sentiment?" He almost used the word *love*.

"Precisely."

They stared at each other for the longest time. The urge to join with her took hold, to push deep inside her body, to experience the sense of contentment he only found in her arms.

"Meet me later tonight." He came around the desk and pulled her into an embrace. "Somewhere quiet. Somewhere private."

A blush touched her cheeks. "Perhaps we shouldn't complicate things any more than they are already."

"There is nothing complicated about our need to spend time together." His words lacked conviction. Their relationship posed a problem on many levels.

"Perhaps we should focus our efforts on solving the mysterious sickness, and in finding your wife's secret lover."

She stared at his mouth and then kissed him.

Her actions and words worked in opposition. The way she grasped his shirt, the way she drank deeply from his mouth as though quenching a thirst, told him she wanted him as much as he wanted her.

Perhaps she needed time to understand these newly awakened emotions. Perhaps they should do as she suggested and focus their efforts on easing their burden. Then he could work on making her position at Everleigh permanent.

Not as his governess, but as his wife.

CHAPTER SIXTEEN

A disagreement between two tenant farmers kept Christian from the house for most of the morning. He promised Rose he would read Cassandra's letters but in truth welcomed the distraction. Upon his return to Everleigh, he spent an hour with his children and fought the urge to take their governess in his arms and convey the happiness filling his heart.

As the day progressed, he managed to sneak a few minutes alone with her. But passions raged almost to the point of no return.

Again, she pressed him to read the letters. Her sudden urgency to help ease his troubles led to a frank revelation. In all likelihood, either Dr Taylor or Reverend Wilmslow had committed adultery, and taken him for a fool. Who else could it be? Both men spent time alone with Cassandra. Both men showed an obsessive interest in searching his house.

Bile burned his throat when he considered how many times they'd sat drinking his port and smoking his cheroots. He used the term *they* and yet one man was innocent. But which one?

After dinner, he entered the study and settled behind the desk, ready to read the letters before Rose returned from putting the children to bed. Staring at the pile on the desk, he picked up the first one to hand, peeled back the folds and perused the words on the page.

Nothing shocked him, not the depths of his wife's depravity or that of her lover. Despite witnessing Cassandra's outbursts and tantrums, he couldn't quite believe she would stoop so low.

The knock on the door brought a welcome relief.

Foster entered. "Excuse me for disturbing you, my lord, but you have visitors."

Christian glanced at the mantel clock. "Visitors? At this hour?" If Wilmslow and Taylor had come to offer an apology, they'd had a wasted journey. He looked for the salver. "No calling card?"

"Lord Stanton assures me he doesn't need one, that you would understand the reason for such an oversight."

Lord Stanton?

Perhaps the earl had called to thank him for fetching the doctor. More likely he'd come looking for his maid.

Christian stood. "You may show Lord Stanton in, Foster." He placed the letters back inside Rose's blue book, for safekeeping. She mentioned something about reading that, too, and he would, but one thing at a time.

Foster announced Lord Stanton and his companion, Miss Asprey. While the lord's dour expression confirmed Christian's fears, Miss Asprey's bright smile put him at ease.

"Welcome to Everleigh." Christian inclined his head. While he preferred to take a friendly, less formal approach, he'd be damned before he'd let them take Rose. "I'm Christian Knight, seventh Viscount Farleigh."

"Forgive us for disturbing you at such a late hour,

Farleigh." Stanton came to an abrupt halt before the desk. "But we have a matter of some importance to discuss."

Panic flared.

Miss Asprey examined Christian's face with curiosity and interest. He supposed a mistress was always looking for her next benefactor should her current lover grow tired and move on.

"Your name is Knight?" Miss Asprey said with mild amusement. "As when the sun has set, or as in the medieval heroes we love to read about in tales of olde?"

Christian frowned. "As in those charged with defending a maiden's honour."

"Splendid." Miss Asprey clapped her hands together. "Now, before we sit, and I recommend we do sit as the matter calls for a calm, logical approach, we must express our gratitude for your help at Morton Manor." She coughed once into her clenched fist.

"Then please take a seat." Christian gestured to the chairs in front of the desk. The ones regularly occupied by Taylor and Wilmslow. "As I'm sure you're aware, the manor is but a mile from Everleigh. I came as soon as I saw the smoke."

"And we are grateful you brought Dr Taylor." Stanton waited for his companion to sit before dropping into a chair. "With his assistance, Miss Asprey has made a speedy recovery."

"I trust your stay at The Talbot Inn is proving satisfactory." Christian sat, too. He suspected they had no desire to pass pleasantries and wished only to address the matter at hand.

Miss Asprey nodded. "Mrs Parsons has been most attentive."

After a brief silence, Lord Stanton cleared his throat. "We

are here to discuss a matter of some delicacy. I don't know you, Farleigh, but they say you're a fair and honest man."

Christian braced himself. This was the moment they demanded the return of their maid. "I try to be. Unless I believe the cause is something worth fighting for." He'd not give up so easily. Besides, Rose hadn't signed a contract, and was under no obligation to go with them.

"We're looking for someone." Stanton shuffled in the chair. "A woman with golden hair and a bright smile to be exact."

What an odd way to describe a servant.

"Her name is Rose," Miss Asprey added.

Christian's stomach performed numerous flips. "You speak of the missing maid?" It was better to come straight to the point.

Lord Stanton frowned. "I think we all know the lady in question is not a maid."

"Indeed." Rose was an angel sent to aid him in his hour of need.

"Look, this isn't easy to say, and so I'll go out on a limb and hope I can rely on your discretion." Lord Stanton sighed. "I'm looking for my sister. Lady Rose Darby. She was staying at Morton Manor and left to go to London but never arrived."

"Lady Rose Darby?" Christian's throat grew tight. A dark cloud descended. He blinked and tried to clear his vision. There had to be a mistake. Surely the earl spoke of another woman, not *his* Rose.

"Yes," Miss Asprey began. "We've been out of our minds with worry. She left determined to reunite with Lord Cunningham, but no one has seen her since."

"Lord Cunningham?" Again, he knew the name, not the man. "Is he a relation?"

"Heavens, no." Stanton gave a mocking snort. "She believes herself in love with him, though heaven knows why. The gentleman is a pompous fool who's happiest when in front of a looking glass."

Christian sat back in the chair and covered his mouth with his hand for fear of cursing. How could Rose be so caring and intimate with him when she loved someone else? A cold chill swept through him. Frost formed around his heart. Soon it would be a thick casing of ice. A barrier against all liars and deceivers.

An uncomfortable silence ensued.

"Well, Farleigh?" The earl narrowed his gaze. "Am I right in thinking you have a lady here by that name?"

Oh, he had a lady in the house called Rose, but clearly, he didn't know who the bloody hell she was.

"The woman you speak of came here five days ago." His voice held no hint of emotion. He kept an indifferent expression, despite nausea crippling him from within. "Mrs Hibbet, my housekeeper, mistook her for the maid I'd hired, even though she was not due to start for another week."

Stanton sat forward. "I suspected as much. My groom, Peters, saw Rose outside The Talbot Inn yesterday and followed her here."

The Talbot Inn? Rose never mentioned leaving Everleigh. But it seems there were a lot of things the lady chose not to mention.

"He said she'd cut her hair," the earl continued in a tone brimming with disapproval. "Hence the reason he took his time before coming to me. Peters spoke to the doctor who confirmed Rose works here."

Taylor? Had the doctor made it his life's mission to cause him misery?

"Rose is no longer a maid." No, she was the ruined sister

of an earl, the one-time mistress of a viscount. "A lady with her intelligence,"—*and cunning*, he added silently—"was better suited to the role of governess."

Miss Asprey looked at the earl and arched a brow.

"Mrs Parsons said you're a widower, my lord." Miss Asprey's tone held a hint of suspicion. If the earl sought a marriage proposal to save his sister's ruined reputation, he could think again.

"These last two years, yes. What of it?" It didn't matter that he cared about Rose. If he took another wife, he needed to be damn sure he could trust her. The stress of living with Cassandra's lies and deceit was enough to last him a lifetime. And his children deserved better.

Stanton fixed him a hard stare. "I'm not asking anything of you, Farleigh, have no fear. Indeed, regardless of what people might say, I would not force Rose to do anything unless she expressly wished it."

Impatient for answers, Christian stood. "Then I shall send for her. She spoke fondly of you. I'm sure she will be only too happy to accompany you back to London."

Christian strode to the door, but the earl called out to him. "Farleigh, I must have your word you'll not mention this to anyone. We must deal with this regrettable situation privately, and with the utmost discretion."

"Of course." He couldn't breathe past the lump in his throat. Beads of sweat formed on his brow. "You have my word." Why the hell would he want to tell the world he'd been taken for a fool again?

"I can only apologise for the inconvenience caused." Stanton sounded sincere. "I doubt Rose was thinking logically when she agreed to work here."

"With the gift of hindsight, I'm sure we would all make

different decisions." Yes, including never hiring a maid without references.

With an urgent need to deal with the matter quickly, Christian strode out into the hall. He summoned Foster and sent him to find Mrs Hibbet.

"God damn," he muttered through gritted teeth as he paced back and forth. He punched the air for good measure. Rose had used him. She'd used his children. And for what? To satisfy a curiosity?

Mrs Hibbet came hurrying down the stairs. "You sent for me, my lord."

"Find Rose," he snapped. Anger whipped disappointment away with a backhanded swipe. God, he had every right to show his disdain for what Rose had done. "She has visitors, come from The Talbot Inn."

"Visitors?" Mrs Hibbet's bottom lip trembled. "Does it have anything to do with that fellow asking questions at the stables?"

"I'm afraid it does. We don't have much luck when it comes to hiring a governess." Christian understood disappointment. This was different. This was akin to the ground trembling beneath his feet, to the whole world he'd come to appreciate suddenly crashing to the ground around him. He sighed. "It seems Rose is to leave us, too."

Rose tucked the children into their beds, kissed their foreheads and bid them goodnight. She slipped out of the room and closed the door gently with both hands. Only when she turned did she notice the figure pacing the candlelit hall. She slapped her hand over her mouth to muffle a shriek.

"Good heavens, Mrs Hibbet," Rose whispered as the

THE DECEPTIVE LADY DARBY

housekeeper stopped and stood there wringing her hands. "What is it? Is something amiss? Please tell me the fever hasn't claimed another victim."

The woman appeared distressed. "Oh, I knew it would happen, eventually."

Rose closed the gap between them and gripped the housekeeper's hands. "Knew what would happen? Is his lordship ill?" Heaven forbid something should happen to Christian.

"No, dear. But he wants to see you in the study right away." Mrs Hibbet shook her head. "Oh, this is dreadful. We've visitors. They've come looking for someone."

Rose took a step back as her heart flew up to her throat. "Visitors? At this time of night?" The words carried a nervous hitch. "Did they give their names?"

She did not need names. The nauseous feeling in her stomach told her all she needed to know. For a moment, her mind went blank, all thoughts sucked into a spiralling cloud of confusion.

"They've come from The Talbot Inn, Rose. They've come looking for you."

Rose's knees buckled, but she managed to remain upright. "I see. Are they with Lord Farleigh now?"

Mrs Hibbet closed her eyes and nodded. "Oh, he'll not recover from this. Mark my words. Things will be worse than before."

Despite Rose's sudden urge to run, she pasted a smile in an effort to ease Mrs Hibbet's anxiety. "Everything will be fine." Oh, if only she could believe that. But the pain in her chest said otherwise. She placed a reassuring hand on Mrs Hibbet's shoulder. "Things will happen just as they should. Fate has a way of organising everything in the end."

"I gave up trusting Fate a long time ago."

Rose hadn't. Coincidence did not bring her to Everleigh. Coincidence had nothing to do with the deep sense of belonging she experienced when held in Christian's arms. This was her predestined path.

"I should go." She simply meant she should not keep his lordship waiting. Still, she drew Mrs Hibbet into an embrace and hugged her tightly. "My mother died a long time ago, but you have given me another glimpse of unconditional love. You love Lord Farleigh like a son. Anyone can see that. Know that I love him, too. Know that I never meant to hurt him."

The words tumbled from her lips without thought or censure, but she felt the truth of them deep in her bones. Tears welled in her eyes, and she hurried away down the stairs before she crumpled into a blubbering wreck.

Once outside the study, she stood there for a moment … waiting for what, she didn't know. She gazed at the long-case clock, listened to the rhythmical tick, wished she could turn back the hands and make everything right again. She looked at the tapestries lining the walls on the stairs, inhaled the smell of polished wood, caught a hint of Christian's musky cologne in the air.

Come what may, her heart would always reside at Everleigh.

Sucking in a breath, she straightened her shoulders and knocked the door. One could not postpone the inevitable.

She waited to hear Christian's voice, wondered if he would give any indication as to his feelings. Instead of calling for her to enter he yanked open the door, and their eyes met.

It was as she feared. Suspicion and disappointment marred those vibrant green gems. He held his mouth in a firm, cynical line.

"Rose. So, it appears the *D* is for Darby." He stepped back and bowed. "Won't you come in?"

She entered the room, and her beloved brother jumped up from the chair.

"Rose!" Oliver rushed forward and drew her into an embrace. He smelt exactly as she remembered, warm, familiar, comforting. He looked at her, regret swimming in his eyes. "Can you ever forgive me for staying away? I would have come sooner had I known of your predicament."

Rose looked up and cupped his cheeks simply to prove he was not a figment of her imagination. "There is nothing to forgive."

Nicole rushed to their side. "Oh, I have been so worried about you. Do you know how many times we've travelled the road back and forth to London? What made you come here?"

Rose glanced briefly at Christian although from the dark look in his eyes she wished she hadn't. She needed to explain it all to him first.

"Yes, why did you not return to London?" Christian's ice-cold tone sliced through the air. "After all, you left Morton Manor with the intention of reaching Lord Cunningham, did you not? He is the man you love, the one you wish to marry?"

Good Lord, no!

Nicole had told him about Lord Cunningham. Oh, he would not understand. "I do not love Lord Cunningham," she snapped. *I love you.* "And I certainly have no intention of ever marrying him."

"Oh, thank the Lord for that." Nicole put her hand to her chest. "The gentleman is a cad. No matter how hard I try, I can find nothing to recommend him. I can't imagine what you were thinking."

"Six months locked in an old asylum can affect one's judgement."

"Indeed," Oliver said, stepping back. "Why else would you take a job as a maid?" He made it sound degrading, undignified, and yet she had never felt so empowered, never felt so needed.

"When I left the manor, I came upon Father's coach at the inn. I assumed he'd come for me." She turned to Nicole. "I wanted to warn you, but got lost in the woods and ended up here. The rest, well … I don't suppose it matters now."

Oliver frowned and then recognition dawned. "You did not know Father had died."

"No. I came back to the manor the following day, but you'd gone."

Christian cleared his throat. "Now I understand why you were so distressed that day. The story about being hired to work at the manor was just that, a story."

The disdain in his voice cut deep. She turned to him, took a hesitant step forward, but Christian stepped back. "I never meant to deceive anyone. You must understand, I didn't know what to do. Had my father found me, he would have sent me back to the manor."

Oliver came to stand beside her. "Lord Farleigh has assured us of his discretion. No one will know you were here. Let us put this unfortunate event behind us and start anew."

Unfortunate event?

Being at Everleigh had changed her in every way. She belonged here. She belonged with Christian.

"We have so much to tell you," Nicole said. "But the most important news is that we're getting married tomorrow, here in Abberton."

"Married?" Rose gulped.

"Oh, Rose, Fate conspired to bring Oliver to me." Nicole looked up at Oliver, admiration evident in her smile. "We've been on one wild adventure this last week. But through all the angst, we found love."

Rose tried to hold back the tears. Nicole deserved to be happy, and Oliver would never find a woman as kind and caring.

One solitary tear trickled down her cheek. "I'm so pleased for you both."

"I'll leave you to continue your conversation in private." Christian shuffled back. He did not sound like himself at all. "I shall be in the drawing room should you need anything further."

"Thank you, Farleigh," Oliver said. "Thank you for coming to our aid, and for taking care of my sister."

Christian appeared indifferent, yet the tension in the air crushed the breath out of her lungs. He stood rigid, his body stiff. No matter how many times she looked at him, he refused to meet her gaze.

"I shall arrange for Mrs Hibbet to help Rose pack, although she came here with very little. I'm sure you want to be on your way. And may I offer my felicitations on your good fortune."

"You're welcome to join us tomorrow. We have no friends or family in the area and would welcome a familiar face in the pews."

"Thank you for the kind invitation, but I fear, in light of this sudden turn of events, I must spend time with my children."

Rose's heart sank to her stomach at the thought of leaving them.

Reality struck her like a sharp slap in the face. The only hope she had of staying was if she married Christian. But he'd made his position clear. Mrs Hibbet would help her pack.

"Can I not at least stay one more night?" She spoke directly to him, and with some reluctance, he met her gaze. "Can I not say goodbye to the children?"

"I shall speak to the children in the morning."

Oliver snorted. "Why would you want to stay? Lord Farleigh will explain that you're not a governess."

Part of her wanted to be a simple governess, with no wealth or home to call her own. She reached out and touched Christian's arm. "I'd like to help them understand my predicament."

"You mean the unfortunate and regrettable situation you find yourself in. No, it's best they hear the news from me." He inclined his head to her brother. "As I said, I shall await you in the drawing room, directly across the hall."

He stepped away, left her hand hanging in the air, and then he was gone.

CHAPTER SEVENTEEN

Christian closed the study door behind him and sucked in a breath. The years spent hearing Cassandra's lies should have prepared him for this moment. He thought he knew a voice filled with falsity. He thought himself a master at recognising those unwitting flicks of the eyes that gave the game away.

But no. He'd come to learn there was no universal dictionary when it came to deceit. Yet the word *fool* was a generic term which defined him in every given situation.

He recalled the moment Rose stood on the steps of Morton Manor, wrapped in his embrace, sobbing into his cravat. The urge to protect her surfaced instantly, and he realised he couldn't fight the connection no matter how hard he tried.

But her sorrow stemmed, not from the family tragedy that left her destitute, but the mistake she'd made in not returning to the manor sooner. And while he'd tried his utmost to persuade her to stay at Everleigh, leaving was always part of her agenda.

The long-case clock chimed the quarter hour, and he

contemplated kicking the blasted thing simply out of spite. His chest felt as hollow as the mahogany casing. And while his heart thumped to the same rhythm as the brass pendulum, he would remain stuck in this moment, never quite knowing how to move on.

He put his hands on his knees and closed his eyes as a deep sense of despair surrounded him—for his own broken heart, and because he knew what this would do to his children.

Anger flared again, and he strode into the drawing room, slammed the door shut and flopped down onto the sofa.

Restless, he jumped straight back up and moved to the row of decanters on the side table. The slight tremble in his fingers reflected the instability of his emotions. Anger gave way to despair. Disdain gave way to sorrow. He grabbed the brandy, splashed a few mouthfuls into a crystal tumbler and gulped it down. Still, the potent liquid did nothing to ease his torment, and so he refilled the glass, eager to do anything to rid his mind of all thoughts.

Frozen in an odd form of stasis, he stared at the pattern on the rug until the shapes blurred into one. Minutes passed. He dissected the events of the last week and cursed Fate's cruel intervention.

The knock on the door startled him. Their eagerness to depart roused his ire. But then Rose had nothing to pack. She'd arrived with a kind smile and a caring heart—or so he'd believed—and another lie to account for her missing luggage.

The caller knocked repeatedly. Christian gritted his teeth and ignored the annoying sound. Stanton could go to hell. He didn't care if the earl thought him rude. He wanted them gone, wanted to regain some semblance of normality.

Normality?

A mocking snort escaped, but he didn't have time to consider the ludicrous thought. The door handle rattled, and before he could blink, Rose entered the room.

Christian's heart thumped in his chest. Even with thin drawn lips and sagging shoulders, she looked angelic. When she walked, her gait appeared clumsy and awkward, as if she carried the heavy weight of her deceit in a sack on her back.

"Christian." She paused. "I hope you don't mind, but I used your paper and ink." With an outstretched hand, she stepped forward. The letters quivered in her trembling fingers. "They're for the children, to explain why I must leave."

He snatched them, noted there were two. "What, do I not deserve an explanation?"

She struggled to look at him. "I'm sorry. I never meant to hurt you." The rapid rise and fall of her chest drew his attention. "At the time, I needed somewhere to stay and well … it was all a terrible misunderstanding."

"Terrible, is that how you describe your time here?" He downed another mouthful of brandy rather than say something he might later regret.

"No, you're twisting my words." Rose shook her head. She placed her hand over her heart. "Wonderful is the only way I can describe my time here."

He wished he could believe her. By God, a huge part of him wanted to trust every word that breezed through those luscious lips. But the lady did not know her own mind. And he couldn't risk his family's stability on a whim.

"I don't know who you are," he whispered.

How could he ever know what was true?

She shuffled closer, reached out to touch him but then dropped her hand. "I'm the same woman you confided in, the one who listened to you and offered advice. I'm the same woman you kissed so passionately. The same woman—"

"Enough!" He raised a hand to silence her. She was killing him. The ice encasing his heart cracked. One more word and he would take her in his arms, forgive every one of her sins. One more word and he'd be doomed to a life borne of deceit. "I'm weary of explanations. We're too different. I'm looking for peace and harmony while you're looking for adventure."

She shook her head again, but he did not give her an opportunity to answer.

"Go now. You have a gentleman waiting for you in London. Only a week ago you believed yourself in love with him." His throat was so tight he could barely speak. "I shall give the letters to the children, explain that you didn't want to leave, but your position in society demands it. No doubt Alice will decide she hates the aristocracy."

A weak smile formed on her lips. "You have the most beautiful children."

"In that, we agree."

"Rose." Stanton cleared his throat to catch their attention. He lingered in the doorway. "We should go."

She shot her brother a hard stare.

"Your brother is waiting." Christian glanced at her hand, thought about bringing it to his lips, but dismissed the idea. "Goodbye, Rose." The gut-wrenching pain in his stomach returned.

"Goodbye, Christian." A tear trickled down her nose and dropped onto her chin. Without warning, she rushed forward and kissed his cheek. "I shall miss you," she whispered and then she ran from the room and closed the door.

Two days had passed since Rose's swift departure.

Leaning back against the wooden shutter, Christian stared out of the study window at the woods separating Everleigh and Morton Manor. So much had changed in such a short time. The house felt empty without Rose. He'd lost the only woman he'd ever wanted. He missed the smell of her skin, the sound of her voice, the touch of her hand. Mrs Hibbet tried her best to entertain the children but an air of despondency had settled, and no one knew quite what to do about it.

He played the events of the last week over in his mind, dissecting each lie, making an excuse for each one. For some reason, he couldn't see Rose in the same light as Cassandra. Had he been too hasty in letting her leave? He should have listened to her explanation.

A knock on the door brought Mrs Hibbet. "Forgive me, my lord. But Jane has returned from her stay in Abberton. Her poor mother passed, and now she's keen to return to work."

"I'm sure you've told her how pleased we are to have her back."

"Well, let's hope we've no bouts of sickness for a while. The bed hangings need cleaning. We've not polished the silver for a month, and Cook wants help to organise the pantry."

Christian raised a brow. "You don't normally give me a breakdown of the household chores. Is there something else you wish to say?"

Mrs Hibbet clasped her hands in front of her. "The children miss Rose. We all do."

"Indeed." He'd had sleepless nights thinking of nothing else.

The children took the news as expected. After many tears,

Alice decided she didn't want to be a lady. Jacob blamed himself and raced off into the garden. Christian found him sitting in the orangery, clutching Rose's letter to his chest. He'd not asked the children to divulge the contents. And he would not read anyone's private correspondence without their permission.

"The children asked me to remind you that you're a Knight. You're supposed to rescue ladies in distress."

"What do you want me to do, Mrs Hibbet? Shall I write to the earl and ask if his sister will work for eighteen pounds per annum?"

"There is something you could do." A blush touched the woman's cheeks. "You could … you could ask Rose to marry you."

Christian gripped the back of the desk chair. "Have I missed something? What makes you think I'm of a mind to marry?"

Mrs Hibbet shuffled uncomfortably on the spot. "We all saw how you were with Rose."

No doubt they'd seen a man with a permanent smile and a mischievous glint in his eye. "And you would see me lumbered with another wife I cannot trust. After what happened with Cassandra, I swore never to marry again." And yet he had considered asking Rose to be his wife. Damn, he would not have taken her virginity without hoping for something more.

"I know Rose isn't who she pretended to be, my lord, but that's my fault."

Rose must have impressed Mrs Hibbet for her to accept responsibility.

"You did not lie, Mrs Hibbet. You accepted Rose's word in good faith. Imagine the devastation if we'd disliked her. Once again, I would have been obliged to marry a woman I don't love. The children would have another mother who cares nothing for their welfare."

The thought sent a chill down his spine.

"But I should have spoken to her."

"I'm the only one to blame for this situation." He'd behaved inappropriately and pressed his advances. "For an intelligent man, I acted like a fool."

"A fool in love," Mrs Hibbet blurted. She covered her mouth with her hand as her eyes grew wide. "Forgive me, my lord. I spoke out of turn. It's just I've been the housekeeper here for all these years and …"

"Emotions are running high since Rose's departure. But we must focus our efforts on solving the problems here." Indeed, he would sit down and read Cassandra's letters, see if Rose was right. "And I have decided not to hire a governess. I shall see to the children's education for the time being."

Mrs Hibbet nodded. "May I say one more thing, my lord, and then I shall not mention it again?"

Christian inclined his head. "Very well."

"Well, it's two things, really. The first is a confession, and then I must tell you something Rose said the night the earl came."

"Go on." The empty feeling in his stomach forced him to breathe deeply. Was this where he discovered he could not trust Mrs Hibbet, either?

Mrs Hibbet rubbed the back of her neck. "I am to blame as much as Rose. I know you don't like us going into the woods but the snowdrops were out, and my mother used to take us on a walk to see them every year."

The woods held no fond memories for him. Then again, the night he'd kissed Rose there would be forever ingrained in his memory.

"What I'm trying to say is, I knew Rose wasn't a maid

come from London. I saw her once, walking near the boundary of Morton Manor. For a moment, I thought I'd seen an angel." Mrs Hibbet's eyes lit up. "And then, just when I thought our problems here could get no worse, she appeared like a glorious vision in the night. That's when I knew the Lord had answered my prayers."

He could not chastise his housekeeper for her lofty ideas. He'd thought the same, too.

"One cannot deny that Rose is a special person." The sudden pang in his chest almost robbed him of breath. "But she had her own reasons for coming here. We should not make more of it than what it is."

"That brings me to my second point." The woman's lips twitched as she struggled to suppress a smile. "Rose told me she loves you, and that she never meant to hurt you."

Christian dug his fingernails into the leather chair. The words were bittersweet. A warm feeling filled his chest, coupled with the pain of regret. Did Rose have strong feelings for him? He would never know.

"It's not too late, my lord. Happen Rose would forgive you anything."

"Thank you, Mrs Hibbet. I shall give the matter consideration." He needed a distraction, something to take his mind off all he'd lost. "I shall take the children for a walk this afternoon. In the meantime, you can find me here."

"Yes, my lord."

Christian dropped into the chair behind the desk, shuffled papers and waited for his housekeeper to leave before a string of curses fell from his lips. With his head in his hands, he considered Mrs Hibbet's comments. Had experience forced him to judge Rose too harshly? In truth, he didn't care if her brother was an earl. His reaction stemmed from jealousy. Who the hell was Lord

Cunningham? And what on earth made Rose believe she loved him?

Christian pressed his fingers to his temples to ease the mounting tension. He couldn't think about Rose, not now. When that didn't work, he opened the drawer and removed Cassandra's letters. Rose had taken her blue diary, the one she'd used to hide the notes. His mind drifted again, and he wondered if she'd written anything about him in her little book.

Was that why she wanted him to read it?

He shook his head. He should stop daydreaming and focus his attention on discovering which one of the bastards had made him a cuckold.

Vulgar was too mild a word to describe the obscene nature of the missives. The content failed to rouse any emotion. Indeed, he felt numb, cold, indifferent. Rose was right. The graphic descriptions bore no resemblance to the passionate moment they'd shared. He'd been right, too. Rose had given everything of herself in that tender moment. Regardless of the other lies, the truth existed in every kiss they'd ever shared.

On a weary sigh, he continued reading about Cassandra's moments of sexual gratification. Every letter said the same. There were no clues to the person's identity. Nothing to lead back to Taylor, Wilmslow or Mr Watson.

The knock on the door drew his attention. Foster entered the room and walked over to the desk, the silver salver balanced on his palm.

"This arrived from The Talbot Inn, my lord. Mr Parsons begs an apology. He meant to deliver it yesterday but his wife misplaced the missive."

Christian took the letter from the salver. "Thank you, Foster. That will be all."

Upon breaking the seal, he looked for a signature and found Rose's name at the bottom of the paper. Instinctively, he brought the letter to his nose and inhaled, hoping to find a trace of her unique scent, something to stir excitement in his chest. When that failed, he brushed his finger over her name, desperate to feel a connection.

Rose.

He scanned the missive quickly, impatient to understand her reason for writing, and frowned. Various quotes from the Bible filled the first half of the page, one from Matthew, another from Isaiah, all relating to forgiveness. At first, he presumed the letter was an apology, but then he noticed Rose's message written at the bottom in a different hand.

As you know, my brother got married today. While there, I took the liberty of confessing my sins to the Reverend Wilmslow and begged him to give me guidance. He noted a few passages to remind me that God forgives all sins if repented. I hope this example of the reverend's writing proves useful in your endeavour to find peace.

Forgive me.

Rose.

Christian sat back in the chair. Instead of celebrating her brother's wedding, Rose had thought of him. A deep ache filled his chest. Mrs Hibbet was right.

He loved Rose.

Even though she'd left, he could still feel her in his heart. So what should he do about it? Perhaps he should find a white charger, ride to London and bring her back. He placed her letter on the desk, his mind distracted with thoughts of rescuing his damsel. But what would he do when he got there? He'd given his friend, Vane, free use of the house in Berkeley Square. And he could not leave the children.

Lost in thought, he stared at the wall until his gaze migrated back to Rose's letter.

Bloody hell!

Christian sat bolt upright. He snatched Cassandra's love note and held it in his left hand, took the example of the Reverend Wilmslow's handwriting in the other.

"They're a bloody match."

Taking a magnifying glass out of the drawer, he scanned them again to be sure.

"That blasted hypocritical toad."

He jumped from the chair, charged from the house to the stables and in fifteen minutes arrived at the reverend's home. After a brief conversation with the housekeeper, he found Wilmslow in St Martin's church practising his sermon.

Christian pushed open the oak doors with both hands and marched down the aisle. The clip of his boots echoed within the stone walls.

Wilmslow's head shot up. "Lord Farleigh? Well, this is a surprise." The reverend's smile faded as he stepped down from his pew. "I trust all is well."

"No, Wilmslow, all is not well." What had Cassandra seen in this lying snake?

"Look, I know we have different opinions about dealing with the sickness—"

"This is not about the blasted sickness, though at least now I know why you're so keen to search Everleigh."

The reverend gulped, and his face grew pale.

Christian glanced at the stained-glass window, at the rainbow of tiny pieces depicting the crucifixion. "I'll not discuss a matter of indelicacy in a house of God. I would ask you to step outside."

The reverend clasped the lapels of his black coat and raised his chin. "The Lord hears everything. There is nothing a man can hide from him."

Christian snorted. Contempt for the reverend oozed from his pores. "Then the Lord must know you're a hypocrite, the biggest sinner in the parish. Now, follow me outside else I shall drag you out."

Wilmslow's bottom lip trembled. He raised his hands to the heavens. "Let your gentle spirit be known to all men. Is that not the way of God? Is there any need for violence?" Wilmslow spoke in the principled tone he used to convey his superiority. "If I have wronged you, my lord, speak of it now."

Christian stepped closer. "Outside!"

"Very well. Very well." Wilmslow clapped his hands to together in prayer. One last attempt to persuade the Lord to intervene. "I shall do as you ask."

Christian turned, stormed out into the grounds and came to an abrupt halt on the grass amid the weathered headstones.

Wilmslow scurried behind. "Wh-what is this about?"

"It's about the letters you wrote to my wife." Christian swung around to face him. "The letters you've spent two years trying to locate in case the whole village should discover the depths of your depravity."

"Letters?"

"I have proof you sent them. I know you committed adultery. What I don't know is how you stand there and preach to the masses every Sunday."

Wilmslow withdrew a handkerchief from his pocket and dabbed the beads of perspiration on his brow. "You've made a

THE DECEPTIVE LADY DARBY

mistake. Everyone knows Mr Watson is the one guilty of the sin you mention."

How fortunate for the reverend that Mr Watson had not lived to defend himself.

"Perhaps I should take the letters to your wife, Wilmslow, see what she makes of my theory."

"My wife is in London, gone to visit her sister."

London? The woman rarely left the village.

"I'll have the truth from you one way or another." Christian shrugged out of his coat and placed it on the ground.

"What are you doing?"

"I am accusing you of adultery. Indeed, after you've fought for your honour, I intend to hire a solicitor to prosecute you for the crime."

"It is not a crime to have relations with another man's wife," the reverend countered.

"No. It's not." Christian was glad he'd read the letters as he recalled the mention of a lewd act conducted in his orangery. "But I can prosecute you for trespass and misuse of my property. As such, I shall press for financial compensation."

The reverend's face turned ashen. A court case would ruin the man in more ways than one.

Christian held up his fists as taught in the boxing salons in his youth. "I seek the truth, nothing more."

Wilmslow swallowed deeply. He glanced back over his shoulder and then once to the heavens. "The Lord tests the righteous and the wicked. How can a man preach forgiveness if he has never sinned?"

"Is that a confession?" If Wilmslow expected sympathy, he'd get none. Christian lurched forward and grabbed the preacher by his high-cut waistcoat. "Let's hear it all."

"It—it started when I attended Cassandra at Morton Manor." Wilmslow's face turned berry red, and his brown eyes flashed with fear. "She complained of hearing the voices of demons in her head."

Christian shook him. "And what, you thought to ride the devil out of her?" He didn't care for his crude comment. He'd not lower himself to Wilmslow's standards. "I think it's time you moved to pastures new."

"But I have repented every day for what I did."

He released the pathetic figure of a man. "You may have the Lord's forgiveness, but you will never have mine." Christian threw his entire body weight into a punch that connected hard with Wilmslow's jaw. The crack echoed through the churchyard. The reverend toppled back and landed between two gravestones.

"That is for hurting my son. Your antics have caused him no end of misery these last two years, and I'll make sure you're never allowed to preach to a congregation again."

"Please, my lord."

Feeling immense satisfaction and an element of relief, Christian stepped back. "And if I discover you had anything to do with Cassandra's death, I'll be back to finish what I've started."

Brushing his hands to show his disdain, he stepped over the reverend's quivering body and strode down the path.

"My lord! Wait! Will you not listen to my explanation?"

Christian ignored the man's cries and protests. He had one more call to make, and so mounted his horse and rode to Dr Taylor's house.

"I'm sorry, my lord, but the doctor got called away on urgent business." The housekeeper wiped her hands on her apron. "There's no telling when he'll be back."

"Away?" Suspicion flared. "Has he gone to see a patient?"

"No, my lord. He's gone to London, something to do with a meeting at the Wishful, no, the Worshipful Society of the Apothecaries. He left early yesterday morning."

Christian swallowed down his surprise. Despite their disagreements, he would have expected the doctor to inform him of his departure.

A strange sense of foreboding took hold.

Was it a coincidence that two people from the same small village had left for London a day after Rose? It seemed there was only one way to find out.

CHAPTER EIGHTEEN

"What on earth made you think you were in love with Lord Cunningham? Look at him prancing about the floor." Nicole gestured to the foppish lord dancing the cotillion with Mrs Webster. "I know I'm not a skilled dancer, but I'm sure you're not supposed to resemble a frog leaping off a lily pad."

Rose glanced at the man she might have married had her father not intervened. Lord Cunningham's chin lacked definition, unlike Christian's strong jaw. And his eyes didn't cause a lady's breath to come in shallow pants. Lord Cunningham's coat didn't cling to the muscles in his arms, and his thighs barely filled his breeches.

"He has a pleasant temperament." Rose had to defend her lack of judgement. "I doubt a harsh word ever falls from his lips. A woman could never disappoint a man like that."

But Lord Cunningham didn't love her, despite his protestations to the contrary. Unlike Christian, he lacked the capacity to care about anyone but himself.

She'd learnt a lot about love during her brief time at Everleigh. While love lived in the heart, it shone in a man's eyes and in the sensual curve of his lips. It was present in his passionate kisses, in the way he gazed into a lady's soul while claiming her body. Some would call it lust. But love didn't fade. Love remained in the eyes as a constant reminder.

Christian.

Her heart lurched. How was she to forget him when he lived inside her? How was she supposed to smile and dance when a ballroom was the last place she wanted to be? But Oliver insisted they make a stand, to allay suspicion and quell the gossips.

"I can think of only one reason why you imagined an attraction to Lord Cunningham. You wanted to escape your father. Cunningham was an easy way out." Nicole always understood. "And while I disagree with your father's method, he saved you from making the biggest mistake of your life."

"I know." Had her father not intervened, she would not have met Christian. "How ironic that I feel a deep sense of gratitude."

Nicole cupped Rose's elbow, and they shuffled back until almost obscured by the giant potted fern. "You would never have known true love had you not escaped from the manor." Nicole's comment caught Rose unawares. "And you do love Lord Farleigh."

"What makes you say that?" Oh, she loved him with all her heart.

Nicole offered a confident smile. "Because now I know what it's like to be in love." With a covert flick of the eyes, she looked across the ballroom at Oliver. "I heard it in your voice when you spoke to Lord Farleigh. The fact you cried for two hours when we left Everleigh was telling, too, don't you think?"

Two hours? She'd cried for days, cried until there were no more tears left to shed.

"And so what I really want to know," Nicole continued, "is what you intend to do about it?"

"Do?" She could do nothing other than pine for a lost love. "All I can do is help him solve the problems at Everleigh." To bring him the peace he deserved.

"I'll not allow you to go snooping around town on your own. If you insist on visiting the places listed in your blue book, then you must take Oliver with you."

By now, Christian would know if the Reverend Wilmslow was the one responsible for sending the vulgar letters to Cassandra. Still, she couldn't shake the feeling that the blue book held some importance, too. Why else would Cassandra hide it in a drawer? That's why Rose brought it to London, in the hope a servant at the address in Bloomsbury might offer an explanation.

"You know what Oliver said. I'm to put the goings-on at Morton Manor behind me and concentrate of settling back into society." But how could she forget all that had happened there? How could she not at least try to help the man she loved?

Sympathy flashed in Nicole's eyes. "It's because he cares. What really matters is your happiness. Let me speak to him. Perhaps I might make him see what helping Lord Farleigh means to you."

Rose captured Nicole's gloved hand. "Thank you. At least if I'm doing something constructive, I might stop crying."

"The only time you smile is when you speak about Lord Farleigh and the children. Come, let us take some refreshment and you can tell me about the day you had a picnic by the lake."

Excitement fluttered in her chest. Talking about her adventures at Everleigh brought the moments to life. "If we wait for Oliver to finish his conversation, we'll die of thirst."

"He's doing what he promised, making sure everyone knows you spent time with him in Italy."

"And what shall I do if someone asks me a question about my visit?"

"Be vague. Mention the spectacular architecture, the warm weather, the insects. Say you came down with a sickness and spent a month in bed."

"Lie you mean?" Lies had cost her everything. And while she knew she should try to forget Christian, she was deceiving herself to think she ever would.

"Sometimes lies are necessary." Nicole spoke with conviction. "I pretended to be a paid companion to escape a cold-hearted brother eager to wed me to the highest bidder. You pretended to be a maid to escape from a father determined to keep you a prisoner. Please tell me what part of that is wrong."

Nicole made deception sound logical. "When you think about it, the similarities between us are striking."

"My case is worse if you consider your brother only learnt the truth after we'd been intimate." A blush touched Nicole's cheeks. "But don't tell him I told you that."

"And yet Oliver did not turn you away." A lump formed in Rose's throat. "That makes my case far worse."

Nicole frowned. Her curious gaze scanned Rose's face. And then she gasped. "You've been intimate with Lord Farleigh?" Despite Nicole's hushed voice, Rose feared the whole world could hear.

"Shush. Why don't you ask the butler to make an announcement?"

"When you say *intimate*, do you mean it in the strongest possible terms?" Nicole wiggled her eyebrows as if it were a covert form of communication.

Rose shuffled closer. "Intimate in the way a wife is with her husband."

Nicole shot back and plastered her hand over her mouth. She took a moment to compose herself. "No wonder you cried all the way home. For heaven's sake, don't mention this to your brother."

"I may be a liar, but I'm not an imbecile." While others would deem her reckless and foolish, loving Christian was the only thing in her life that felt right.

"I know you speak highly of Lord Farleigh, but trust me, a gentleman would not take a woman of your calibre to his bed and then let her leave." Nicole clutched Rose's arm. "Lord, I may punch him if I ever see him again."

Having witnessed Nicole punch the guard at Morton Manor, she prayed Christian was agile and light on his feet.

The low hum of voices in the room suddenly grew in speed and pitch. Rose peeked around the potted fern curious as to what had captured the crowd's attention. Two gentlemen and a lady stood at the large wooden doors leading into Lord Warner's ballroom.

The lady to their right gasped. "Goodness, Felicity, it seems the night won't be so tedious after all. Please tell me he's not a mirage. Please tell me that's Vane. I've waited two seasons to try my chances with him."

"Step in line, dear." The woman's companion snorted. "The vultures are already circling. See?" Numerous ladies edged closer towards the new arrivals. "I see he's brought his sister. Terrible shame what happened. I fear for any man who so much as looks at her in the wrong way."

"They say one night with Vane and a woman is ruined for any other man."

"I wouldn't know, but like you, I wouldn't mind finding out."

While the ladies' conversation proved entertaining, Rose wasn't looking at the gentleman with the devilish grin. Nor did she care much for the woman with hair as dark as ebony. The other gentleman stole her attention. The one with green eyes that held her spellbound. The man who caused her body to flame at the merest glance, caused her heart to pound wildly in her chest.

Rose tapped Nicole on the arm. "You know you want to punch Lord Farleigh." She focused on the magnificent vision before her. "Well, I think you may have your chance."

CHAPTER NINETEEN

"Next time you lend me the use of your house, have the decency to warn me you might visit with a whole entourage in tow." Ross Sandford, Marquess of Trevane, known to all as Vane, brushed his hair back from his brow. "How the hell do you sleep when they make such a racket?"

"I would hardly call two children and a housekeeper an entourage." Christian scanned the sea of heads looking for Rose. "Be thankful my son likes you else you might wake in the morning to find those ebony locks scattered about the bedchamber floor."

Vane snorted. "Only your son would have the nerve to attack a man twice his size."

"Is that supposed to be a compliment?"

"Were you not the only boy in school to put Haystack Henry on his arse?"

Christian chuckled. "Someone had to fight for those too weak to defend themselves."

Two ladies sauntered past, their eyes glistening as they feasted on Vane's masculine form.

Vane observed the crowd and turned to Christian. "Good

THE DECEPTIVE LADY DARBY

God, if it weren't for you I'd be at home." The words burst through gritted teeth. "Do you see what you've done to me? Every lady with loose morals wants to eat me alive."

"And all the rakes and rogues have rushed to hide behind the curtains, trembling with fear."

Vane raised a brow. "You're the only man who could make light of my situation and not get thumped."

"I meant nothing other than I admire your ability to deal with scoundrels in the only manner fitting." It had taken every ounce of strength Christian possessed not to beat the reverend to a pulp. "Of late, my method for dealing with vermin is to pretend they're not there until they've eaten a hole in my breeches."

Vane offered his arm to his sister, Lillian, and they stepped into the ballroom amid shocked glances and excited whispers. "You have to convey a respectable demeanour. You have children to consider. I have none. It makes a vast difference." Vane's mouth twitched at the corners. "But I'd rather not see your bare behind if it's all the same."

"You don't know what you're missing."

"I've seen your pert buttocks more times than I care to count. May I suggest you save that pleasure for your lady love when we find her?"

Lord Warner's ball was just one event on a long list of possible places Rose might be. But a spark of energy in the air stirred Christian's senses, and he knew with certainty that he'd come to the right place.

"Had you sent me round to question Stanton's butler," Vane said, "I doubt he'd have remained tight-lipped for long."

Lillian chuckled. "My brother is renowned for his powers of persuasion."

Christian had to admit to being shocked when he called to see Rose, only to discover she'd gone to a ball. After a brief tussle with his pride, he understood the earl's urgency to introduce Rose back into society.

"Is that why you insisted on coming with me? Did you hope to persuade the lady to give me another chance?"

"I came because I had no desire to spend the next few days listening to you pining for your lost love. Someone had to make sure you didn't throw yourself in the Thames in a fit of desperation."

Christian appreciated his friend's directness. He'd always been able to talk to Vane. Despite years of separation, the conversation felt natural. And Vane never lied.

"Trust me. I'd have barged into every ball and soiree until I found her." He'd thought of nothing else since the night she'd left Everleigh. He couldn't forget the words she'd whispered before running from the drawing room and out of his life. Rose's safety was his primary concern, and Dr Taylor's timely visit to London proved worrying.

"I think it's rather sweet," Lillian said, her eyes wide and bright. Most ladies who'd suffered as she had would hang their head in shame. But then most ladies did not have Vane for a brother. "You must care for the lady a great deal. Is this not the first time you've been to town in years?"

"Like your brother, there is nothing here for me now. I'm only grateful you're receiving invitations else we'd still be loitering on the front steps."

Vane cast him a sidelong glance and winked. "What makes you think I had an invitation?"

"But this is the third ball we've attended tonight. Our hosts waved us in without comment."

"I don't need an invitation, Farleigh. No sane gentleman would dare question my right to be here." Vane gave a weary sigh. "Now, I shall take Lillian for a stroll in the garden while you search for your lady. I find I'm somewhat blind when it comes to noticing debutantes and so will be no use to you now."

Debutantes? By society's standards, Rose was his mistress. "I'll come and find you when it's time to leave."

Vane inclined his head and proceeded towards the doors leading out onto the terrace. God help anyone who made the slightest comment about his sister. Christian was surprised Lillian had come. But the siblings had spent two years abroad, and Lillian was not one for hiding in the shadows. Vane sought any opportunity to ruffle the feathers of those who dared look down their nose at her.

Left alone, it didn't take Christian long to find Rose. From the moment he entered the ballroom, he'd sensed her presence. Indeed, when he looked straight ahead, their gazes locked.

His heart swelled, and his knees almost buckled. Why the hell had he let her leave?

Rose cast him a warm smile.

Christian stopped a foot away and bowed. She offered him her hand, and he brushed his lips over her knuckles as he'd wanted to do at their first meeting.

"Lord Farleigh, I must say I'm shocked to see you. You assured me you rarely leave Abberton and yet here you are in a ballroom in London no less." She gestured to Miss Asprey standing at her side. "And of course, you remember Lady Stanton."

While mildly flirtatious, Rose's tone lacked the warmth of feeling to which he was accustomed. Was he too late? Was he misguided in thinking she felt something, too?

"May I offer my felicitations on your recent marriage."

"Thank you, my lord." Lady Stanton cast him a hard stare. "While we are all guilty of leading with the heart, at some point we must act responsibly."

Christian understood the message clearly. "Hence the reason I stand before you tonight."

The lady remained at Rose's side, though turned away and feigned interest in the ridiculously large potted fern.

The first few strains of a waltz punctured the air.

"Would you care to dance, Rose?" He despised the formality of it all when all he wanted to do was take her in his arms and kiss her deeply. "Please tell me I'm not too late and that you have space on your card."

"Dance? I assume you're here because there are things you wish to discuss."

"I hadn't planned on talking, at least, not just yet." He hoped the words struck a chord, that they reminded her of the intimate moment they'd shared in his study.

Recognition flashed in her eyes. "Then I hope you are as skilled at dancing as you are other things."

"Thankfully, I'm able to master anything when I'm with you."

Her blue eyes sparkled as they journeyed over him. "May I say you look rather dashing in evening attire."

Rose looked stunning in the pastel-blue gown. "You always take my breath away, even when you have ash on your chin."

She smiled. "You remembered."

"I will never forget." His breath came quickly as his heated blood surged through his veins. "Dance with me, Rose." *Forgive me for letting you go.*

She offered her hand, and he led her out onto the floor. Taking her in his arms soothed his fears. She belonged with him, he'd known it since the day she strode into his study pretending to be a maid.

For a few minutes he didn't speak, but let the music wash over him, savoured the instant feeling of contentment as her body glided in tune with his. Rose was his peace, his harmony.

"Tell me you hold no affection for Lord Cunningham." Before he allowed himself to hope, he had to know the truth. "Tell me he means nothing to you."

She stared into his eyes. "My heart is yours, Christian. After all that happened between us, I'm surprised you need to ask."

He felt foolish. "I didn't know what to think. You gave yourself to me freely though I've spent the last few days questioning whether I'd misread the signs."

"You misread nothing." A blush touched her cheeks. "I wanted you then, as much as I want you now."

Good Lord, if only they were somewhere private. He firmed his hold on her hand as energy sparked between them. The urge to crush her to his chest proved overwhelming.

"Christian, you're holding me too close." The whispered words breezed past his ear. "Someone will notice."

"Forgive me." He slackened his grip. "The last few days have felt like a lifetime. The house is empty without you. The children are miserable, and Mrs Hibbet mumbles to herself at every given opportunity."

"And what about you?"

"I need you, too. I'm empty, miserable and have no one to talk to."

She caught her breath. "Christian, I—"

The dance came to an abrupt end, and they parted. With no option but to escort Rose back to her brother, he waited for Lord Stanton to berate him for being far too familiar.

"Lord Farleigh, I trust it's been a while since you danced and consequently have forgotten what is deemed an appropriate distance." Lord Stanton straightened to his full height. "How is Rose able to settle back into society when you're determined to make a spectacle of her?"

Christian inclined his head. "As you say, after such a long stint in the country, I find my skill is somewhat lacking when it comes to dancing."

Stanton stepped closer and bent his head. "My sister does not need any more upset."

"Oliver, please," Rose whispered.

"No, Rose, he needs to know. He needs to know that you cry yourself to sleep at night. Don't think I don't know. Don't think I can't hear you."

Christian's tongue grew thick as a pang of self-loathing hit him hard in the chest. He turned to look at Rose though he directed his reply to her brother. "I shall make it my life's mission to ensure she has no need to shed a tear again."

A foppish gentleman approached and cleared his throat to gain their attention. "Lord Stanton, I wonder if I might have the pleasure of asking Rose—"

"Bugger off, Cunningham." Stanton didn't bother to make eye contact with the dandy.

So, this was Lord Cunningham. What the hell was Rose thinking when she imagined herself in love with him? Heaven help the man when it came to undressing. It would take him a week to untie the ridiculous knot in his cravat. Christian breathed a sigh of relief when he considered the competition, but that didn't stop him wanting to throttle Cunningham until the fellow's cheeks turned blue.

"But I wanted to ask Rose—"

"Leave, Cunningham, else you'll feel my shoe up your behind."

"There is nothing to say," Rose interjected when Cunningham lingered like a bad smell. "During my absence, I've come to realise we're not suited."

As Christian had no right to comment, he glared at Cunningham until the lord scuttled away.

"Now," Stanton began, "I suppose it's too much to hope you're only here for that little blue book, Farleigh."

Rose stiffened. "Does it matter why he's here?"

"Blue book?" Was Stanton referring to Rose's diary, the one she used to hide the letters? "I am not in the habit of reading a lady's personal reflections."

"I'm referring to the one she found at Everleigh." Stanton glanced at Rose with some disapproval. "The one she should have left there. The one she had no right to take."

Rose turned to Christian and placed a hand on his sleeve, much to her brother's chagrin. "Perhaps we should take a stroll around the garden."

Panic flared. If she'd lied to him about another matter, he wasn't sure how he'd react.

"We'll accompany you outside." Lady Stanton took hold of her husband's arm. "It's clear you have things to discuss that requires time away from the ballroom."

Stanton gestured for Christian to lead the way. "You may walk a few feet in front, but no more. I'll not have people gossiping about Rose."

Christian offered Rose his arm and led her out onto the terrace. They descended the stone steps leading into the well-lit garden. Christian waited until they'd settled into a relaxed pace before asking the question plaguing his thoughts.

"Why didn't you mention the book before? You had every opportunity to do so. And what is so important you would bring it with you to London?"

"I did mention it. If you recall, I brought the book down to the study along with the letters, but you distracted me."

An image of her lying naked beneath him flashed into his

mind. "Granted, I had more pressing matters to attend to at the time."

"The following day, I asked you to read it after you'd studied the letters."

After that night in his study, he'd struggled to think of anything other than Rose. While he'd tried to read the letters, he wanted nothing to rid him of the warm, fuzzy feeling in his chest.

"Now I come to think of it I do recall you mentioning the book. But that still doesn't explain why you brought the diary with you to London."

She paused for a moment before speaking. "It's not a diary but a ledger. It contains at least twenty names including Miss Stoneway, and payments ranging from thirty to two hundred pounds. In the back is a list of addresses, mostly here in London."

"And you found this at Everleigh?" He might have suggested it belonged to his father had it not been for Miss Stoneway's name. His father died long before the woman was a patient at Morton Manor.

A cool breeze drifted over them, and Rose shivered. Christian contemplated draping his arm around her shoulder, but he glanced behind only to meet Lord Stanton's beady stare.

"I didn't find it, Christian, Jacob gave it to me. He stole the book from Cassandra along with the letters."

What would Cassandra want with such a thing? "And you're certain it's not a diary or a list of people Cassandra met at Morton Manor?"

"No, it's a record of payments made."

"Perhaps the ledger is the property of Morton Manor, and Cassandra stole it for some reason." Cassandra often behaved irrationally, acted out of spite. "Perhaps she used it to bribe one of her lovers."

"Oh, did you get the note I gave to Mrs Parsons?" Rose gripped his arm in a sudden flurry of excitement. "She promised she'd send it up to the house."

"I did, and you were right. Whether Mr Watson and Cassandra were lovers remains to be seen, but the Reverend Wilmslow is the one who wrote the letters."

Rose stopped abruptly and turned to face him. He could see her pulse beating hard in her throat. "Oh, Christian, I'm so sorry." She placed her hand on his chest, and for a moment he forgot where he was. "Have you spoken to him?"

Behind them, Lord Stanton coughed discreetly.

Christian clasped Rose's hand, placed it in the crook of his arm and continued walking. "He admitted to having relations with Cassandra. The man took me for a fool. The business about poisonous plants was merely a ploy so he could search the house."

"The children mentioned that the reverend sat with them when they were ill. When he thought they were asleep, he tidied the room."

"Tidied the room?" Recognition dawned. Damn it all. He should have done more than punch the man. "Cassandra must have told him that Jacob had stolen the letters. No doubt he was desperate to find them before I did."

"But you know what that means?"

Oh, he knew. Other than daydreaming about Rose, he'd spent the journey to London considering all the problems at Everleigh. "That the sickness in the house has nothing to do with dangerous spores hiding amongst the linen." His mocking tone conveyed an element of embarrassment, too. He'd been blind. A damn fool.

"Worse than that, Christian. I believe the tonics and

tinctures make the staff ill in order to give the reverend access to the house."

"That means Wilmslow has been poisoning my staff."

"Perhaps not Wilmslow, is it not Dr Taylor who administers the medicine? Are the concoctions not made by his housekeeper?"

The heavy feeling in his gut told him Taylor was involved. But why? "What has the doctor to gain?"

"Money? You do pay him for his services?"

Dr Taylor struck him as a man too proud to use underhanded methods to gain money. "Not always, he's refused payment many times, in part because he is just as frustrated as I am when it comes to the lack of progress made. Or so he appears."

Rose sighed. "The doctor is guilty of something. I suggest we visit an address listed in the back of the ledger. I had my sights set on the one in Bloomsbury. If we ask the right questions, we may get answers."

A sudden chill passed over him. Rose's inquisitive mind might lead her to make enquiries on her own. "Promise me you won't do anything without me. Do not go tearing around the city, knocking on doors."

How could he trust her word?

Christian came to an abrupt halt outside a stone memorial surrounded by iron railings at the front and a tall topiary hedge to the rear. Lord Stanton stopped walking and remained a few feet behind.

"You must give me your word, Rose." Panic infused Christian's tone. "Do nothing without me. Let me examine the book before we make any rash decisions." Taylor was in London for a reason. Had Cassandra stolen the book from him? "Promise me."

She looked up at him, her blue eyes wide, her lips parted.

"I promise to wait for you. I know you think my word means nothing, but that's not true. The only reason I broke my vow on the night of the fire was that I couldn't bear to think of you hurt and alone." Tears welled in her eyes.

"Do you know why I came here?"

She shook her head.

"I did not come to find a silly book, or to traipse around looking for answers to the mysteries of Morton Manor." Blood rushed through his veins at far too rapid a rate. "I came here for you. Nothing else matters to me. Everything else is a mere pebble in an ocean when I consider how close I came to losing you."

Rose sucked in a breath as her hand came to rest at the base of her throat. "But I lied to you, just like Cassandra."

"You're nothing like Cassandra."

Lord Stanton exhaled deeply, and Christian resisted the urge to turn around and tell him to bugger off. But it was Rose who reacted.

She glanced beyond the iron gate, and then at her brother. "We're going to read the inscription on the memorial stone." She didn't give Stanton a chance to reply.

The hinges creaked as Rose opened the gate and slipped inside. Christian followed.

"I expected it to be a memorial to the fallen heroes of the Warner family." Rose stepped closer and peered at the inscription. "But unless they had ancestors named Hyperion and Arion, I highly doubt it."

While curious about the meaning behind the names, he couldn't tear his gaze away from her. She wandered around to the back, to the part hidden from view.

"Come and look at this. They're not names of people, but horses."

Christian followed her and was about to examine the

markings when Rose jumped into his arms and kissed him. There was no time for a slow melding of mouths. Indeed, her tongue skimmed the line of his lips, seeking entrance. He cupped her cheeks, and tilted his head to delve deeper, tried to swallow down her moans of pleasure. Dainty hands moved over his chest, grabbing at his coat, pulling him closer. The scent of roses filled his head while the sweet taste of her mouth seduced his senses. God, her lips were hot, passionate, demanding. When he kissed Rose, the rest of the world melted away.

They broke on ragged breaths, touched foreheads and closed their eyes.

"How long does it take to read a few lines?" Stanton said. "A man was born and died, what more is there to see?"

"Leave them alone," his wife whispered. "Just give them a minute."

A shriek pierced the night air, the sound accompanied by raised voices.

"You might want to come and look at this, Farleigh. You're missing the night's entertainment."

Christian opened his eyes and caressed Rose's cheek. There was only one diversion he sought. Who needed jugglers or fire eaters when the woman before him stole his breath?

"If you don't come now, Trevane is liable to murder a guest, perhaps even two."

Christian groaned. Bloody hell. Vane's scandalous past followed him wherever he went. The man held his temper in check with the flimsiest thread. One wrong word or insult and Vane would rip the place apart.

"Forgive me, Rose, but I am somewhat responsible for Lord Trevane this evening." Christian had not seen his friend for years, but the bonds formed at school and in those formative years proved unbreakable.

"Come then." She stepped out of their hideaway and led him to the gate. "You're not a man who shirks his responsibilities."

"Don't ask me how it started." Stanton gestured to the commotion near the steps leading to the terrace. "In all fairness, your friend attempted to walk away."

The crowd dissipated to offer a clear view of Vane, his hands gripping the lapels of a gentleman's coat as he held the fellow a foot or more off the ground. Vane looked set to rip the man's throat out with his teeth. No one would dare step forward to stop him.

"I must take him home before he beats everyone here to within an inch of their life. I'm not really sure why he insisted on coming." Christian wasn't sure why Vane had asked to stay at his house in Berkeley Square when he had a property in London.

"His sister looks distraught." Rose placed her hand lightly on his back. "We can continue our discussion tomorrow."

Christian brought Rose's hand to his lips and planted a quick kiss on her knuckles. "I shall call on you at two. We can study the book and decide how best to proceed." He stared into her eyes. "And there are things I want to say that require privacy."

"Until tomorrow." Rose smiled. "Go now. Save your friend."

CHAPTER TWENTY

R ose sat at the dining table, buttering her toast and sneaking covert glances at Nicole and Oliver. They sat next to each other as opposed to opposite ends of the table, their chairs so close their arms touched. Oliver muttered something in her ear and smiled. Nicole blushed but shot him a look that said she was game for whatever it was Oliver had suggested.

The affectionate display warmed Rose's heart. Even in her wildest dreams, she'd never imagined seeing Oliver happy, never imagined ever seeing Nicole again. And now they were a family.

Other than the clink of cutlery on china plates, the house was quiet, at peace. And yet Rose glanced at the door, waiting for a roar of disapproval to ring through the corridor, for her father to come bursting into the room and berate her for some imagined misdemeanour. She could picture his face, all red and puffy, his eyes bulging from their sockets.

"What time did Lord Farleigh say he'd call?" Oliver's voice broke her reverie.

"I think he said two o'clock." The distraction helped to

calm her racing heart. "Although with the commotion in Lord Warner's garden, I may have misheard. Either way, I have no plans to leave the house today."

"What does he want?" Oliver held her gaze while he sipped his coffee.

Nicole gave a bemused chuckle. "You're a man, Oliver, what do you think he wants?"

The cup rattled on the saucer as Oliver placed it down. "A man doesn't come to town after all this time unless a lady has given him some incentive. Are you going to tell me what happened during your stay at Everleigh? And I don't mean you played with the children and ate cake."

It crossed her mind to lie, or to evade the question. But after her experiences at Everleigh, she'd made a pact with herself to tell the truth. "Do you really want to know?"

Oliver sat up straight. "I do."

"I fell in love at Everleigh." The truth of her words filled her chest, the sensation all warm and fuzzy. "I fell in love with the house, with the children"—a chuckle left her lips —"even with Mrs Hibbet." How she wished she was back there, running around the lawn wearing her blindfold, holding secret meetings with Christian in the study.

"And what of Lord Farleigh?"

Rose paused as an image of Christian's handsome face filled her head. She could almost smell his cologne, smell the unique scent that clung to his skin. "Oh, I am so in love with Lord Farleigh it hurts."

Nicole's beaming smile stretched from ear to ear. "Perhaps it was just as well you did get lost. I have a strange suspicion he feels the same way."

A weary sigh left Oliver's lips. "Well, I suppose I'd rather see you wed to Farleigh than Lord Cunningham. I assume he will approach me to ask for your hand."

"I have no idea what he will do." Rose bit into her toast, her heart feeling suddenly light and free.

"Perhaps I should pay him a visit—"

"No." Rose shot out of the chair. "Lord Farleigh must make the decision on his own, without coercion." He'd been pressured into marriage before and come to regret it. "Promise me you'll say nothing. Promise me you won't try to force his hand."

"Let's see what the day brings." Nicole patted Oliver's arm. "I'm certain, come tomorrow, this will prove to be a pointless conversation."

Rose settled back in her chair. The clock on the mantel chimed eleven. Good Lord, at Everleigh she'd have eaten her breakfast and done a host of chores by now.

They continued their meal in silence until a knock on the door brought Bradbury carrying the salver. "A letter has arrived, my lord, addressed to Lady Rose."

"Lady Rose?" Oliver took the note and scanned it before handing it across the table. "Thank you, Bradbury."

"Shall I wait for a reply?"

Rose shook her head. "I shall call you if I need you."

The butler bowed and left the room.

As soon as the door clicked shut, Oliver sat forward. "Is it from Farleigh?"

Rose ignored Oliver's hard stare. "Won't you at least give me a chance to open it?"

Her heart leapt as she studied the folded paper with her name scrawled neatly on the front. She flipped it over and broke the seal. Unable to contain her excitement she read it quickly, but couldn't quite believe the words as they formed in her head. Her smile faded, the corners of her mouth pulled down by the weight of her burden. The sudden need to breathe deeply came upon her, and she put her hand to her throat and gasped.

"What is it, Rose? Is it Farleigh?" Oliver would not rest until she'd offered an explanation. "By God, if he's playing games with—"

"No, it's not from Lord Farleigh." In truth, she didn't know who'd written the note. She swallowed deeply though the large lump in her throat remained. "Just give me a minute to compose myself, and I'll tell you."

The tick of the mantel clock pierced the prolonged silence.

"Well, what does it say?" Oliver modified his tone, concern now the overriding emotion. "You can tell me."

Rose sighed. Oh, she should lie, but only a fool would tackle this problem alone. "It says I'm to come to the Chelsea Physic Garden at two o'clock today. That I'm to wear a coat and breeches, as women are not permitted entrance. That I'm to bring the blue book." She closed her eyes briefly. "Should I fail in the task, Lord Farleigh and his children will suffer a fate similar to that of his late wife."

Nicole's mouth gaped open.

Oliver scrunched his napkin in his fist as he stared at her. "Who the devil sent it?"

"I don't know." No one would sign their name to something so threatening. "But he goes on to remind me that a man must watch what he eats and drinks. Poison is an invisible enemy often consumed without knowledge."

"The Physic Garden is well known as the garden of the apothecaries. They study all means of plants there with a view to creating new medicines."

And tonics and tinctures, no doubt.

Rose's heartbeat pulsed hard in her throat. Someone skilled in botany was responsible for the illness at Everleigh.

But how was she to pass for a gentleman of science? "What if they see through my disguise and turn me away?"

Oliver slapped his palm on the table, shaking the delicate china. "Don't think for one moment I'll let you go gallivanting off on your own."

What was it about men and power? After a two-year absence, did Oliver think it was acceptable to charge into her life, firing demands? "It is not your choice to make."

"Does this have something to do with the sickness you mentioned?" Nicole said, not giving Oliver an opportunity to respond.

Everything came back to the sickness. Everything came back to the reverend's need to search the rooms at Everleigh. "In a way, although I believe there is also a connection to Morton Manor."

"Morton Manor?" Nicole frowned. "Will we ever be able to put that place behind us?"

"Perhaps only when we discover the true value of the blue book. At first, I suspected Lady Farleigh had a gambling habit, and that it was a record of her creditors. But now it is evident that someone deems it important enough to threaten murder."

Nicole exhaled. "So, what are we to do?"

Rose recalled the words she'd read three times now. "Under no circumstances am I to contact Lord Farleigh. I'm to go to the garden alone. The instructions are clear."

Oliver threw himself back in the chair. "And if you think I will let you walk out of here to meet someone capable of these vile and vicious taunts, think again." He paused and thrust his hand through his mop of ebony hair. "I've failed you once before. I'll not fail you again. If you insist on going, then we'll come with you."

"But you can't. What if he has a boy watching the house?"

"He?" Oliver arched a brow. "You're certain this person is a man?"

It was not her place to accuse anyone, but she knew she would be meeting either Dr Taylor or Reverend Wilmslow. "I'm certain. Besides, women cannot access the garden."

One question plagued her thoughts. How did the culprit know she had the book? She'd walked out of the house with it in her hand, but the staff at Everleigh had always assumed it belonged to her. After her brother's wedding, she'd taken a moment to scour the names on the tombstones in the churchyard in Abberton, looking for a correlation between the names in the book and those of local parishioners. But Reverend Wilmslow had been deep in conversation with Oliver and Nicole.

Nicole cleared her throat. "You'll not like what I'm going to say, but the book does not belong to you. Should Lord Farleigh not have a say in what happens? Isn't he the one who's suffered at this man's hands?"

If Rose acted on her own without seeking Christian's counsel, what then? How would he ever trust her again? "You're right. But Lord Farleigh will do everything in his power to prevent me from going."

Oliver snorted. "In that case, I find I like him a little more."

Anger flared. "No part of this is amusing, Oliver. Two women died. The staff at Everleigh suffer from a constant sickness. Lord Farleigh has spent two years living under the misconception that he is somehow to blame for it all."

Oliver raised his hand. "Forgive me. Let us not argue. Our time is better spent formulating a plan. Although I am opposed to this meeting in the strongest possible terms, I can see you have limited options."

Nicole gazed up at Oliver and smiled. "It's simple. Rose leaves in a hackney cab, and we leave in the carriage half an hour earlier. We call for Lord Farleigh and explain the situation, visit the garden and act as patrons. I assume the garden is open to the public?"

Oliver nodded. "Yes, but it's as Rose stated. Women are not permitted entrance."

Rose scanned Oliver's broad chest. "And therein lies another problem. Where are we to find a coat and breeches to fit?"

"Two coats and breeches," Nicole corrected as she cast Oliver a sidelong glance. "Don't think for a moment I'm waiting in the carriage."

The hackney jerked to a stop in Swan Walk, outside the tall gates leading to the Chelsea Physic Garden. Rose climbed down to the pavement and paid the driver who wasted no time in flicking the ribbons and charging off in search of his next fare.

She tugged on the cravat, tied so tightly she had empathy for those poor souls in Newgate waiting to swing from the gallows. Old stockings padded the hessian boots to account for them being too big, and the thin length of rope tied around her waist worked to keep her breeches up.

There were few houses in this part of town, and although the quiet street was untouched by the hustle and bustle of city life, the stench of the river hung in the air as a constant reminder.

"'Ere, sir." A boy pushed away from the stone wall and

came sauntering over, his faded top hat balanced precariously on his head. "Would you be the gent looking for a cure to end all sickness?" He waved his walking cane at the iron gate like the men who stand outside tents at the fair and lure you in with a promise of a mystical sight from the Orient.

Rose cast him a curious glance. "And what would a boy of your age know about it?" Oh, heavens, her voice sounded croaky rather than manly.

"I know if you've had the pox for a month likely it won't kill you. I know not to eat stew from a man with black fingernails."

Despite the grave nature of her situation, Rose couldn't help but smile. "I'm assured the garden is a treasure-trove for an apothecary eager to learn more about medicinal plants."

"It is if you've got the key." The boy winked.

Rose peered through the iron bars at the empty gravel path. "Is the garden closed today?" Having not the slightest interest in medicine, and being entirely the wrong sex, she'd had no cause to venture to the garden before.

"The apothecaries and their apprentices have been and done their daily scribbling." The boy pushed the rim of his shabby hat up with the tip of his cane. "Sometimes a gent pays to study alone if he's got the funds and the curator's got gambling debts to pay."

"I see." A sense of trepidation washed over her.

The boy stepped forward and unlocked the gate. "I'm to see the book before I let you inside. Master's orders."

Rose reached into the pocket of her coat and removed the blue ledger. The boy flicked his finger, a sign to say he wanted to look inside. She showed him the pages of names, and he nodded as if it were an entrance ticket to a one-time show.

"Do you always do what your master tells you?" Loyalty was often decided by whoever offered the biggest bribe.

"I do if I want to eat." He gestured to the gate. "You're to wait under the cedar tree near Sir Sloane."

"Sir Sloane?" Was that the name the villain used to disguise his identity?

"The statue. Follow the path to the middle. Look for the ugly gent with a wig."

"Are you referring to the statue or your master?"

The boy shrugged. "You'll see."

Rose opened the gate and stepped inside. The boy closed and locked it before pushing the key back into the fob pocket of his fancy waistcoat. The green garment with brass buttons caught her attention, not because a boy of his ilk couldn't possibly afford such a piece, but because both the top and bottom buttons were missing. However, before she could ask him anything he moved away from the gate, out of view.

Rose stared through the black metal bars. Locked inside the garden, she contemplated how Christian would gain entrance. The irony of the situation was not lost on her. She'd broken free from her previous prison, but would she escape this one?

Well, there was only one way to find out.

Just like the night she'd stumbled upon Everleigh, the gravel crunched beneath her feet as she hurried along the path, past the beds of herbs and plants. Standing five feet wide and twenty high, one could not miss the white figure on the stone plinth. Two cedar trees flanked the walkway, and Rose stood and waited for Taylor or Wilmslow to arrive.

She did not have to wait long.

A figure appeared from behind the tree: a gentleman only a few inches taller than the boy. Rose scanned the line of his jaw and the breadth of his chest as he approached. A frisson of fear shuddered through her upon witnessing the stranger. When one knew their quarry, it made negotiation easier.

"Lady Rose, it was good of you to come." The woman's voice pierced the tense air. "But then I suppose you had little choice in the matter. Few women understand what it is to love a man, few would be willing to do anything to keep him safe."

Rose stared at the face beneath the top hat, wracking her mind to think where she'd seen this woman before. With porcelain skin and ebony hair tied back in a queue, she had a childlike quality somewhat similar to Alice. Her eyes were the darkest brown though they appeared as cold, black pools devoid of life.

"I've seen you once before but cannot think where." It wasn't at The Talbot Inn or Morton Manor. So where?

"Then I am at an advantage." She gestured to the path leading south towards the river. "Let us take a little walk."

Oliver mentioned that the apothecaries transported certain herbs and plants from exotic locations directly to the gate leading from the Thames. "Where are we going?" Heavens, if this woman had a barge waiting, Oliver and Christian would never find her.

"To one of the potting rooms. Even though the garden is closed to visitors temporarily, we wouldn't want to attract any undue attention."

She spoke so calmly, with a serene quality that belied the evil mind lurking beyond the fake facade. "And what are we to do there?"

"We will examine the book away from prying eyes."

Prying eyes? There wasn't a soul in the garden. Only the faint hum of bees and the crisp sound of their footsteps broke the silence. "Is that why we're wearing these ridiculous clothes?"

"Men like to think they have the monopoly on everything." They passed beneath the thick boughs of the cedar trees, and the gate leading down to the river came into view. "They like to make rules and preach about their moral superiority. If a lady is lucky, she might find one who is not a fake or fraud."

When Rose thought of Christian's fine qualities, she considered herself amongst the luckiest of ladies. She only hoped he could find a way to rescue her from this mess. The sight of the river in the distance, coupled with the slow advance along the narrow path, roused images of walking the plank. At some point, she expected to feel the tip of a sword pressed into her back, to feel the murky water filling her lungs as she tried to stay afloat.

They approached the row of red-brick buildings to their left. Rose stopped abruptly. "What assurance do I have that you'll not harm Lord Farleigh and his children? What assurance do I have that I'll leave this garden alive?"

The woman smiled. "This was never about Lord Farleigh. We want the book that's all."

"We?" So the lady had an accomplice. The identity of the perpetrator was not the mystery. It was Taylor or Wilmslow … or maybe both. The reason behind their scheme is what baffled her.

"As I said, a woman will do anything for the man she loves."

Rose examined the woman's features, and recognition dawned. She tried to suppress a gasp, but it burst from her lips. She had seen this woman once before, in the churchyard of St Martin's on the day Oliver and Nicole married.

"Then I fear your affection is misplaced, Mrs Wilmslow."

CHAPTER TWENTY-ONE

M rs Wilmslow gave a sly chuckle. "I knew you'd work it out, eventually. You're far too smart for a maid, though in coming here you're clearly far too senseless for a lady."

Christian and Oliver were due to arrive any moment. Rose just needed a little more time. "As you said, often a woman will do anything for the man she loves. What a shame your husband sought fulfilment elsewhere."

"Indeed. Men can be rather shallow, don't you think?" Mrs Wilmslow appeared unperturbed by her husband's adultery and gestured to one particular door. "Shall we?"

"Now I would be rather foolish to step inside there." Rose glanced at the small brick building. "I'm afraid we will have to conduct our business out here."

The arrogant grin on the woman's childlike face faded. "No, we won't. Did you hear news of the recent poisoning? With the extortionate price of sugar, a confectioner added arsenic to his sweet treats. Children cannot tell the difference and gobble them up without thought or question."

Rose clenched her jaw. She'd only punched a person

once. Baxter had deserved more than a thump, and so did Mrs Wilmslow. "What sort of woman threatens small children? Lord above, your husband is a reverend." Was there something in the air in Abberton that turned normal people into crazed fools?

Mrs Wilmslow screwed up her pretty nose and bared her teeth. "Get inside." With a flick of the wrist, the leather sheath slipped out from the end of her coat sleeve, and she drew the knife in one swift movement. "I'll not tell you again."

Sunlight glinted off the metal blade, but Rose dismissed the sudden fear clawing at her throat. She had yet to play her ace card in this game of wits, and so had to trust that Fate would see things right.

Mrs Wilmslow opened the door, tugged the sleeve of Rose's coat and forced her inside.

A sweet, aromatic smell filled the air, something strange, something Rose couldn't quite place, though it came from the potted plants on the table to the right. Various herbs hung from a drying rack on the ceiling. A magnifying glass, jars full of soil and various scientific instruments lined the shelves.

Mrs Wilmslow pushed her towards a crude wooden chair positioned in the centre of the room. "Sit."

Rose dropped into the chair and waited for direction. A heavy silence ensued. Mrs Wilmslow's breath came quickly as she focused her attention on the door.

"Don't you want to see the book?" Rose scanned the room, looking for anything that might serve as a weapon.

"All in good time."

It didn't matter to Rose how long they waited.

The clip of booted footsteps on the stone floor in the building next door captured her attention. A creak of a rusty hinge preceded the crunch of gravel. Mrs Wilmslow's eyes lit up as a dark shadow appeared in the doorway. She rushed over and crushed the newcomer's mouth in a kiss that spoke of lust and desperation.

Rose sucked in a breath as the gentleman dragged his mouth from Mrs Wilmslow's ravenous lips and stepped into the room.

"Ah, Rose, and so we meet again."

"Are you here to join the party, doctor?" Though events were proceeding as Rose expected, the lack of emotion in Taylor's cold blue eyes confirmed he was a man determined in his evil course.

The doctor partially closed the door. "You could have avoided all this if only you'd left the book at Everleigh."

"But how did you know I brought the book to London?" She had not seen the doctor since the day he'd escorted her back to the house. And after today, she hoped never to see him again.

"Servants talk. You'd be surprised how easy it is to gain information in my profession."

"Lord Farleigh's staff would never betray him." She knew all the servants at Everleigh; they respected Christian and were loyal to a fault.

Taylor smirked. "No, not intentionally. They're just simple folk, easy to confuse, easy to manipulate. Had you been a little more discreet when you left, I would not be standing here now."

Those last few moments spent at Everleigh were a blur. She'd fought an internal battle, contemplated professing her love, struggled with the pain brought about by Christian's expression of indifference. She'd snatched the book in a hurry, and hugged it to her chest as she waved a teary goodbye to a handful of servants.

"And pray what brings you here?" Disdain marked her tone now. "What is so special about a few words and numbers that would make a man disregard his integrity?"

Taylor jerked his head back but then laughed. "Do you think integrity puts food on the table? Do you think that having ethical principles makes it easier to find your way in the world?"

"So this is about money?" The need to know why burned in Rose's chest. The look of adoration in Mrs Wilmslow's eyes forced her to doubt her initial assessment. "Or is it about love?"

Taylor cast Mrs Wilmslow a sidelong glance. "It's about doing what is necessary to survive."

From the quality of the doctor's clothes, the man was by no means struggling.

"And so you've spent two years persuading Lord Farleigh's staff to drink your mysterious potions, making them sick, making them better again." No doubt using skills he'd acquired in the apothecaries' guild. "Why? To survive?"

"Why do you care?"

Rose lifted her chin. "A woman will do whatever it takes to protect the man she loves. In coming here, I think I deserve an explanation."

Taylor folded his arms across his chest and gave a mocking snort. "Do you really want to know?"

"Would I have asked if I didn't?" She tried to keep her voice even, tried to disguise the tremble that conveyed fear. If Taylor told her the truth, it meant he had no intention of letting her leave.

"Very well." The doctor held out his hand. "Pass me the book, and I shall tell you."

Rose reached into her coat and removed the small ledger. Dr Taylor's eyes brimmed with excitement and perhaps a hint of relief. He stepped forward and snatched it from her hand. A brief silence ensued while he scanned the pages, though he muttered a curse when he came to the paper pocket at the back and found it empty.

"What's wrong?" Mrs Wilmslow asked as Taylor rifled through the book.

With a growl of frustration, he held the ledger at one corner and shook it violently as if he were throttling the life out of some poor creature. "Where is it?" Taylor's expression darkened.

"I—I don't know what you mean." And she didn't. Truly.

"Where's the damned letter?" Taylor skimmed through the pages one more time, tore the pocket from the back cover, scrunched it in his hand and threw it to the floor. "Don't play games with me."

Confused, Rose wasn't sure how to answer. "Are you referring to the letters written by the reverend and sent to Lady Farleigh?"

"Obviously not," Taylor snapped. "Why would I have any interest in Wilmslow's immoral antics? What I want is the letter from Miss Stoneway's aunt!"

Rose put her hand to her chest. "On my life, I have not seen the document." Panic flared. She'd spent twenty minutes copying every address listed in the back of the book, and the names of every person mentioned. Were her efforts in vain?

Mrs Wilmslow turned to him. "Mr Watson must have removed it, hidden it somewhere else."

"Impossible." Taylor threw the book onto the wooden table, knocking over a pot of soil. "I ripped the manor apart before Stanton purchased the damn place. It has to be at Everleigh."

"I can assure you it is not. I found the book in my room, hidden underneath the chest of drawers." She knew not to mention Jacob. "From the dust and cobwebs, it had been there for some time."

"That blasted bitch," Taylor spat. He flung his top hat at the wall and shoved his hands through his mop of golden hair, tugging at the roots as if determined to pull out every strand.

Mrs Wilmslow placed a hesitant hand on his arm. "Perhaps this is good news. Perhaps Watson never got around to giving it to Lady Farleigh, and the letter perished in the fire."

"But you searched both bodies." Taylor spoke without thought.

A gasp of horror burst from Rose's mouth. "You killed Lady Farleigh and Mr Watson?"

Taylor glared at her. "I may be guilty of fraud, but I'm not a murderer."

Mrs Wilmslow grinned. "Lady Farleigh was already dazed from the effects of the laudanum when she arrived at the cottage." Arrogance dripped from every word. "And Mr Watson certainly didn't expect me to wallop him with a cudgel."

The woman was insane, a prime candidate for Bedlam. If anyone deserved to be locked away in Morton Manor, it was Mrs Wilmslow.

"But why set the cottage ablaze? What possible reason could you have for killing two innocent people?"

"Innocent? Watson was a thief and a traitor," Mrs Wilmslow scoffed. "Lady Farleigh was a jezebel who seduced my husband. No woman wants to suffer that sort of humiliation."

Taylor brought Mrs Wilmslow's hand to his lips and pressed a kiss on her knuckles. "It doesn't matter. Once we've dealt with this, we'll be free to leave Abberton for good."

And with any luck, they were destined for the scaffold at Newgate.

"What are we to do now?" Mrs Wilmslow's eyes shone with affection for the doctor.

Taylor took hold of the woman's chin. "We have the book. Now no one can trace the relatives. There's no proof I took money to falsify documents."

"And what if someone finds the letter?"

"Without the book, the authorities will struggle to gain evidence. Miss Stoneway is no longer with us. And I doubt the aunt would confess to fraud now Mr Watson is dead."

Had they forgotten she sat there listening to every word?

"And what about me?" Rose prayed that Christian arrived soon. This sorry pair had already killed three people. One more would hardly make a difference. "Am I to suffer the same fate as Miss Stoneway?"

Dr Taylor turned to face her. "Miss Stoneway died of natural causes brought about by her condition, although I must admit I'm rather thankful. I'm afraid your fate lies with that of Lady Farleigh."

Lord, he really was a cold-hearted blackguard. Mrs Hibbet would forever punish herself for her failure to notice the signs.

Rose steeled herself. "Well, we have a problem on numerous counts." She glanced briefly at the silver blade in Mrs Wilmslow's hand. "I think your plan may have a few flaws."

Taylor snorted. "There is little point trying to bide time. Unfortunately, I cannot allow you to leave."

"Then I take it your offer of marriage no longer stands." Rose knew it had been a ploy to gain her trust.

Mrs Wilmslow's face turned beetroot red. "You asked her to marry you? What about me?"

"It was merely a comment made in passing."

Rose frowned. "So I'm not the only intelligent woman in Abberton?"

"Playing games will not save you now," Taylor said, ignoring both her question and Mrs Wilmslow's angry stare.

"Perhaps not, but I copied every address before I left home this afternoon."

Taylor paused. "Out of context, the names and addresses mean nothing." His rapid blinking suggested otherwise.

"My brother read your note this morning. He knows where I am and will be here any minute." Well, she prayed he would. The roads were a hazard day and night. Stray sheep and cattle, carriages with broken wheels and spooked horses were just a few problems one might encounter.

Mrs Wilmslow flashed the knife. "Then we'd best get on with it before he gets here. Lucky for us, the gate is locked."

Rose sucked in a breath. "And what of the brass buttons found on the victims? Lord Farleigh has them as evidence." She said it to stall them, but the look of shock on the doctor's face convinced her the buttons held some importance.

"Brass buttons?" Deep furrows appeared on Taylor's brow. He remained silent for a moment. "Describe them."

"Don't listen to her. We should put an end to it now." Mrs Wilmslow glared at the doctor. "Before the earl comes."

"Wait." Taylor shot forward, gripped Rose's elbow and dragged her to her feet. "What buttons?"

Rose struggled to catch her breath. "The ones engraved with the sun and a unique leaf pattern. Lady Farleigh had one in her hand. The other lay amid the leaves next to Miss Stoneway's body."

Mrs Wilmslow tugged the doctor's arm. "We must leave now. I think I hear something. If the earl finds us here, we'll both hang."

Taylor pushed her away with his arm. He pulled his watch from the fob pocket of his waistcoat and showed Rose the gold case. "Are they like this?"

The intricate scrollwork matched the buttons perfectly. "Yes, they are exactly like that."

With a loud exhalation, Taylor released Rose's elbow, and she stumbled back into the chair. He turned on Mrs Wilmslow like a rabid dog in the fighting pits. "You bloody bitch."

With wide eyes, she shuffled back until she hit the edge of the wooden table. "Why would you speak to me like that? Are we not in this together?"

"Tell me! Tell me why. What did you hope to gain?"

"I don't know what you're talking about." Mrs Wilmslow clutched the knife to her chest. "She's poisoning your mind. How can Lord Farleigh have the buttons when you lost them here in London?"

"Did I though? Is that not what you wanted me to think? When I packed my valise, my waistcoat had six buttons. When I unpacked, two were missing. You were in my bedchamber that afternoon. You had ample opportunity to steal them while I slept."

"But why would I do that?" Panic infused her tone, and she struggled to hold his gaze.

"To frame me for the murders you committed." He stepped back and dragged his hand down his face, but then his eyes grew wide. "Good God, you killed Miss Stoneway."

Rose glanced at the half-open door and debated whether to run. It was only a matter of time before Christian arrived, but with the volatile mood in the air, she decided not to take the chance.

"You killed Miss Stoneway?" Taylor repeated.

Mrs Wilmslow's hands shook. "I did it for you. What if Mr Watson gathered enough evidence to go to the magistrate?

What if she made it to Everleigh and convinced Lord Farleigh that she wasn't mad at all?"

"Damnation, do you know what you've done?" Taylor gestured to the blade in the woman's hand. "Give me the knife, Abigail."

Abigail? It didn't sound like the name of a murderess. But it was fair to say, Mrs Wilmslow's logic had abandoned her long ago.

"No, I don't trust you. I'm the only one alive who knows the truth of what you've done. Why do you think I planted the evidence?" She spoke so quickly it was difficult to follow her ramblings. "For security. Because all men are liars and cheats. You're going to use me and discard me and—"

"Just give me the damn knife and let us think of a way out of this mess."

"Step back." Mrs Wilmslow jabbed the knife at the doctor. "I'm leaving. You can deal with this on your own."

"Like hell you are!" Dr Taylor lunged forward and grabbed her wrist. A scuffle broke out. They pushed and shoved, knocked a glass beaker onto the floor and it shattered into a hundred pieces. "Stop fighting me and listen to sense."

Rose shuffled to the right, eager to escape the small confines of the room. She'd take her chances. But mayhem ensued as the pair wrestled for control.

Then a guttural growl put paid to their wild tussle. Mrs Wilmslow charged at the doctor and drove the blade deep into his chest.

CHAPTER TWENTY-TWO

C hristian opened the carriage door and vaulted down to the ground. "Move the cart out of the way else I'll smash the blasted thing to pieces." In anger, he kicked the apples strewn across his path, much to the horrified gasps of the passersby.

The grey-haired man doffed his shabby hat. "I can't, my lord. The wheel's come off, and it won't budge."

Stanton marched around the carriage. He took one look at the mess on the road. "Jackson, climb down and help us with this damn thing."

The coachman obliged. Between them, they carried the cart and set it down on the pavement. Stanton jerked his head to Jackson who happened to understand the silent nod and so removed a few coins from his coat pocket and thrust them into the old man's hand.

"Much obliged to you, my lord." The man beamed and flashed them a mouth full of rotten teeth. "And may the Lord bless you all this fine day."

They climbed into the carriage, relieved to hear Jackson

crack the reins and to feel the violent rumble of the wheels as the conveyance picked up speed.

Christian whipped his watch from his pocket. "Rose has been alone with Taylor for almost twenty minutes." He stared at the delicate gold hands, convinced they were moving faster than usual. Why hadn't they called for him sooner?

"Taylor? You're sure the doctor is the one responsible for sending the note?" Stanton raised a dubious brow. "The man is so considerate, so generous to his patients."

"What other explanation is there?" Deep down, Christian had always known something wasn't right. He blamed himself. They'd had him chasing his tail for nigh on two years. But then who would suspect a reverend of adultery? Who would suspect a doctor of murder? "Taylor's not what he professes to be, of that I'm certain."

A heavy silence filled the small space. Jackson's impatient cries to those who happened to get in their way conveyed the sense of desperation hanging in the air.

"We're nearly there." Lady Stanton kept her nose pressed to the window, only moving to rub away the patch of mist that appeared every few seconds. "Did Jackson not say it was the next road after Paradise Row?"

"The entrance to the garden is on Swan Walk," Stanton replied.

Christian closed his eyes briefly. "I still can't believe you let her go alone. What the hell were you thinking?" Images of Rose lying face up in the shrubbery flooded his vision.

"What else could I do? She's not the timid woman she was before my father locked her in the manor. And I couldn't take the risk of her sneaking off without my knowledge."

Lady Stanton dragged her gaze from the window and gave her husband a reassuring smile. "Rose is determined to solve Lord Farleigh's problems. Yes, I'm worried, but I can't help but admire her tenacity."

The lady's thoughts mirrored his own. Rose risked her life to bring him peace. And by God, he would worship her with every breath in his body until the end of his days.

"We're here," Lady Stanton cried, opening the door before the carriage rumbled to a stop.

"Wait!" Stanton grabbed his wife's arm. "Just because you're wearing breeches doesn't mean you can leap out of a moving carriage."

With a huff of impatience, Lady Stanton waited, though the last few rolls of the wheels seemed to take forever. As soon as their feet touched the pavement, they made a dash for the Physic Garden.

Christian reached the iron gate first only to find it locked. "The garden's closed today. Are you certain we're at the right place?" He rattled the metal bars and peered through the gaps at the deserted path. Panic surfaced.

"Here, let me try." Stanton stepped forward and fiddled with the handle. He put his hands on his hips and frowned. "So how did Rose get inside?"

Christian glanced down the length of Swan Walk. Other than a boy lingering near an oak tree and a woman pushing a perambulator, there wasn't another person on the road. "You're certain the note said Chelsea? Are there other botanic—"

"This is the right place," Stanton interjected.

"When you've finished debating will one of you give me some assistance?" Lady Stanton stood before the wall, the toe of one boot wedged into a gap between the brickwork, her fingers lodged into another gap higher up. "Hurry, before someone sees us and goes looking for a constable."

"Good God, woman, are you planning to scale the wall?"

Stanton strode over to his wife. "When we return home, remind me to hide all the spare pairs of breeches."

The lady sighed. "Take hold of my foot and push me up."

With no time to argue, Stanton gave his wife a boost, and she hauled herself over the wall.

A few moans and groans accompanied a dull thud. "I'm over, but I may have killed a plant in the process."

"Don't move until we join you." Stanton turned to Christian. "She's liable to go tearing off looking for Rose."

Christian scanned the height of the wall. "You go next. I don't need your assistance."

Stanton blinked in surprise as his gaze drifted over the breadth of Christian's chest.

"School pranks," Christian continued, "you know how it is." Once, he'd climbed from the roof down to the lower floor to seek revenge on Haystack Henry.

Stanton was heavier than expected but one good push and the earl cleared the wall, too. Christian followed Lady Stanton's lead and used the gaps left by the missing mortar as footholds.

"Did the note say where Rose should meet Taylor?" Christian brushed the dust from his hands as he scoured the garden. Rows of beds lined the walkways, each one filled with unusual plants and herbs.

"No, but I don't suppose there are many places for a person to hide." Lady Stanton walked a few paces along the path. "But from the stench in the air, it's clear we're close to the river. Perhaps there's a—"

A high-pitched shriek captured their attention.

"Rose!" The sound of a woman's mournful wails held Christian rooted to the spot.

"This way." Stanton pointed south, and they took flight along the path. With the heavy crunch of their boots on the gravel, the whole of London would have heard them coming.

They followed the cries to a row of brick buildings, the door to one stood ajar. Christian thrust out his arm, a gesture to urge his companions to stop and tread carefully.

"Shush," he whispered, and they crept closer to the door. "We don't want to startle Taylor."

The loud din inside the building obliterated any other sound. Cries of despair followed bouts of angry curses.

"You did this," a woman yelled, "meddling and poking your nose in where it doesn't belong."

"Don't just stand there," Rose said. Hearing her voice calmed Christian's racing heart. "We must call for help."

"Why could you not leave things alone? Look! Look what you've made me do."

"It is of no importance now. You must check his pulse. You must try to stop the bleeding."

Lady Stanton put her hand to her mouth and coughed. Perhaps she still suffered from the effects of the smoke inhaled at Morton Manor. But one cough led to another, and another.

"Who's there?" The woman peered around the door but shot back into the room. "Don't come any closer else I'll put a knife through your maid's heart, too."

Christian looked at Stanton. No one knew quite what to do.

A scuffle broke out inside the building. Rose groaned. The woman cursed. A chair scraped along the floor. Rose appeared in the doorway. Her frantic gaze met his, and Christian's heart dropped like lead into the pit of his stomach.

The woman held Rose around the neck, the edge of a shiny blade pressed to her throat.

"Move away," the woman cried, shoving Rose forward.

A single drop of blood trickled onto the collar of Rose's white shirt.

"Let her go." Christian spoke as calmly as he could, given the circumstances. "Leave here, and we'll promise not to follow you." It was a lie, but he'd come to learn that sometimes they were necessary.

The woman snorted as she shuffled to her left. "We're leaving by barge. Once I'm safely away, I'll let your maid go." That was another lie.

"Do what she says." Rose's hoarse voice conveyed fear. She kept her head stiff and rigid as she spoke. "One of you must attend to Dr Taylor."

Taylor?

Stanton looked at him and raised a questioning brow. "Is he alive?"

"Barely."

It was only as the woman continued her movement towards the path that they saw her face clearly. Christian recognised her instantly.

Mrs Wilmslow?

It took every effort not to gasp and call her name. What had this got to do with the reverend's wife?

Lady Stanton raised a hand. "May I attend to the doctor?"

"Leave him." Bitterness infused Mrs Wilmslow's tone, and she pressed the knife against Rose's porcelain skin to show she meant business. "It's too late now."

They stood helplessly and watched the reverend's wife drag Rose onto the path.

"We must do something," Stanton said through gritted teeth.

Rose disappeared behind a stone pillar, and they followed slowly behind. The walkway led down to a gate and a flight of stone steps giving access to the river. From what he'd heard, the apothecaries transported herbs and plants via a barge to other botanic gardens and nurseries in the district, took delivery of new specimens transported from far and wide.

As they moved closer to the steps, a vessel bobbed into view. Clearly, Mrs Wilmslow had missed the flaw in her plan. How was she to loosen the boat's moorings when she needed both hands to hold Rose?

A crippling sense of panic burst to the fore. What if Rose seized the opportunity to break free, and the woman lashed out? As he watched Mrs Wilmslow open the gate and descend the steps, Christian's blood rushed through his veins at such a rapid rate it affected his vision.

Christian tapped Stanton on the arm. "We must close the gap if we have any hope of ensuring Rose's safety."

Stanton nodded, and as Mrs Wilmslow stared at the iron ring embedded into the stone wall, wondering what to do about her dilemma, they quickened their pace.

Mrs Wilmslow looked up, her eyes suddenly bulging with terror. Christian thought her fear stemmed from their sudden advancement, but a shuffle of footsteps and a mournful groan caused Christian to glance back behind him.

Dr Taylor approached, shambling like a man who'd downed copious amounts of brandy, and whose limbs had a mind of their own. Blood stained the front of his waistcoat and trickled through the gaps between his fingers where he clutched his chest. Christian was not a doctor, but he knew the look of death. The doctor's sallow skin held a bluish tint, and his sunken eyes were glassy and unresponsive.

Lady Stanton gasped. She took two steps towards the doctor and hesitated as if expecting Mrs Wilmslow to protest.

Mrs Wilmslow's frantic gaze shifted back and forth between the doctor and the iron ring. Her arm sagged, the knife no longer pressing into the delicate skin at Rose's throat. But then the doctor dropped to his knees, and another heartfelt wail burst from the woman's lips.

"Oh, what have I done?" In her distress, Mrs Wilmslow stumbled back and slipped on the bottom step. The knife fell from her hand and landed with a clatter. Arms flailing, she tried to keep her balance and grabbed the back of Rose's coat for support.

"No!" Rose's eyes were wide, her mouth agape.

Christian stared in horror. Time slowed. Rose was falling, clutching at nothing, almost suspended in the air.

"Rose!" Christian darted forward, as did Lord Stanton.

Mrs Wilmslow hit the water first, banging heads with Rose who fell on top of her. The almighty splash sent waves rippling across the surface. Watermen stopped rowing as they passed although no one called out to offer help.

"Rose!" Christian shrugged out of his coat, threw his hat to ground and raced down the steps. Rose tried to keep her head above the water. Again, her hands came up as if stretching for the sky. There was no sign of Mrs Wilmslow.

"Help! Christian! She's pulling me down." Rose disappeared beneath the circle of white foam.

"Good God, she can't swim," Stanton cried.

"I know." Without another thought, Christian dived into the murky Thames.

Beneath, the water was a cloudy green yet surprisingly clear. His eyes stung, and it hurt to keep them open. He spotted Rose, writhing and wriggling to free herself from the coat. With her eyes closed, Mrs Wilmslow showed no sign of distress. Perhaps the bang on the head had knocked the fight out of her. Indeed, when Christian wrapped his arms around Rose and tugged, the woman relinquished her grip, and sank serenely to the bottom.

With Rose in his arms, he swam the few feet to the surface and spat out the foul taste of the river.

Lord Stanton stood on the bottom step in his shirtsleeves, ready to jump in. "Thank the Lord," he gasped, and he waved them ashore as though the thought of swimming to safety hadn't occurred to them.

Christian reached the steps, and the earl grabbed Rose by the arms and pulled her out.

"What about Mrs Wilmslow?"

Christian glanced back over his shoulder. "I'll go back for her."

"No." Rose coughed and sucked in a breath. "I—I can't lose you, Christian."

But despite all Mrs Wilmslow had done, he could not leave her there. He returned to the water and dived down. He could see the woman's lifeless body, but couldn't hold his breath long enough to reach her.

He returned to the bank and Stanton hauled him out. "No luck?"

Christian shook his head and collapsed on the steps next to Rose, his clothes sodden, his breath coming in painful pants.

Rose scrambled to his side, stroked his face, pushed the wet strands of hair off his forehead. "Say something. Tell me you're all right."

"I'm fine, but I was too late to save the reverend's wife." Guilt flared until he noted the red line marring the skin at Rose's throat. Then he pushed all grim thoughts aside.

Sitting on the top step, Lady Stanton sighed. Blood covered her hands and breeches. "It's too late for the doctor, too."

Lord Stanton found his coat and shrugged into the

garment. "We need to inform the authorities. For the life of me, I have no idea how we'll explain this mess."

"It shouldn't be too difficult to gather proof of the doctor's nefarious dealings." Rose took hold of Christian's hand and held it tightly. "After all, we still have the blue book and the note requesting I meet him here. The mere fact he paid for private use of the garden creates suspicion."

"We'll leave together and go straight to Peel. As Home Secretary, I believe he'll have a vested interest in our case." Lord Stanton withdrew his pocket watch and checked the time. "It shouldn't be too difficult to locate him at this time of day. And that way the matter will be dealt with swiftly and with the utmost discretion."

Christian hoped Stanton was right. Peel was considered a fair man though one obsessed with combating crime in the city. "On the way, I want you to tell me what the devil Mrs Wilmslow had to do with it all."

Rose nodded, but her gaze drifted to the body sprawled across the path. "What about Dr Taylor? We can't leave him here."

Lord Stanton shrugged. "Then we have no choice but to take him with us."

Rose shivered visibly. "You forget, the gate's locked. The only way out is by boat."

"I found this in the doctor's pocket." Lady Stanton opened her blood-stained hand to reveal a small iron key. "I presume it's for the gate."

"Let us hope so. After all that's happened we deserve some luck." Christian stood, took Rose's hand and brought her to her feet. "Come. The sooner we get this business dealt with the sooner we can move on with our lives."

Christian caught himself. Could this truly be the end of his problems? After seven years spent in a miserable marriage, and two years spent living with the threat of constant sickness, he'd lost all hope of ever being happy again.

Everything changed the day Rose came into his life.

His throat grew tight when he thought of how close he'd come to losing her. Rose was his friend, his love, his everything.

He recalled something she'd said at Everleigh. *Often our greatest teachers are the ones who cause us the most pain.* Now he understood Cassandra's lesson. She had shown him all that love was not. Only now could he appreciate the value of sacrifice. Now he could appreciate the beauty of true love.

CHAPTER TWENTY-THREE

It was seven o'clock by the time Rose and Nicole left Peel's office. Through the patches of fog, a warm orange sky spoke of the sun's slow descent. Thankfully, the testimony of two peers proved more than adequate to appease Peel. Indeed, the gentleman seemed more interested in the fraud committed at Morton Manor than the fact the reverend's wife had killed a doctor in the apothecaries' garden.

Peel sent a constable around to every London address listed in the blue book. It soon became evident that some patients at the manor had not been mad at all. Greedy people often resorted to underhanded methods to rid themselves of their unwanted relatives. Peel agreed that the doctor could not have acted alone when he took the bribes. And the consensus was that Mr Watson, at one time, must have been his accomplice.

As Oliver's carriage rattled through the London streets, Nicole sat at Rose's side, gripping her hand as she'd done many times during the six months spent together at the manor.

"I'll be glad to be out of these ridiculous clothes and in a warm bath." Nicole's weary tone conveyed the stresses of the day.

Rose glanced down at the faint blood splatters on her breeches. She grimaced when she inhaled, and the vile stench of the river invaded her nose. "I don't want to go home."

Nicole turned to her and frowned. "You don't?"

So much had happened in the last week it was hard to think clearly, but one thought remained constant. She loved Christian. The only place she wanted to be was in his arms. "Take me to Berkeley Square."

"But Oliver insisted we return home and wait for him there. They could be with Peel for hours."

"Berkeley Square *is* my home, as is any place where Christian happens to be."

Nicole scanned Rose's coat and breeches and screwed up her nose. "But you need to bathe. You need clean clothes."

Rose shrugged. "Mrs Hibbet will see to it all." When Christian told her he'd brought the children and his housekeeper with him to London, Rose's heart soared. "Please, Nicole. I want to be there when Christian comes home."

Nicole pursed her lips and nodded. "Who am I to stand in the way of true love?"

Christian hadn't told her what number Berkeley Square, only that he had a house next door to Lord Marlborough. Nicole refused to allow Rose to knock on doors while wearing a gentleman's coat and smelly breeches and so they waited in the carriage while Jackson made the rounds.

Eventually, he returned to the carriage and opened the door. "It's this one, my lady."

Rose hugged Nicole before alighting and mounting the three small steps. She expected to see the butler, but Lord Trevane stood at the door in his shirtsleeves.

"Lady Rose." Trevane inclined his head but smirked as he perused her unconventional attire. "I received a note to say Farleigh won't be back for a few hours."

"I know. He asked me to wait here until his return." It didn't matter if she lied to this man. "I thought I might spend time with the children."

Trevane raised a brow. "You wouldn't happen to have a calming influence by any chance? Three glasses of brandy and still the noise is deafening."

Rose smiled as she imagined mayhem within. "The only way you'll find out is if you let me inside. Or are we to spend the evening conversing on the doorstep?"

Trevane stepped aside and gestured to the hall. "You're certain you wish to enter the house while I'm in residence?"

Rose's heart raced. Trevane knew how to intimidate without saying much at all. "I assume your sister is here," she said, marching past him.

"Do you think that will stop the gossips?" He closed the door and then inhaled deeply. "Good God, you smell as though you've spent a week sleeping in the gutters."

Heat flooded her cheeks. "I've been swimming in the river, though not out of choice."

Trevane stared at her neck and narrowed his gaze. "And if that wasn't foolish enough you thought to enter the home of two unmarried gentlemen, without the aid of a chaperone."

Rose waved her hand down the front of her coat. "As you can see, my sense of propriety abandoned me long ago. And as you obviously enjoy playing butler will you not at least offer to take my hat and gloves?"

Trevane's eyes flashed with amusement. "Now it's clear why Farleigh dragged me around half the ballrooms in London to find you. Originals don't come along often. But allow me to point out that in your effort to appear scandalous you seem to be minus both items of apparel."

"Rose! Rose!" The children's excited voices rang through the house. "Rose is here." They came bounding down the stairs, their little legs moving so fast they were liable to fall. "Rose."

Trevane winced. "I'll be in the drawing room, cradling a decanter of brandy if you need me."

Jacob reached her first and flung his arms around her waist. Alice was but a second behind. "We missed you," they both cried.

Rose closed her eyes and hugged them with every ounce of strength she had left in her body. She knelt down, cupped their tiny faces and kissed their cheeks.

"We kept your letters." Alice's innocent blue eyes widened. "And we did what you said."

Jacob raised his chin. "I filled a glass with brandy without spilling a drop and brought it to Papa."

"That is a feat. Crystal decanters are extremely heavy."

"And I brought him a flower from the garden and left it on his desk."

Rose's heart swelled. "And did he appreciate your small gestures of love?" She'd hoped the tasks would distract their minds and make them focus on the one person who truly loved them and was always there.

Alice nodded. "Papa told Mrs Hibbet he'll teach us our sums from now on."

"That's wonderful."

"I'm sure we'll have another governess soon." Jacob conveyed a relaxed, carefree air, exactly as a child unburdened with problems ought to be. "Papa sometimes mumbles to himself and stares out of the window, and then he forgets what he's told us."

Tears formed in Rose's eyes. Happiness blossomed in her chest. This was where she belonged.

"Are you crying because of that terrible smell?" Alice pinched her nose. "I know I said I don't want to be a lady but breeches pong."

"They do." Rose chuckled. "And so I suggest you stick to wearing dresses."

Mrs Hibbet rushed down the stairs. She took one look at Rose and sniffed. "Oh, saints preserve us, we'll need a ton of soap to rid you of that awful smell."

Alice giggled. "Rose needs to look pretty for when Papa gets home."

The thought of spending time alone with Christian caused Rose's stomach to flip.

Mrs Hibbet clapped her hands. "Come on now. You two run along upstairs. Rose needs to bathe. I'm sure she'll come and read to you when she's clean again."

The children stood at Rose's side and took a hand each. Clearly, they had no intention of leaving.

Mrs Hibbet shook her head but smiled. "It's good to see you back, my lady."

"Thank you, Mrs Hibbet. In my heart, I never left."

"We're not expecting his lordship home for a few hours. By that time, we'll have you washed and dressed and looking your best."

Alice squeezed Rose's hand. "I've got a pretty pink ribbon you could use for your hair."

"That sounds lovely. Pink is my—"

Lord Trevane yanked open the drawing room door, and they all jumped. "There are rooms in the house. Must you loiter in the hall?"

Mrs Hibbet smiled sweetly. "We're heading upstairs now, my lord, and shall leave you in peace."

Trevane nodded and returned to converse with his brandy.

Mrs Hibbet ushered them all upstairs. "We'll speak to Lady Lillian and see if she can lend you something to wear for the time being."

Rose had been keen to meet Lady Lillian Sandford ever since hearing snippets of gossip at Lord Warner's ball. Regardless of what people said, Rose trusted Christian's judgement when it came to picking friends. Besides, after the events of the last week, surely Rose held the title of the most scandalous lady in all of London.

"You'll like Lillian," Alice said, knocking on a bedchamber door. "She's kind and funny and loves to eat cake."

Lady Lillian opened the door. She smiled warmly at Alice but took one look at Rose's filthy clothes and matted hair and gasped. "Good heavens. What happened to you?"

"Rose has come for a bath," Alice said as though she regularly brought in waifs and strays off the street.

Mrs Hibbet stepped forward. "Forgive us for disturbing you, my lady, but we're in desperate need of a dress."

A smile touched the corners of the lady's mouth, she reached out and grasped Rose's hands. "Oh, I was hoping to meet you. Lord Farleigh has told me so much about you." She winked at the children. "And I'm told you love sweet treats, too."

At the mere mention of sweet treats Rose's heart lurched. "As to that, I think we should all refrain from such things for a day or two." When everyone looked at her with some confusion, she added, "I heard tell that there's a problem with contaminated sugar."

Mrs Hibbet jerked her head back. "Contaminated with what?"

"I'm not sure." Over the top of the children's heads, she mouthed, "Arsenic."

"Goodness gracious." Mrs Hibbet put her hand to her chest. "Then I'd best mention it to Cook."

"I'm sure there's nothing to worry about, but I suggest she replaces her current stock as a precaution. I'm sure Lord Farleigh will say the same when he returns."

Mrs Hibbet hurried to the stairs. "Lady Lillian will look after you, and I'll get a maid to come and light the fire and have the tub brought up, and some water heated."

Still gripping Rose's hands, the lady pulled her into the bedchamber. "I've fresh water in the bowl so you can wash your face. And you can change into my bathing gown while you wait." She scrunched her nose. "The sooner you change out of these clothes the better."

The children were right. Rose felt an instant connection to Lillian. She possessed a serene quality that put one at ease. While her brother's hard stare could frighten the devil, her hazel eyes brimmed with compassion. Even so, she possessed a regal air, aided by the conservative cut of her high-collared dress.

A maid appeared at the door. "Come now, children. Mrs Hibbet said I'm to settle you in your beds."

Jacob looked most put out. "But we want Rose to read to us."

"I'll come and see you once I'm out of these smelly clothes." Rose kissed both children on the forehead and with some reluctance they followed the maid.

"They've done nothing but talk about you since they arrived," Lillian said helping Rose out of her coat. "I don't mean to speak out of turn, but I think their father has told them he's come to take you back to Everleigh." She threw the coat to the floor and then looked Rose in the eye. "Will you go with them?"

Rose didn't need to time to think. "In a heartbeat."

Lillian smiled. "That's what I hoped you would say. I believe Mrs Hibbet loves you as much as the children do."

Rose fiddled with her cravat but struggled to pull the silk free of the knot. "My brother prefers the fancy styles, though they're a devil to untie."

"Let me try." Lillian stepped forward. "There are not many brothers who would allow their sister to don gentlemen's attire."

Rose recalled Oliver's growl of disapproval while finding her suitable clothes. "I'm afraid he had no choice in the matter. Nothing would deter me in my course."

Lillian untied the knot and jerked her head back. "Heavens, where have you been?"

"I took a dip in the Thames, though it wouldn't have been so bad if I could swim. Christian … I mean Lord Farleigh rescued me. He truly was the hero of the hour." And the love of her life.

Lillian dropped the cravat on top of the coat and ambled over to the window. "What's it like?" She pulled the curtain to one side and stared down at the street below. "I mean, what's it like to feel loved and cherished?"

How could one answer such a question?

"Do you mean by a man?"

Lillian nodded. "I'm sure you've heard talk of my scandalous encounter with a rogue. With my ruined reputation, I don't hold out much hope for a love match."

Rose could feel the pain behind Lillian's words. "There are good men in the world, ones willing to look beyond society's rigid rules." Men willing to forgive a lady's mistakes.

"When my brother finally stops blaming himself for what happened and allows me some space, the best I can hope for is a gentleman in dire need of funds." She gave a weak chuckle. "Forgive me for rambling on. It's just that it's been an age since I've spoken to anyone other than my brother."

Rose sat down on the stool next to the dressing table and tugged on her boot. "From what I hear, your brother is rather protective." While waiting in Peel's office, Christian spoke fondly of his friendship with Lord Trevane. "Though I'm sure he has your best interests at heart."

With a sudden gasp, Lillian shot back from the window. She stood frozen for a moment, her eyes wide as she gulped.

"Is everything all right?" Rose yanked off one boot, and it landed with a thud on the floor.

Lillian jumped. "What? Yes. It's nothing. A carriage stopped outside, and I thought it might be Lord Farleigh, but it's moved on now."

As an expert in lies and deceit, Rose suspected the lady was not being entirely honest. Indeed, she would have pressed her further had Mrs Hibbet not arrived with a maid and two footmen in tow.

"All sorted in the kitchen." Mrs Hibbet stepped aside as the footmen came into the room carrying a copper bath tub. "After the sickness at Everleigh, it's best not to take any chances." Mrs Hibbet scanned Rose's dirty breeches. "The water is almost ready. Let's get you out of those clothes before his lordship returns."

The room erupted in a sudden flurry of activity. There was no time to continue her conversation with Lillian or probe her further about what she'd really seen outside.

Christian would be home soon, and Rose would be ready and waiting for him when he walked through the door.

CHAPTER TWENTY-FOUR

Christian's carriage rolled to a stop outside his house in Berkeley Square, but he chose not to alight. He needed a few minutes alone. The day had brought one shocking revelation after another, and yet it all amounted to the same thing in the end: greed.

Accepting one's fate and making the most of opportunities were said to be the secret to happiness. Dr Taylor might have found a miracle cure for the pox had he focused on his skills in botany. But a bitter heart is its own poison. Every wicked deed is like another dose.

Christian closed his eyes as his head fell back against the squab. He waited to feel a crippling bitterness, too, and yet love was the only sensation burning in his chest.

Sucking in a breath, he opened the door and jumped down to the pavement. The soft glow of candlelight broke through a gap in the drawing room curtains. Hopefully, someone was waiting to share a brandy with him, even if it was Mrs Hibbet.

Bamfield opened the front door as Christian approached.

"Welcome home, my lord." The butler took his hat. "Have you eaten? I can arrange for a light supper."

"There's no need. I had dinner with the Home Secretary." Indeed, Christian had sent for a clean change of clothes. Still, the smell of sewerage clung to his nostrils.

The butler inclined his head. "Lord Trevane is in the drawing room should you wish to join him."

"Thank you, Bamfield." The butler opened his mouth to speak, but Christian tapped him on the upper arm. "Get yourself off to bed. It's been a long day, and I shall retire shortly."

"But, my lord, you have—"

"Don't fret, Bamfield. I shall snuff out the candles." Christian strode into the drawing room to find Vane, minus his boots and cravat, sprawled out on the chaise. Something troubled his friend, but Christian was so absorbed with his own problems he'd not had a chance to broach the subject.

"I'm awake, Farleigh," Vane said as Christian crept closer to the chaise. "Fetch a glass and have a drink with me." Vane sat up and dragged his hand through his hair. "There's enough left in the decanter."

Christian poured them both a brandy, handed Vane a glass and then dropped into the seat opposite.

Vane took a swig. "I believe congratulations are in order."

"Congratulations? Are you referring to my problems at Everleigh?" Christian frowned. His note made no mention of the doctor, only that he was meeting Peel.

"I am referring to your upcoming nuptials."

"Do you know something I don't?" While he had every intention of asking Rose to marry him, the words had not yet left his lips.

Vane gave a devilish grin. "Your lady love is upstairs and has been waiting for hours."

Christian's heart skipped a beat. "Rose is here?"

"Indeed. Lord and Lady Dovecot were passing as she entered, and I gave them a little wave. As my reputation is not without blemish, if you don't marry her I'll have to." Vane swallowed a mouthful of brandy. "I don't suppose it would be a hardship. The lady is rather unconventional, just the sort of wife a man in my position might find appealing."

Christian raised a challenging brow. "Be thankful you're my friend else you'd be on your arse for that comment."

"Be thankful you're my friend else I'd have pressed the lady for a little more than a smile." Vane sat forward. "Rest assured, Farleigh, your love has spent the evening with my sister, your over-friendly housekeeper and those bundles of noise you call children."

"Is Rose with Lillian now?" The urge to dash upstairs proved overwhelming.

Vane shrugged. "Everything went quiet almost an hour ago." He stared at the amber liquid in the glass. "Although that might be down to the brandy numbing my brain."

Christian considered his friend. The man was punishing himself for something. It could only be his failure to protect his sister.

"What happened to Lillian, it wasn't your fault, Vane."

Vane shot out of his seat. "Damn right it was. I might have fought the war, but Lillian bears the battle scars." He dragged his hand down his face. "I seem to have a knack for ruining the only women I've ever cared about."

Women? Despite his many encounters, Vane could mean only one other person.

"You're not to blame for Miss Darcy's fate, either."

At the mere mention of her name, Vane sucked in a breath. A darkness passed behind his bright blue eyes.

Whether it was pain or a warning to tread carefully, Christian didn't know.

Vane turned his back and strode over to the decanters on the side table. "Why are you wasting your time here with me, when the answer to all your prayers is waiting for you upstairs?"

Christian sensed his friend retreating. The barriers were up. Not even a horde of vicious Vikings could break their way through.

"Will you be all right here alone?"

Vane cast him a sidelong glance. "Alone is the safest place *to* be."

After the horrific events of the day and the years spent worrying about his troubles, Christian had no desire to sit and wallow in Vane's misery. "Then I shall bid you goodnight."

Vane raised his glass in a toast. "For what it's worth, I'm pleased everything has worked out well for you."

Christian inclined his head and slipped quietly out into the hall. It took every effort not to charge up the stairs. But what was the hurry? He had the rest of his life to love Rose.

After checking the only available rooms and finding them empty, a sense of panic took hold. He checked his bedchamber, hoping to find Rose sprawled naked in his bed, but no. And so he opened the door to the children's room and peered inside.

The sight stole his breath.

Drawn by the beauty of the scene, he stepped into the room. Rose was curled up on Alice's bed, her arm draped over both children as they lay huddled beside her. In sleep, they looked content. Their soft, peaceful breathing warmed his heart, and he simply stood there staring for the longest time.

The light patter of footsteps behind forced him to glance over his shoulder.

Mrs Hibbet entered the room. "Now there's a sight to behold, my lord," she whispered. "Happen I was right. The Lord sent us an angel."

Christian struggled to contain the sudden surge of emotion. "You're always right, Mrs Hibbet."

"Not always. Dr Taylor had me good and proper. And to think I drank his potions."

Guilt flared for his failure to spot the signs, but he pushed it aside. The past mattered not. "Let's not think about the doctor anymore. The man has taken up enough of our time."

Mrs Hibbet nodded. "Well, I best move Jacob into his bed else he'll have a crick in his neck come the morning."

"I'll wake Rose." Christian moved to the side of the bed. "Rose." He placed a hand on her arm and shook her gently. "Rose."

Her lids fluttered open. She blinked numerous times and then her eyes met his. "Christian, when did you get home?"

"Half an hour ago."

"Is everything all right?" She sat up and eased herself off the bed, trying not to wake the children.

Christian caught her by the elbow when she nearly tumbled. "Everything is fine. But there are things we need to discuss. I'm afraid they cannot wait until the morning."

"Oh, I see." Her tone held a nervous edge. She glanced at the bed. "Let me settle the children, and I shall join you in a moment."

Mrs Hibbet came forward. "I'll see to things up here. You go off now." The housekeeper ushered them out of the door and closed it behind them.

"Come." Christian grabbed Rose's hand and pulled her along the corridor. As they passed his bedchamber, he took a quick peek over his shoulder before opening the door and dragging her inside. He kicked the door shut.

"Christian," she gasped.

"This isn't the time for talking, Rose." He crushed his mouth to hers, delving into its warm depths in the hope of satisfying the clawing need within.

Passion burned instantly, soon reaching the point of no return.

With frantic hands, they stripped each other naked, sank to the floor despite there being an oversize bed a mere foot away.

He wanted to pleasure her until dawn, but the urgency to claim her body took hold. "Rose, I imagined this would be a slow, languorous affair where I would … good God."

Rose wrapped her thighs tightly around him and grabbed his bare buttocks. "Don't wait, Christian."

She didn't need to tell him twice. He entered her in one long fluid movement. The muscles in her core gripped him like a glove. Everything about this woman felt right.

"I'm afraid I couldn't wait even if I wanted to. Love, I've waited for you my whole damn life." They were one now, and nothing or no one would ever change that.

"I'm yours, Christian. I always will be."

His heart swelled, which was a feat considering every drop of blood in his body filled his cock.

"I love you, Rose." He loved the way she looked at him with desire swimming in her eyes, the way she welcomed him into her body, made all his cares slip away. He loved the way she cared for his children, how she gave everything of herself and expected nothing in return.

A whimper escaped from her lips as he thrust hard and deep. "I—I have loved you from … from the moment you wiped ash off my chin."

He rose above her, and she looked up at him, love and lust evident in her eyes.

"Marry me."

A smile touched her lips, one that turned into a sweet moan when he pushed inside her. "Yes," was all she managed to say.

Christian withdrew slightly. "Then we'll leave for Scotland tomorrow?"

She raised her hips and took him deeper into her core. "Yes."

While he wanted to race to the rooftops and share his good fortune with the world, he focused his efforts on pleasing the woman clutching him tightly and panting his name.

She writhed beneath him, arched her back and pressed her breasts against his chest. And then she was shaking. Her body clenched around him, drawing his release from him in powerful jerks and shudders.

Their breathless pants filled the air. Beads of sweat trickled down the line of his back, and he collapsed at her side, exhausted.

"Do you know the first thing I'm going to do when I get you back to Everleigh?"

Rose threw her arm across his chest and smiled seductively. "Has it anything to do with the rug in the study?"

"No. There'll be no more rushing to the denouement, no more uncomfortable places. I intend to spend many hours worshipping you in a plush bed."

"Oh, I rather like frolicking in the study. I like the spontaneity of it all. And the fear of getting caught adds to the excitement."

"There's nothing to stop us fitting in a few study sessions in between."

"Or a few midnight strolls in the woods."

Christian waited for the frisson of fear to strike, but it didn't come. When he thought of the woods, he imagined chasing Rose, pressing her up against a tree and claiming her mouth in a wild and passionate frenzy.

"So what is the first thing you intend to do with me?" Rose asked.

"I intend to teach you to swim." He kissed her on the forehead. "I'll not risk losing you again."

Rose chuckled. "Am I to learn to swim with or without clothes?"

He stroked her back, cupped one soft buttock and squeezed. "With clothes until you've mastered the art, without when you want to take me to the lake to work on your strokes."

A satisfied sigh left her lips. "I'm so happy, Christian, I could burst."

Christian pulled her on top of him and kissed her tenderly on the lips. The feel of her warm body against his sparked his desire. "You're all I've ever wanted, the angel I dreamed would one day come and save me."

"An angel? Am I not the damsel who came to save the knight?"

"Love, a damsel is a naive maiden. After all we've shared, I'd hardly call you innocent." He wrapped his arms around her and kissed her again. "But you're right. You saved me from myself. From a miserable, lonely existence and so you may claim your reward."

"Then I claim you, Christian Knight, as my husband, lover and friend."

Christian pressed his growing erection against her stomach. "I shall be forever your servant, my lady, and am ready to do your bidding."

Rose chuckled. "Good, you can start by sweeping the grate."

Scotland proved to be the perfect place for a wedding. Not only did it give them the opportunity to put the events in the apothecaries' garden behind them, but Christian refused to marry in Abberton while Reverend Wilmslow remained there. And, of course, the children thought of it as an exciting adventure.

Even so, when the gates of Everleigh came into view, they all sighed with relief.

Rose clutched his arm. "Oh, it's so good to be home."

"I hope Foster's kept the staff working hard in my absence," Mrs Hibbet said.

Rose shrugged. "I don't care if the house is in chaos, with a full complement of staff we'll soon have everything right again."

"When are our swimming lessons starting, Papa?" It was the fifth time Alice had asked in the last hour.

"If it's dry tomorrow, we can take a picnic to the lake." He glanced at Jacob and raised a brow. "We'll look for a spot where you can both touch the bed."

"The bed?" Alice screwed up her nose. "Fish don't sleep."

"They do," Jacob protested. "But they keep their eyes open."

Rose turned to Christian. "I think you need to hire a governess posthaste."

Having received the news that their master had married, the servants lined up to greet Rose as mistress of Everleigh. She accompanied Mrs Hibbet on her inspection of the house while Christian settled in the study and sifted through his correspondence. One particular letter caught his attention, and after breaking the seal and scanning the missive, he sent for Rose.

"I've received a letter from Vane."

Rose narrowed her gaze. "Judging by your solemn tone, I assume it's not good news."

Christian shook his head. "Lillian is missing."

"Missing!"

"Vane wants to know if she said anything to you when you met her at the house in Berkeley Square."

"No." Rose put her hand on her chest. "She asked a few questions, vaguely touched upon her ruined reputation. Perhaps she went to stay with a friend or other relative. While it's clear her brother cares for her, his need to protect her must be suffocating."

Guilt drove Vane to behave as he did. "I'll ride to London tomorrow and see if there's anything I can do."

Rose gave a weak smile. "Of course."

He handed Rose the letter. She scanned the first few lines and looked up. "But this is dated ten days ago. There's every chance he's found her."

Christian rifled through the rest of the letters littering his desk before finding another written in Vane's flamboyant script. He tore it open. "This one's dated a week ago." The first few words calmed his racing heart. "It's all right. He knows where she is."

"Oh, thank heavens. Now I've got you all to myself, I can't bear the thought of you leaving."

Christian offered a devilish grin. "When I'm done with these perhaps you should come here and sit on the desk, let me admire those new stockings that cost a small fortune."

The letter in his hand shook as he imagined a rather erotic scene. The next few lines wiped the smile off his face.

Christian swallowed as he absorbed the words on the page. "Good Lord!" He fell back in the chair, dragged his hand down his face and reread it.

"What is it?" Rose stepped closer to the desk.

"Surely not?"

"Christian?"

"Sorry. Vane knows where Lillian is because she's been kidnapped."

"Kidnapped? By whom?"

Christian read it once more just to be certain. "By a blasted pirate."

Thank you!

Thank you for reading *The Deceptive Lady Darby.*

If you enjoyed this book please consider leaving a brief review at the online bookseller of your choice.

Read the next book in the series
The Scandalous Lady Sandford

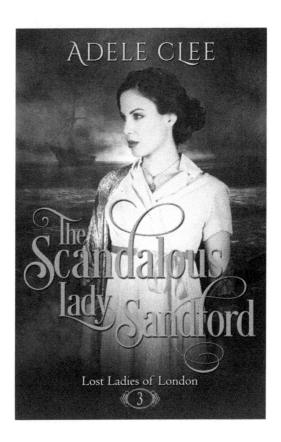